Rock & Roll Rip-Off

by

RJ McDonnell

© 2010

Killeena Publishing

2nd edition
This book is a work of fiction. Any similarity to real people,
alive or dead, is purely coincidental and not intended by the
author.

Printed in the United States

ISBN: 978-0-9814914-9-3

www.rjmcdonnell.com
rj@rjmcdonnell.com

Cover by Maryann Nebraski of Morison's Memories

Chapter 1

Some people are meant to get second chances while others are not. Leandra Lundquist felt entitled to a major break after 21 years of being bitch-slapped by the hand of fate. All of that would change today.

The old Leandra would never take advice from her ex-con older brother, John. The notion of jeopardizing the pharmacy job she'd held since 10th grade would have been inconceivable a year ago. Blackmailing a young pharmacist into ordering a massive shipment of pseudoephedrine would have been beyond consideration for a girl who made it to adulthood without a detention or a parking ticket.

But misfortune had collected in her life like plaque in an imperiled heart. Her fairy godmother was looking more and more like her real-life alcoholic mother. Staying the course seemed like a death sentence. John was right. If she didn't take control of her own destiny it would take her down like a rip current at Wind & Sea Beach.

At 10:20 AM an unmarked white truck pulled up to the loading dock at Popakalitis Pharmacy. A buzzer sounded behind the pharmacy counter.

"Leandra, you're needed in the back," called Myron Rosen, a 50ish pharmacist who was filling prescriptions while three customers waited.

"This is a pretty big order for a neighborhood store," remarked the driver.

"Poppy's either getting a great deal or we're in for a wicked cold and flu season," Leandra replied.

Due to the size of the shipment, the loading dock door wouldn't close completely. Leandra signed the electronic receipt tablet.

"Sorry about the way I had to stack the pallets, but there's just no room."

"Don't worry. I'll take care of it," she said.

After the driver pulled away, Donnie Daniels, one of John Lundquist's former prison buddies, ended his phone call and walked into the pharmacy. He wore a baseball cap low on his forehead and had been growing a beard since he agreed to help. John had given him a drawing that noted the location of the store cameras. He walked a well-planned route with his head down.

'Hey, could somebody give me a hand over here," he called to the pharmacist.

"We're a little busy right now," Myron replied.

"My mother's out in the car in a lot of pain. We just came from the doctor's office and she needs a knee support, but I don't know what'll fit her." Donnie's voice was both tense and loud.

Myron walked to the storeroom door and called for Leandra to come out and help.

"We just got a big delivery," she complained.

"It'll wait, Leandra. I want you to take care of this man first," he said, pointing at Donnie.

While she answered Donnie's many questions, John and Leandra's musician boyfriend loaded the band's equipment truck with the pseudoephedrine. After a few minutes, Donnie and Leandra saw the truck drive past the front of the store.

Donnie shouted, "So you think my mother's too fat to fit into any of your braces!"

"I didn't say that," Leandra replied. "I just suggested we go out to your car and measure her knee so we get the right fit."

"Fuck you, bitch! I'm outta here!" Donnie angled his cap at the door camera and stormed out.

Leandra said to Myron, "I swear I didn't call his mother fat."

"He was a jerk. Don't worry about it."

Five seconds later Leandra screamed, and Myron rushed into the storeroom. "We've been robbed!" she cried.

Chapter 2

Leandra began calling her boyfriend Rock Star after his group won a San Diego Battle of the Bands competition. Actually, she agreed to go out with him for the first time shortly after Poppy asked him how he would be spending his millions once he became famous. She considered him an adequate male partner, though not her ideal mate. But he was physically attractive and could very possibly provide her with a first-class ticket out of her unbearable life.

The Rock Star dropped John off at his part-time job, and drove the drugs to the home of meth cook, Nelson Tabor. At 7:00 PM Leandra received a call from her boyfriend, whose voice was anxious and shaky.

"Leandra, I'm in my car outside your apartment. Can you come down here right now? We need to talk."

She lived in a three bedroom apartment above the six car garage of her mother's obnoxious, bed-ridden employer, Mrs. Winthrop Ballington. Leandra's body tingled with fear when she hung up the phone. It was a feeling she hadn't experienced since she was nine years old and climbed much too high in an elm tree just as the wind started to gust. Leandra drew the curtain back from the kitchen window and looked down, expecting to see a police cruiser next to her boyfriend's car. Her fear was unfounded.

"What happened?" she asked, closing the car door.

"I drove to a dumpy-looking house on the other side of Valley Center that smelled like roofing tar. The chemist met me at the door wearing really thick glasses that made his eyes look huge. I asked if he was putting on a new roof. He said he owns a small roofing business. He doesn't do many jobs, but said it masks the chemical smell and helps him to clean the money."

"That's pretty smart," Leandra said.

"While we were unloading the truck, Tabor said, 'I understand you're a musician,' and I told him I'm in The Tactile Tattoo. He saw us in Escondido a few times. He was acting all buddy-buddy, and asked if I wanted a little taste of his product. I told him no thanks, I was paranoid enough driving all that shit up to his house."

"What did he say?"

"He said, 'Suit yourself,' but I think he was disappointed – like maybe he'd have something on me if I got high with him."

"Are you reading minds now?" Leandra asked.

"No. Anyway, twenty minutes later I was driving down the hill between Valley Center and Escondido when a K-9 police cruiser pulled out of Lake Wolford Road and followed me all the way to the light at the entrance to the freeway."

Leandra's tingling sensation returned. She shifted in her seat to look directly into his eyes.

He continued, "While I sat at the light in the left turn lane, the cruiser pulled a little past me in the next lane. All of a sudden the police dog started to bark, and I realized I should have rolled up my windows when I had the chance. I was sure the dog got a whiff of the drugs."

"Oh my God," Leandra said.

"Both of the cops were looking over their shoulders at me when the one in the passenger seat pointed at me and yelled, 'Bitch must be in heat.' At first it didn't make sense. Then I looked to my left and saw a young girl barely holding on to the leash of a female German Shepherd." He took a deep breath. "After the light turned green, I drove to the bottom of the entrance ramp and puked into my soda cup."

"Poor baby." Leandra stroked his hair. "But the truck was empty by that point. What could they find?"

"Have you ever watched an episode of CSI?"

"I've seen enough cop shows to know about *probable cause*."

He said, "The truck was used in a crime earlier in the day. Don't you think the cops canvassed El Cajon Boulevard around the pharmacy? If anybody saw me pull out of the alley, I'm sure an APB went out on the truck."

"It's not like the band's name is on the side. It's pretty ordinary looking. Even if they pulled you over they'd still need a good reason to search it."

He reached into the back seat and pulled a metal briefcase onto the console. "Do you mean like seeing this on my front seat?"

Leandra opened the case and gasped. "We did it!"

"I still hate the way we got it."

"Don't worry about it. The pharmacy's insured. Myron blames himself for calling me out of the storeroom to deal with Donnie. We're in the clear."

"I got a bad feeling about that meth cook. I think his story about only selling to a bunch of computer nerds is a crock of shit. I'm gonna have nightmares where I see those magnified eyes looking down at little kids on a playground."

"It's all up here," she said, knocking lightly on his forehead.

"Maybe we should watch his house for a few days and see where he goes."

Leandra replied, "Don't be stupid. You should concentrate on the new album and stop being such a worrier. I think I know how to straighten you out."

"How?"

"My mother's asleep and John's out. Let's take the money upstairs, spread it all over my bed, and I'll screw your brains out. I guarantee you'll sleep like a baby tonight."

"Yeah, let's get our DNA all over it. Now who's being stupid?" he asked. Leandra didn't reply.

"Actually, I'm handing it over to Dr. DD in about an hour. I better get going."

"I'm sure your manager can wait for your night to have a happy ending."

"I'm too nervous. If there was any other way of making our second album happen, I would have turned around the minute I looked in Tabor's eyes."

Cupping her fingers around his chin, Leandra brought his attention back to her. "I know you think Dr. DD is a great guy.

5

But he's a lot older than us and I don't trust him. How about if you call me just before your meeting and leave the phone on?"

"Don't ask me to do that, Leandra. I told him that the bribe was just between the two of us."

"I just stuck my neck out a mile for you today. I could still get in trouble."

"You said everything went great. I thought we were in the clear."

"Poppy still hasn't seen what was stolen. Parker Willis is going to take a lot of heat for ordering all of that pseudoephedrine."

"What do you think Parker's gonna say?" he asked.

"Poppy usually orders about 25 boxes at a time. If there's a big sale he might order 100. Parker's going to tell him he saw that it was the final day of a big sale and tried placing an order for 100, and accidently added a zero."

"I'm surprised the manufacturer didn't catch it."

"Parker said that pharmaceutical sales reps have incentive contests for big product promotions, and an order of that size could put a rep over the top. That's why he waited till the final day of the sale to place the order."

"At least you can be pretty sure Parker's not going to tattle on you after you took those pictures of him snorting coke off of the pharmacy counter."

"You wouldn't think so, but who knows what somebody's going to do under pressure. It's just like the situation with Dr. DD. If something unexpected happens with the record executive, he could end up screwing us."

"What good would it do for you to listen in?"

"I'll record it. We can make him live up to his commitment if he starts getting hinky on us."

"I trust Dr. DD. I made a big withdrawal at the karma bank today and don't think I should push it any further."

"Last year you asked me to marry you and I said I didn't think you were ready for the commitment. Marriage is a partnership that involves a lot of compromise. If you want me to feel you're any closer to being ready, I need you to compromise on this one."

He rested his head on the steering wheel and closed his eyes. Leandra remained silent.

He said, "Don't make any noise. Don't make any copies of the call. Don't tell anybody we did this. And, the recording gets destroyed when this is over."

"You got it, Rock Star. Now gimme a kiss."

He buried his fingers in her long, thick, strawberry blond hair and kissed her with a passion that bordered on desperation.

Chapter 3

Dr. Damien Dumajian ran his music management company from an upscale office suite in the Golden Triangle section of La Jolla. True to his word, Leandra's boyfriend called her just before entering the suite.

"Judging from your luggage I'd say you're either ready to move forward with the album, or you're taking a vacation," said Dr. DD.

"It's been a long day. I just wanna get this over with."

Leandra heard the briefcase snap open. "I should be able to arrange a meeting with the executive later this week. How are you coming with the compositions?"

"We're working on the 10th of 12 cuts." After a brief pause he added, "I wish we didn't have to do it this way."

"I concur with your assessment. The instrumentation on that first album was top of the line. Make sure you keep Marni away from the creative process this time."

"She really is an asset to the band."

Leandra heard a couple of drawers close. Dr. DD said, "Before I take that briefcase, I insist that you listen to me read the review that killed your first album."

"I was hoping to make it to my grave without hearing it again."

"Let us call this preventive medicine." Dr. DD picked up a single sheet of paper, rose to his feet, cleared his throat, and began.

"The pre-release hype coming out of Dannick Records for the debut album of The Tactile Tattoo was intense. They told us that the instrumentation was technically very tight, and they were right. They told us that lead singer, Marni Hawley, is as

beautiful as Ashlee Simpson, and has the voice of an angel, and they were right. They didn't tell us that her lyrics sound like they were written by a stoned 13-year-old. Unless you're a masochistic insomniac who lies in bed longing for the days when you rode the short bus, stay away. I played it for a couple of friends, who said they wouldn't buy this album if it was being sold for half-off at the dollar store, and they were right."

"Are you one of those guys who think artists need to suffer to do their best work?"

Dr. DD replied, "There won't be a third opportunity for your band. Hell, there wouldn't be a second without that briefcase. The record industry has fallen upon hard times. Fans who aren't pilfering shared files are buying 99 cent downloads instead of $15.99 CDs. I know that Marni has been using classic mystery novels as the basis for each song, and I loved the two cuts that you put on the demo. But I don't trust her judgment on the other 10 songs."

"She read that review to the band the day it came out. It was the most humbling experience of her life."

Dr. DD said, "I heard she rolled the magazine up into a mini-bat and swatted a bust of Paul McCartney through your living room window."

"All of the new songs are outstanding – lyrics and all. Feel free to pop by our practice room anytime."

"I'll do that. Don't be surprised if your producer, Tony Zembrano, insists on some input. I'm sure his bosses will be questioning his judgment about offering your band another contract. Don't make waves in the studio."

"As far as I'm concerned, he already had his input when he forced us to come up an extra $40,000 to pay for the two studio musicians."

"They'll be with you for about four months, including the practice sessions, test gigs, recording sessions, and promotional tour. I'll make sure you maximize the return on your investment by securing top quality personnel."

"I hope so."

"Remember, this is just between the two of us," said Dr. DD.

"You've been great. I'd never do anything to hurt you."

Chapter 4

Two days later Leandra was preparing to open the store when Parker Willis arrived. "What did Poppy say about the order?" she asked.

"He wanted to know why I ordered so many boxes. I stuck with our plan."

"Did he buy it?"

"I think so. Now he merely thinks of me as stupid and incompetent."

"Poppy is a very nice and forgiving man. Just don't behave like a self-pitying dickhead and he'll eventually get over it," she said.

"We'll see."

"Are you sure there won't be any investigators from the FDA or DEA?"

Parker said, "The controls on pseudoephedrine were put in place to keep meth cooks from getting their supplies from local pharmacies. The focus was on the retail buyers. The pharmaceutical lobbyists made damn sure their distributors and retailers wouldn't be hurt by the legislation that made it a controlled substance. The only investigation will involve local narcs looking for drug thieves."

Shortly after the store opened, Leandra reflected on her original plan before dating the Rock Star. During her first year of employment she decided that a younger version of Poppy would make an ideal husband. She fanaticized about marrying a handsome young pharmacist who would earn over $100,000 per year. Both of Poppy's associates were too old for her. But when Parker came along, she seriously considered dropping the Rock Star and returning to Plan A.

Unfortunately, Parker reminded her of the snobs she knew in high school, who looked down on the white trash girl that lived in servant's quarters over a rich bitch's garage. Snapping a picture of Parker with a rolled-up $20 bill in his nose gave her a thrill unlike anything she had ever experienced. Adrenaline was clearly her drug of choice.

Leandra received a call from her boyfriend that evening. Twice she reassured him that all was well at the pharmacy.

She asked, "What's happening with the record company?"

"Dr. DD called today and said we start working with the studio musicians on Monday."

"Tell me again why you had to hire those two guys?"

"When Tony presented the album concept to his board, they said that mystery novels are full of suspense and intrigue. They felt that it called for more than three instruments to create that effect."

"I'm off on Monday. Mind if I tag along?"

"You can tag along every day."

Chapter 5

The band leased a practice room at Sterling Studios on South Hill Street in Oceanside. The building looked like a warehouse with multiple loading docks on either side of the main entrance and across the entire back of the T-shaped facility. The main entrance housed a reception area where a clerk/technician sat behind a display case and sold guitar strings, drum heads, cabling, and various replacement parts for amps and PAs. Sterling Studios also included a small recording studio for demo discs, and 12 practice rooms leased by area bands.

The Tactile Tattoo is comprised of Marni Hawley on vocals, Garvey Thompson on drums, Chris Barnett on lead guitar, and Jake Fuller on bass. Garvey, Chris, and Jake live together in an apartment building on the north end of Oceanside, less than a mile south of the Camp Pendleton Marine Base. Marni lives with her parents in a Solana Beach home overlooking the Pacific, about seven miles south of Oceanside.

Dr. DD worked out a payment plan with the bribed record company executive. Tony Zembrano would be receiving the payments in five increments to make sure he held up his end of the agreement at various crucial phases. Dr. DD also took charge of paying veteran keyboardist Max Varner, and rhythm guitarist, Pedgy Peterson.

On June 21st Leandra was with her boyfriend when Dr. DD introduced the band to Max and Pedgy in the reception area of Sterling Studios. Both men were in their 40's and well built. Max was tall with dark hair and a goatee. Pedgy was five inches shorter with hair that was obviously dyed blond.

"I take it Pedgy isn't your given name," commented Chris.

"Frank Zappa hung that one on me just before he died. I was doing some studio work for him and he changed one of his

13

compositions to feature my arpeggios. After that he called me Pedgy and it stuck."

Max said, "You could do a lot worse than getting your handle from a legend. I knew a metal drummer with a big nose who was nicknamed *Dickface* by a roadie who found him passed out drunk in a compromising position with a groupie."

Pedgy replied, "Sure, Dickface Denton. I met him at an Ozzfest backstage party a while back. I think he drank his way out of the business."

Dr. DD said, "Actually, he drank his way into the hereafter three years ago."

"How about if we show you our practice room?" Chris asked.

The walls of the 20' x 15' room were covered in posters, with each of the four band members decorating one wall. The drums were on a riser against an interior wall. Matching floor lamps with copper colored cut glass stood on either side of the risers, compliments of Marni's mom. The lead singer's mic was out front, in the middle. Chris was behind her on the right and Jake on the left.

Dr. DD wore an off-white suit, tailored to minimize the effects of 59 years of rich meals. His perfectly manicured, snow-white beard and full head of slicked-back hair gave him a look that couldn't be missed in the most crowded of concert venues.

He said, "The band wants Max on the far left and a little behind Jake. Pedgy, you're on the far right. That should put you far enough away from Garvey that his pranks won't make you quit on us before the album gets cut."

"Pranks?" Garvey asked with a devilish grin.

Dr. DD rolled his eyes at Garvey and said, "I can't stick around for your first session. I'll just say a few words, and let you get to work.

"You four have never worked with studio musicians before, so I want to clear up a couple of common misconceptions. First, these guys aren't interested in becoming permanent members of your band. They're going to be working with you on a contract basis before you go into the studio. During this time, I want you to develop a synergy and come together as a group. I expect Max and Pedgy to help write themselves into your songs. But these guys understand that they're *your songs*, and you have the final say on all compositions."

"That said, keep in mind that your label insisted on their presence. If you minimize their role, you could very well sabotage the project."

"The other misconception is that contract musicians are the hired help. They're not your gofers. Treat them with the respect they deserve and you'll end up with a better album. Any questions?" After a brief pause he said, "Good." Dr. DD then pivoted on his shiny, black Bali shoes and walked out the door.

Over the next few days the studio musicians successfully blended into the band. Max invited them all to his annual snowboarding weekend at his home in Big Bear, where about 200 musician friends gathered each year for what Max called his "Winter Woodstock." Max also told them about his five kids and how he planned to finance their college tuition by eventually selling off his treasured music memorabilia collection. He went on to note some of the unusual and sometimes outrageous items in his collection.

By the end of the week the band started playing local gigs to help assimilate the new musicians and gage fan reaction to the new material. Leandra arrived during the first set of a Friday night show in downtown San Diego. She was excited to see how the band had progressed since adding the studio musicians. Everyone sounded fine except for the Rock Star, who was a little too fast and a little too loud.

At the break he ran to her table, pulled her to her feet, and anxiously said, "We've got a problem."

Outside the venue he asked, "Did you see this morning's paper?"

"What did I miss?" she replied.

"There was an article about a kid overdosing on meth at a

junior high in Escondido," he said.

"That's what you're so upset about? Last month I was stocking shelves at the pharmacy when I overheard a couple of guys talking. The one asked how the other's daughter was doing in school. He said she was the only one in her class who wasn't on meth. It's been all over the place for a long time. You've got to forget about it"

"That's not the end of it. I was totally freaked out by the time I made it to band practice. Before we got started, I was at my footlocker when Max came over and asked me for an autograph. I grabbed a piece of paper out of the footlocker, thinking it was the back of a piece of sheet music. On my way home I realized it was the invoice I pulled off of one of the pseudoephedrine boxes that I carried into Tabor's garage."

"Why did you save it?" she asked.

"I didn't want to just throw it in a waste basket where somebody would find it, and I knew I couldn't play if it was sitting in my pocket, so I stuck it in my locker. I have the only key to the padlock. I wanted to put that experience behind me so badly that I guess I just forgot about it being there."

Leandra wanted to go off on him for being such an idiot; to tell him she should have broken up with him when his first album bit the big one. But she realized that he would keep his mouth shut and never implicate her as long as his love remained strong.

"We have to get it back," she said.

"I'll ask him for it tomorrow," he said.

"If you do that he's sure to take a close look. Do you think he kept it in the practice room?"

"He doesn't have a locker. He's a major collector and told me he has a den filled with display cases and a basement filled with autographs and memorabilia at his house in Big Bear. I told you about being invited to his snowboarding party next winter."

"Do you think it'll just get stuck in a box somewhere?" Leandra asked.

"I hope so," he replied.

"But if the album takes off he might put it in his den for everybody to see."

"What do you think we should do?"

"Let me think about it. Give me a call tomorrow after your practice, and don't worry. We'll figure it out and everything will be fine," she said.

"I love you, Leandra."

"I love you, too."

Chapter 6

The following morning, Leandra paced around the apartment trying to figure out what to do. She often paced when she was nervous. John had been sleeping on the couch since their mother had converted his room into a storage area shortly after he was sent to prison. Like most sixty-year-old homes with hardwood floors, a cacophony of squeaks followed Leandra as she walked. After fifteen minutes of the horror movie soundtrack, John got off of the couch.

"What the hell is bothering you?"

One of the things she had been thinking about was whether or not to confide in her brother. Prison had definitely changed him. He used to be a carefree guy who paid too much attention to his own entertainment and too little attention to the laws of the land. But he had always been a decent older brother until he ruined her high school experience by going to prison. Since he returned, John acted like he was mad at the world and cared only about getting away with things. He talked about getting over on his parole officer, his boss at the garage, the cop who busted him, the people who mistreated him in prison, and almost everybody who came in contact with him. His personality change was equaled by his physical metamorphosis. His 6'2" frame went from slightly overweight to well defined muscles.

Although he never gave any indication, she couldn't help but wonder if he was planning on getting his hooks into the money that she and her boyfriend were sure to come into in the near future. But all of her plans might fall apart if that invoice was discovered. Leandra proceeded to tell him the whole story.

John said, "I know I made high school extra hard for you when I got busted right after graduation. It was bad enough that our father never came back from that hunting trip when you were in 7th grade. But to start 9th grade with all of those silver spoon assholes reading about your brother in the paper, it had to be hell. I want to make it up to you. Find out where the invoice is and I'll get it back."

The following day, the Rock Star called Max from Leandra's room using the speaker function on her phone. He learned that Max would be taking his family back up to Big Bear for the upcoming 4th of July weekend.

After he departed, Leandra conveyed this information to her brother. John said it was a sure thing that Max would bring the receipt and any other memorabilia he had collected recently to his home for storage.

"How can you be sure he's going to bring it with him?" she asked.

John replied, "Because Max thinks of this stuff as his retirement fund. To him it's money in the bank. Why would he make a trip to the bank and not make his deposit? Tell your boyfriend to get Max's address off of the band contract."

"When will you go in?"

"I'll give it a couple of days in case his wife decides to stay a little longer to do a project. Is the band going back to work right after the 4th?"

"The 4th is on a Sunday. The band is off on the 5th, and start at noon on the 6th."

"I'll wait till the 8th, case the house, and go in the same day."

"Do you want me to help?" Leandra felt her adrenaline surge as she asked.

"No," he said.

"Why not?"

"You're the only one in this family who hasn't screwed up their life yet. As your big brother, I intend to see that it stays that way."

"Who will you get to help you?"

"I'll use Donnie again."

Leandra said, "I wasn't very impressed with him at the

pharmacy. The instant he yelled, 'Fuck you, bitch,' every customer in the store immediately looked at his face."

"Are you kidding? I saw him when he walked out the door. His baseball cap was pulled down so low I was surprised the button on top didn't pop right off. He did fine."

"What's he going to want for his trouble?"

"I'll let him take some of the collectable crap as his end for helping out," he said.

Ten days later Leandra was in her bedroom reading a magazine when she heard a knock on the door. She opened it and John stood in the hallway holding the invoice.

"Could I interest you in an autograph?"

She snatched it out of his hand and gave him a hug. "You're wonderful."

"Don't say I never did anything for you."

"After all of the years I've been doing Mom's job as the crone's cleaning lady, it's about time somebody did something for me. How did it go?"

"Smooth as a Brandy Alexander," he replied. "Nobody home, no neighbors, no witnesses, it couldn't have been better."

"Great," she said with a smile. "I'll sleep a lot easier tonight."

"By the way, you were wrong about Donnie. As soon as we loaded up the truck, I was ready to get the hell out of there. But Donnie remembered to check this year's autograph box and found the pharmacy invoice."

"Maybe I misjudged him."

John produced a cigarette lighter from his pocket. "Shall we put this little matter to rest forever?"

After they walked into the kitchen, Leandra crumpled the invoice, tossed it in the sink, lit it on fire, and let out a big sigh as it burned.

"I'm so glad I'll never have to worry about that damned invoice again."

Chapter 7

I walked into my detective agency on Monday morning with high expectations. My assistant, Jeannine Joshlin, received a call from a professional musician on Friday and scheduled a meeting for 11:00 AM. The fact that I didn't recognize the musician's name meant little, since stage names are a common practice. I spent the weekend wondering if my work on the Doberman's Stub case had landed me a referral to another headliner.

"Did you find anything about our musician on the Internet, Jeannine?"

"I sure did," she said. Her manner conveyed that she was having a good day. "Do you want me to bring my notes into your office?"

"Give me a couple of minutes to check my messages," I replied.

My office looked as neat and clean as humanly possible. That's one advantage to having an assistant who suffers from obsessive-compulsive disorder. I once saw her cleaning the *Do Not Remove Under Penalty of Law* tag under my desk chair.

I punched-up voice mail and heard my girlfriend, Kelly, say: "Jason, I thought of something that might be really fun for our Wednesday night date. Call me at lunchtime." The last time she used the phrase *really fun*, I ended up being one of two guys suffering through a baby shower.

Jeannine walked in with a file folder in her hand. She is tall, blond, and exceptionally beautiful. If not for her neuroses she'd be every guy's dream girl.

"Are you ready for me?" she asked quietly.

"I can't wait. What's his real name? Who does he play with now? Tell me everything."

Jeannine carefully opened the file folder, withdrew a single typed sheet, and read: "*Max Varner is a career studio musician who plays keyboards and occasionally tours with the bands he helps in the studio.*"

"Like Chuck Lavelle, who toured with the Stones and Clapton?"

She ignored my question and continued. "*Mr. Varner played on nearly 200 albums over the course of his career.* When I Googled his name, the best description came from RocknItOnline.com. It said: *Max Varner is a musician's musician. He's an excellent keyboard player with a knack for making fast friends and quickly adapting to a wide range of musical stylings. If your band is about to go into the studio and you need a keyboard player who sounds like he's been playing with you for years, Max is your guy.*" Looking up from her report Jeannine asked, "Does that sound right to you?"

"Unfortunately, yes. He's a career backup musician who never broke out with his own band. I guess we'll find out why in a few minutes."

At precisely 11:00 AM Jeannine showed Max and his wife, Ellen, into my office. Ellen carried a sleeping two-year old boy. I thought that Max looked like Dave Matthews with a goatee.

I asked, "What brings you in to see me today, Max?"

"This," Max said, handing me a ten-day-old copy of the Big Bear Gazette with the headline: *Resident Musician's Home Burglarized.* The sub-heading read: *$2.3M Music Memorabilia Collection Stolen.*

I asked myself how a career studio musician could afford a $2.3 million dollar collection of anything? Max and Ellen were perfectly content to sit and watch me read the entire article.

"It must have been one amazing collection to be worth that much money."

"I realized pretty early on in my career that I wasn't going to be a star. By the age of 25, I came to grips with that reality, but I still had a burning love for music."

Ellen said, "He was going to quit the business for his family's sake, but I wouldn't let him do it. I knew it would be a struggle, but I also knew that an important part of Max would die if he stopped doing what he loves."

"Most studio musicians don't earn much money, and Ellen and I wanted a big family," Max said.

"We have five kids," she added.

"So anyway, just when I was about to move my keyboards into the garage, I got a call to perform on an album for a major label. The band was great, and I got paid well to do a tour. But I realized after talking to those guys that I needed to be putting money away for my kids' future. When I got back to Southern California, I drove straight to my agent's house to thank him for all of his help and to tell him I was calling it quits."

Ellen said, "He knew that if he went home I'd just try to cheer him up and talk him out of it, especially since he just earned almost $8,000 in a month."

"My agent insisted we go to the neighborhood pub to talk things out, and I agreed. His car was in the shop, so we took mine. He mentioned the incredible amount of clutter all over the back seat. I told him that at least I had a lot of great souvenirs to remember my time in the music business."

"Luckily, Gary was a serious collector and recognized the value of Max's treasures," Ellen stated.

"We were also lucky Gary's an honest man. He could have asked for everything I had in that car as a way of thanking him, and I would have walked the whole collection into his garage on the spot."

"So, you figured a way to build up a nest egg and keep working as a musician," I offered.

"Exactly," Max said. "While most people collect autographs and autographed guitars, I also collect off-beat stuff like chipped cymbals, old wah-wah pedals, stage-worn costumes, hair extensions, and things like that."

"Did you get documentation?" I asked.

"Letters of authenticity and videos of musicians autographing their instruments and other memorabilia," Ellen said with a sparkle in her eye. "It's a very unique collection."

Max reddened and said, "I had a codpiece, autographed boxers, a pointy bra worn by you-know-who, and other weird stuff like that."

"Wow!" I exclaimed. "Did you have many items from major stars?"

"Hell yes," he said. "I got a ton of equipment and apparel from my studio gigs. The stars realize that I don't get any royalties from their recordings and a lot of them heard about how I collect these things to send my kids to college. Besides, most of the big stars get that stuff for free."

"But the majority of your career has been in the studio," I clarified.

"It has. But I tend to make friends quickly and most of them know what I'm doing. So they save me lots of goodies."

"We have a weekend-long snowboarding party every year and invite all of our friends. Last year we had over 200 people show up," Ellen said.

"They treat it like my birthday and give me memorabilia presents," he added.

"You also got lots of good stuff from guys on their way up," she stated.

"We kept our best stuff in display cases in the Rock Room of our house. The crooks took everything in that room and some of the boxes full of autographs and autographed pictures in the basement," Max said, then stared at his shoes.

"Do you have a burglar alarm?"

Ellen replied, "We do, but it wasn't on that day."

"Why not?"

"Max has been playing with The Tactile Tattoo out of Oceanside. He's been working with them in their practice room before going into the studio. Our family tries to spend as much time together as we can, so we took a summer rental in Oceanside. Our oldest son, Carl, has been staying in Big Bear to take summer school classes at the community college in San Bernardino. He forgot to turn it on."

"I told her Carl was too young to stay by himself for the whole summer, but she said it would help him grow into a man."

I could sense this was a sore subject and didn't want them

getting sidetracked. "I thought studio musicians usually spent just a few hours with a band before recording."

"The songs weren't finished and none of them had ever written for keyboards before. I've known the band's manager, Dr. DD, for quite a while. He told me that he wanted me to build some rapport with the band, and make sure I had a lot of input on writing myself in."

"Was the collection insured?"

"That's an even sadder story," Max replied. "We were able to afford the down payment on our house by selling a piece of the collection five years ago. I liked the memorabilia dealer we worked with, so a couple of months ago I hired him to appraise the collection. He came out just before the Oceanside gig started and spent three days doing a complete inventory of the collection, including every autograph."

"There were over 2000 autographs," Ellen said, looking at the baby as he started to fuss.

Max said, "He came up with an appraised value of $2.3 million about three weeks before we got hit."

"We were in the process of shopping insurance companies when they cleaned us out." A teardrop formed in the corner of her eye, and her son reacted to his mother's unsteady voice by wailing. Ellen stood up and said, "I'll take him outside till he settles down."

"Ellen said, 'they.' What makes her think there was more than one burglar?"

Max replied, "The cops found two sets of footprints where they loaded their vehicle. The chief thinks it was a rental truck or a large van based on the tire tracks."

"Did he say anything else worth noting?"

"I'm sure he did, but I was so upset at the time that I don't recall the details."

"How old is Carl?" I asked.

"He turned 19 in March."

"Is there any chance one of his friends had something to do with this?"

"I hope he's a better judge of character than that. But at his age you sometimes learn by your mistakes. He's just starting to break away from the nest. Carl's trying hard to be his own man, and I'm sure his friends are doing the same thing. When he was in high school, and I knew the parents of all of his friends, I would have said no to your question right away. But now that he's going to school in San Bernardino, I don't know most of his new friends."

"Is he a musician like his old man?"

Max said, with a touch of sadness in his voice, "He can't play a lick. Back in the days when he should have been learning an instrument, I was shuffling around doing tours, hoping I'd get discovered. Ellen thinks Carl sees music as robbing him of a father. I just think some people take to it and some don't."

We concluded our meeting by agreeing on my rates. "Big Bear is three hours away. The burglars could have gone in any direction. Why did you come to me?"

Max replied, "Three reasons. First, I'm working in San Diego County, so it's convenient for me to work with a local. Second, my greatest fear is that my collection will cross the Mexican border and I'll never see it again. I figured, since your county is so close, you might have a contact with the border crossing cops and tell them to keep an eye out. And third, I did a little studio work at Cerise Records and read about you solving the murder that happened there last year. I'm hoping you'll be able to help me, too."

When we walked into the waiting room we saw Jeannine stooping behind the toddler, picking up bits of Animal Crackers while Ellen pleasantly chatted with her. I could see why Max and Ellen were well-liked, and wished I could have assured them that the collection would be returned. But in this case, their popularity could very well be a curse. It meant that the suspect list started with the 200 attendees from last year's party, and also included past guests, local friends, a certain memorabilia dealer, and the student population of a community college.

"I'll keep you posted on any significant developments," I said.

Chapter 8

I made it out of the foothills by 10:00 AM on Tuesday and started up the mountain toward Big Bear. There are two routes off of Interstate 10 leading away from the coast. One road is shorter, but incredibly twisty. The other is longer, but decidedly safer. Until I started my detective internship at age 25, I played in a rock band called Tsunami Rush. I made several trips to Big Bear during the snowboarding season to play the ski lodges and area clubs. The band always took the long route, so I decided to try the shortcut since it was summer.

As I stress-tested my Acura RXS through the pine covered mountains, I wondered what kind of reception I would receive at the Big Bear police station. Max called last night and left a message that I could stop by the stationhouse any time before noon. You never know what you are going to find at a small town police station. Sometimes you get Andy of Mayberry and sometimes you get Andy Hitler.

Noticing the slow pace and tranquility as I made my way through the adjacent town of Big Bear Lake, I got the feeling I was missing something special by living in the city. I thought about a psychology class I took at UCSD. The professor talked about how animal studies consistently demonstrated that overcrowding caused several of the animals to develop severe psychological problems. Small town people always seemed more relaxed and open. Walking through the front door of the police station, I was yearning for a piece of Utopia.

The desk sergeant asked, "What do *you* want?" in a very abrupt manner.

"I'm here to see Chief Carson. My name is Jason Duffy." Schnell, Andy.

"Stay where you are. I'll find out if *he* wants to see *you*."

A minute later the sergeant hung up the phone, pointed at a

single door to the left side of the front desk, and bellowed, "Go straight through that door."

The chief was in his mid-fifties with salt and pepper hair, and a build that suggested he had been holding a desk job for several years. "You must be Jason Duffy. I'm Chief Carson. Max called me yesterday after he hired you. He needs all the help he can get finding that collection before it gets fenced."

"I'm glad you feel that way. A lot of policemen don't care to collaborate with private investigators."

"There's only so much I can do for him from here. There are no music memorabilia dealers in Big Bear, not even a pawnshop. Whoever stole that collection is going to try to move it in a big city."

"I'm sure you're right. Let's just hope whoever did it headed west. Any chance it was a local?"

"It's possible, but I don't think so. Max and Ellen have done a lot for the community in the five years they've been here. People know them, and I'm sure many have been entertained at their home," he said. "But they also have a huge party every year for friends from the music business - hundreds of them. I'm afraid our list of suspects is immense. That's one of the reasons I'm glad you're helping out. I can check the local B&E suspects, but I'll need your help with the party people."

"Do any of the B&E suspects look promising?"

"I know most of them pretty well. It's gotten to the point where I can walk onto a crime scene and say, 'this was the work of the Johnson brothers,' or 'Larry the tweaker was in this room.' The mug book ain't that thick in this neck of the woods."

"Any chance it could have been done by kids?"

"I don't think so. Max and Ellen have a well-stocked bar. That would have been the first thing to go if the perps were kids," said the chief.

"I understand their son, Carl, forgot to turn on the alarm. Could he have been in on it, or maybe one of his friends from the college?"

"I've known Carl since the family moved here. He's a good

29

kid. He's into cars and snowboarding. He's worked at Sam Weller's gas station since he was 16. I've had at least one conversation with the boy every week for the last four years. If my daughter wanted to date him, she'd have my blessing."

"I guess that's about as strong an endorsement as a dad can give."

"Wanna take a look at the scene of the crime?"

"Definitely."

As we exited, the desk sergeant asked, "Is the PI behaving himself, Chief?"

"We're going out to the Varner house. Don't call unless it's an emergency," the chief replied. When we got outside he said, "Don't let Reid bother you. During ski season, when we have a jail full of young men drunk on beer and testosterone, it's very handy having an asshole on the team."

I decided at that moment that I was going to enjoy working with Chief Carson, and would go along with his gut feeling about Carl. We headed toward Bear Mountain, one of two ski lodges in town. About a mile from the lodge we turned onto a dirt road and made our way past two A-frame homes before turning into the driveway of a well-maintained, ranch-style home.

"Let's go inside first," he said.

Chief Carson punched in the security code. "Max called me with the code this morning." He led the way through the living room into a large den toward the back of the house. "This is Max's version of the Hard Rock Cafe."

I entered a room filled with empty display cases and track lights aimed at nothing. Max wasn't exaggerating when he said the room was cleaned out. The burglars took everything.

"I wish I had a picture of what it looked like before the break-in."

"Ask Ellen, she's got a bunch. Max has a great sense of humor. He used the track lights to illuminate pieces of equipment that were mounted in frames with funny captions he thought up. Every few months he'd feature different pieces under the track lights, all with captions, and one was funnier than the next."

The chief led us into the basement where six file boxes sat on shelves. "These are all autographs-only files. All of the autographed-picture files are gone."

I said, "Max told me they took this year's autographs-only box as well."

"They realized that when they got outside."

"What do you mean?"

"We found a bunch of the autographs in the lawn."

I finished snooping around the basement. "Can we take a look at where you found them?"

When we got outside, Chief Carson showed me where the vehicle tracks were located and where they found the autographs strewn about. I walked a circle around the area the chief had pointed out. Not far from the driveway, the west side of the lot was bordered by a white picket fence. This seemed unusual, since the fence did not extend all the way around the perimeter. When we got closer, I realized the fence was there due to a significant drop-off of about fifty feet to the adjacent lot. I stared out at the pines below, trying to think if I was missing anything that would cause me to make another six-hour round trip, when my eyes rested on an odd looking shadow in one of the pine trees. I changed positions a couple of times to get different angles, but the color of the shadow kept bothering me.

"What is it?" asked Chief Carson.

"I'm not sure."

I pointed out what had caught my eye. The chief spotted it, walked back into Max's house, and emerged with a fishing pole. Demonstrating some very deft casting skills, he reeled in the suspicious shadow ten minutes later. It turned out to be two black ski masks tied together.

"Could they be from the last ski season?" I asked.

"These are new."

"It looks like the burglary would have been a robbery if Carl had been home."

"Carl's lucky to be alive," said the chief.

Twenty minutes later we pulled into the parking lot of the police station. Chief Carson asked, "How about having some lunch before heading down the mountain?"

"I'm in. Where should we go?"

"Mario's, across the street, is always good. Are you up for Italian?"

"Let's do it."

As we walked to a far table, most of the patrons said hello or nodded at the chief. We were seated in a somewhat isolated nook, affording as much privacy as possible within the confines of the room.

After we placed our orders I asked, "Have you had any robbers wear ski masks this year?"

"We've had a few gas station and convenience store stick-ups. One perp wore a ski mask, but he's been incarcerated since April."

"Do any stores in Big Bear sell ski masks in the off season?"

"Probably about four in Big Bear Lake and six in Big Bear City," he stated. "I'll check them out. Do you really think they would've waited to get up here before buying their masks?"

"Not many California stores carry them in mid-summer."

"Then it's worth the time to ask a few questions," he said.

"How about the gas stations? It's a long run up here. I'm sure trucks and vans burn a lot of gas making the climb to 7500 feet."

"I talked to all of the gas station attendants on duty that day, and had them send me a list of credit card purchases. We don't get many visitors over the summer. If they bought gas here, it was a cash transaction."

I scanned the room and noted a young man with a shaved head, seated alone at a table for two, staring at us. Nodding in his direction I said, "Somebody seems pretty interested in our conversation."

"If you were here looking for an ax murderer I'd introduce you."

I said, "Armed robbery can be tough on the nerves. Do you think it's worth checking with the bartenders and liquor store clerks to see if any strangers stopped by?"

"You wouldn't think they'd be that careless. But I could spend a week talking about the total morons I've busted over the years. I'll let you know how it goes," he said. I paid the bill and parted company in the parking lot of the stationhouse.

The interior of the Acura was at least 120 degrees, so I rolled down the windows and cranked the air conditioning to full blast. I popped a Doberman's Stub CD into the sound system and turned it up so it could be heard over the air conditioner. I cruised about five miles before starting down the giant slalom course known as Route 18. When I began my descent down the mountain, the shiny black pickup truck that had been six car lengths behind me was now right on my bumper. I looked in the rear view mirror and saw the skinhead from Mario's shaking his fist.

Transfixed by this unexpected development, I inadvertently allowed my speed to build to ten miles an hour past what was reasonable for a winding road that is totally devoid of guard rails. I realized there was no way I could touch my brakes without having the pickup plow into the back of the RXS. As I glanced to my right to look at the severity of the drop-off, the skinhead leaned on his horn, snapping my attention back to the maniacal expression on his face.

I glanced again and saw at least a thousand-foot drop-off. I looked in the rear view mirror and the black pickup was gone. A moment later the truck roared out of my blind spot and cut sharply in front of me before completing the pass. Instinctively, I hit the brakes and swerved to my right. The RSX left the pavement and, upon hitting gravel, went into a double 360 spin. Then the car stopped. My brain wasn't processing what had happened. I was expecting to see my life flash before me en route to meeting my maker. But instead I was sitting in the middle of a landing the size of a small parking lot, rimmed by large boulders.

I barely had time to come to the realization that I was in a *turn-out,* where trucks in low gear pull over to allow faster vehicles to pass, when I saw the skinhead roaring directly at me. I reached for my snub-nosed .38. The skinhead cut his wheels hard so that the driver's side of the truck skid to within a few feet of my window.

Just as I was about to aim and fire, the skinhead screamed, "Doberman sucks!" Then he spewed gravel 50 feet and roared back up the hill.

I got out of the Acura, walked to the back of his car, and pulled the Doberman's Stub bumper sticker off in one mighty yank. Now that I knew how the psychotic population felt about the group, I thought it wise to remove the target. My friend Michael gave it to me shortly after becoming a member of the band. I was never a bumper sticker kind of guy, and felt the stickerless look was more conducive to undercover operations.

Chapter 9

I barely crossed the threshold of my agency on Wednesday morning when Jeannine shot out of her chair holding a pink message. "Max Varner wants you to call the minute you get in the door."

"What's going on?"

"Somebody tried selling part of the collection to a vintage guitar dealer here in San Diego."

I had Max on the phone in two minutes. "I hear we have a lead on the collection."

"It's gonna be all over the state in no time. I'll never see it again."

"Actually, this could be a break for us. If they had a contact on the black market the collection would simply disappear. Now we know they have to expose themselves and take chances if they want to cash in. That will help us tremendously."

"Do you really think so, or are you just trying to make me feel better?"

"What's the name of the dealer?" I asked.

"Callison's Vintage Guitars & Memorabilia, on 7th Avenue."

"Who did you talk to?"

"Detective Darden. He told me not to go over there."

"I'll drop by and see what I can find out."

An hour later I walked into Callison's. "Are you with the police, or the media?" asked the owner, who had a squint that Popeye would envy.

"Neither," I replied, handing him a business card. "I work for the owner of the collection." This got his attention.

"Those were some impressive items. Are you sure they're authentic?"

"Didn't the police tell you? The owner is a musician who worked with all of those guitar owners," I said, knowing that any dealer would love a connection in the business.

"Who is it?"

"I can't tell you without his consent, but I'm sure he would be very grateful for your cooperation. Would you please tell me what happened?"

Mr. Callison was in his late sixties, and in no hurry to rush into the story. "How grateful?"

"I guarantee you he'll make a personal appearance, and sign any item here in the store. I wouldn't be surprised if he threw in a big bonus if your information aids in the recovery of his collection."

Mr. Callison adjusted his wire-rimmed glasses and moved slowly to his desk. He removed a pad and pen, handed them to me and said, "Write it down and sign it."

"No problem," I replied. The old man would probably be up half of the night hoping he would be meeting a future member of the Rock & Roll Hall of Fame.

I handed my promissory note to the proprietor. "Tell me what happened."

Callison gave my signature a hard squint. "Yesterday afternoon, around three o'clock, a man walked into my store with a large duffel bag, and asked if I was a buyer as well as a seller. I said yes, and he opened the bag. Inside was three guitars autographed by well-known musicians, and a DVD of each signing."

"Did he have anything else in the duffel bag besides the guitars?"

"He also had a couple of autographed bathrobes from some hotel and a pair of autographed panties that were so tiny I couldn't make out the signature with my magnifying glass." Callison's face flushed.

"I take it those are some pretty unusual items for your store."

"I read about the bathrobes and undergarments about two weeks ago when Detective Darden sent a fax telling me to be on the lookout for a long list of items."

"And the panties stood out because they were so unusual?" I asked.

"The bathrobes rang a bell, and I knew I was looking at part of the stolen collection."

"What did you do?"

"I told him his collection was very valuable and I would have to call a potential buyer before I could commit that kind of money."

"What did he say?"

"He seemed a little suspicious, but he was also pleased that I recognized the collection's value. I was hoping his greed would keep him around while the cops made their way over here."

"What spooked him?" I asked.

"The only thing I can figure is that I'm a little hard of hearing and my friends tell me I tend to speak louder than I need to, especially when I'm nervous."

"So, you think he overheard your conversation with the police?"

"That had to be it. By the time I got off of the phone he was gone."

"What did he look like?"

"He was white, mid- to late twenties, about six feet tall, and in good shape."

"Is it possible he was a musician?"

"It's possible, but I didn't recognize him. I've been looking at guitar and music magazines for years and I still have a pretty good memory," he said.

"Could he have been from a new group?"

"I guess it's possible. But I got the feeling while he was emptying his duffel bag that the collection meant nothing to him. I have a hard time believing a guy who spends years learning an instrument would be so indifferent to the treasures he just dumped on my counter."

"I wish I could agree with you. But I've read too many interviews with musicians who have no concept of the history of the music business or the people who paved the way for them to make millions," I said.

"Sadly, I know you're right."

"Did the cops have you go through the mug books?"

"That's one collection I hope I never have to look at again."

"Anybody look familiar?"

"I couldn't be sure. My glasses are set to reading length. Everything outside of two feet looks fuzzy," he said. "I keep my driving glasses in my car."

"Anything distinctive about his voice, the things he said, or the way he said them?"

"He was a smoker. I could smell it on him. I didn't tell that to the cops, do you think it's important?"

"If you talk with Detective Darden again, let him know. Anything else?"

"If I think of anything I'll give you a call," he said. "When can I expect to hear from your client?"

"Would you rather I ask him to call you soon, or do you want to wait and see if your information helps lead to an arrest?"

"The sooner the better," he replied, rubbing his palms together.

At 5:00 PM I picked Kelly up at her condo for our weekly Wednesday night date. The *fun* thing she wanted to do was to visit friends who recently set up a glassblowing studio in an annex built onto their detached garage. I agreed that it might be fun, but told her about the case and that I needed to attend the Tactile Tattoo concert at a venue an hour outside of San Diego. Reluctantly, she agreed to postpone the glassblowing outing, hopefully to a month when standing next to a 2000-degree oven would be less oppressive.

We picked up our tickets at the *Will Call* window and met Ellen Varner in the *Family & Friends* balcony box to the right of the stage, shortly before the first song. The box held two tables. We were at the front table, and would not have to worry about being overheard by the band girlfriends, seated behind us, when we got into the topic of band mates who might be suspects.

"Is Max OK?" I asked. "He sounded pretty stressed when I talked with him yesterday."

"He was hoping the burglars would sit on the collection long enough for them to be caught."

"I went to Big Bear yesterday and took a look around with Chief Carson."

"Did you find any clues?"

"I got a very strong feeling that whoever did it knew exactly what to look for. That means it was probably a neighbor, a musician, a friend of one of the kids, or someone who attended one of your annual parties."

"Oh my," she said. "It's hard to imagine any of those people being involved."

"Chief Carson thinks your son is a great kid, and feels most of his friends are kids from high school. Does Carl have any friends from San Bernardino who strike you as capable of doing this?"

"I don't think so. The chief is right. Carl's a good boy, and he still associates with the friends he had in high school. Same with our other kids," she said defensively.

To settle Ellen down I drew Kelly into the conversation, and focused on the show when the band started. After the first set, the lead singer picked up a piece of sheet music from a stool and led the band backstage.

I said, "Max seems to be a very likeable guy, but bands have squabbles all of the time. Sometimes musicians work on projects, or play gigs, and get stiffed on the pay. Nobody works in this business without making a few enemies along the way. Can you think of anyone who had a problem with Max?"

"Max played in a few bands when he was in his late teens and early twenties. You're right. Bands have infighting and break up all of the time. Sure there were some hard feelings along the way," she said. "But after our second child was born, Max got a chance to do some studio work, and everybody loved how quickly he could adapt to all kinds of music. He could've had his pick of bands, but chose to go in a direction

39

that offered a steady paycheck as a contract musician."

"So, no potential enemies come to mind?"

She replied, "There was a young guitarist with a big drug problem that Max got bumped from a steakhouse commercial. He filed a complaint with the union, and went off on Max pretty hard while clearing out of the studio."

"Do you think he could be a possibility?"

"I don't think so. I understand he got into rehab and is now doing all right with a solo career in New York."

"Can you think of anyone who might still be holding a grudge?"

"Now that you mention it, there's a guy who hates Max with a passion."

"What happened?" Kelly chimed in.

"A couple of years ago, Max did a tour with a band that had just cut their first album. The leader was a drummer named Jimmy Marcello, who was trying to save money on the tour by using his cousin to hook up the electrical and run the soundboard.

"The CD went to the top of the charts when the president's daughter told a White House reporter that they were her favorite band. A gig at the Kennedy Center in D.C. was added to the tour. Along with the daughter, the president and first lady were also in attendance. Jimmy had his cousin add some sound enhancement electronics to Max's keyboard and organ. He told Max he was going to announce the dignitaries before the first song by saying 'I'd like to welcome the president and his continued support of our band, as well as the first lady, on this very special night.' Jimmy told Max to start playing *Hail to the Chief* when he said the word 'continued.' But when Max hit the first note, the whole sound system blew out, as a stunned crowd just heard Jimmy say, 'I'd like to welcome the president and his cont–'"

"I saw that on CNN at least 20 times," I said.

"The tour was immediately cancelled. CDs were pulled from shelves at all of the major retailers, and the band called it quits a few weeks after the incident when their music was banned on most FM channels."

"Jimmy blamed Max?" I asked.

"Jimmy tackled Max backstage and started swinging. Max said it took six security guards and a Secret Service agent with a pistol to get Jimmy off of him and out of the Kennedy Center."

"Has he ever threatened Max since then?"

"For about three months after the incident he called and sent letters saying that Max ruined his life. I can't believe I didn't think of him before this."

"When is the last time you heard from him?"

"The calls lasted about three months. We thought he got over it and moved on."

"Maybe he adopted the adage: *Don't get mad, get even.* Are you sure he got out of the music business?"

Ellen said, "There were quite a few reporters backstage who saw Jimmy go nuts on Max. Between the perceived insult to the first lady and the unwarranted attack on Max, Jimmy was blackballed."

"Any idea where he is now?"

"Max has a friend in the musicians' union front office. I'm sure he could get you Jimmy's last address."

"Did Jimmy know about the collection?"

Ellen sat silently, looking up and to her left. After a minute she said, "I remember Max telling me he once said, 'You're here to get autographs, I'm here to re-write rock & roll history.' I'm sure he knew."

When the show was over I introduced Max to Kelly, and mentioned the Jimmy Marcello incident. "I can't believe I didn't think of him right off the bat. Not only does that guy hate me, he told me I owed him for ruining his life. I'll call my friend at the union first thing in the morning and try to get his address."

"Find out if he had any friends or relatives on his insurance form who might know where he is now," I said.

"Will do," said Max, and he waved goodbye.

During the ride home Kelly said, "Something interesting

41

happened while you were at the snack bar."

"What's that?"

"You saw the band girlfriends sitting at the next table, right?" she asked.

"I thought I was pretty discreet. I only glanced when you were turned away. You know how I value my shin skin."

"Very funny," Kelly deadpanned. "Anyway, when the band took a break they all went over to that table, including Marni, the lead singer. After the hugs and kisses, the boys started talking shop, and the strawberry blond gave Marni a little nod. She then discreetly passed her a paper that was folded in her hand."

"Did you see what was on it?"

"I did. She walked around our table and, with her back to her band mates, she unfolded it. I think it was a sexy female model in a Calvin Klein ad."

"Interesting," I said.

Chapter 10

I have been known to arrive late for work on mornings after date night with Kelly. During the school year, when Kelly is teaching second grade, I usually roll in a few minutes after 9:00. When she's on summer vacation, I rarely make it to the office before 10:00. Today was no exception. By the time I arrived, Jeannine had placed color-coded pushpins in a giant map of San Diego that hung on a corkboard in my office. Each pushpin held a small circular sticky with a number printed on it. There appeared to be 27 in all. Neatly pinned to the corner of the map was a typed legend, noting the names of collectibles and memorabilia dealers, musical instrument shops, and eBay consignment companies.

Jeannine was quite excited about her project. "What do you think?"

"It's terrific, Jeannine." In spite of her many obsessions and compulsions she is very bright and beginning to think like a detective. "I take it we're contacting the dealers nearest to Callison's to see if the crooks will try again."

"All but three have fax numbers. I thought you might want to send them a memo," she said, handing me a piece of paper. "I took the liberty of typing up a little general information flyer. What do you think?"

"It's a good idea, but let's add that the collector is a professional musician, and offer a four-hour personal appearance for any dealer who provides information that leads to the return of the collection."

"Ooh! I like that. Should I put Max's name on the flyer?" she asked.

"Not if we actually want any phone calls. Let me take a look at it before you send it out."

I called Max and asked him what he learned about Jimmy

Marcello. Fortunately, Jimmy continued his medical benefits through a union program until his new employer covered him. He went to work for a welding shop in Long Beach. I took down the address and was on my way, hoping to arrive before Jimmy went to lunch.

No such luck. Traffic was painfully slow and I didn't get into Long Beach until 12:30 PM. I found the welding shop, noted the *Closed till 1:00* sign on the door, and located a deli about a half-mile down the road. By the time I returned, all welding operations appeared to be at full speed. I asked a huge guy, who bore an eerie resemblance to Uncle Fester of the Adams Family, where I could find Jimmy Marcello. Without speaking, Fester nodded at a body builder who was clamping a piece of metal into a vise.

"Jimmy, I'm Jason Duffy. An old friend of yours got robbed, and I'm here to see if you know anything about it."

"Are you a cop?"

I flipped my credentials at him and said, "Private investigator."

"Not interested," he said, and went back to work.

"We can talk about it here and get it over with in five minutes, or I can call the detective in charge of the case, and he'll give you a ride to his stationhouse in San Diego. We can do it fast or we can make a day of it – your choice, Jimmy."

"Who got robbed?" he asked.

"Max Varner."

Jimmy got very agitated and loud. "That motherfucker! He ruined my life! If I was the one doing the robbing there'd be a homicide detective here instead of you!"

"Calm down, Jimmy. I just want to ask you a few questions."

Several of Jimmy's co-workers formed a circle around us and waited to see what would happen.

"Don't tell me to calm down! You're helping the guy that killed my chance at fame and big money! You're helping the guy that made me a welder instead of a legend!"

"C'mon Jimmy. All he did was start to play *Hail to the*

44

Chief on cue. You're the one who dropped a C-bomb on the first lady."

The co-workers roared with laughter. Jimmy shook off his work gloves and charged like a wild animal. We crashed hard on the concrete floor and I was briefly stunned when my head struck the base of a well-anchored workbench. I tried struggling to my feet, but before I could get all the way up, Jimmy locked me in a sleeper hold that completely cut off my air supply. A couple of large, dark spots clouded my vision and I felt my arms lose their grip on Jimmy. As I was about to pass out, I heard a loud metal clank and a thud. The next thing I knew I was falling to the floor. I squeezed my eyes shut tight. When I opened them, Jimmy Marcello was lying next to me unconscious.

I looked up and saw Uncle Fester holding a gigantic wrench. Addressing his fellow workers he said, "Ain't nobody gettin' killed around here as long as I'm foreman. Now get back to work."

"Thanks," I said, and gingerly struggled to my feet.

"You can thank me by not pressing charges," he replied. "Jimmy's a freakin' lunatic, but he's also the most productive guy in the shop. He works at 100% all day long and hasn't missed a day since he started."

"What about two weeks ago? Has he taken any vacation time?"

"He's the first one here in the morning and the last to leave at night. Even though we give an hour for lunch, he takes about 15 minutes, and only breaks to piss."

"How long has he worked here?"

Fester replied, "About a year, maybe a year and a half."

"No vacations?"

"No vacations, no absences, no doctor's appointments, no taking kids to the orthodontist, no chiropractic appointments, and none of any of the other bullshit excuses I get from most of these other guys," he said, raising his voice for their benefit.

"Thanks. You saved my life," I said, and extended my hand.

Fester squeezed it a bit too hard. "It's been a pleasure. Now

45

do me one more favor and never come back."

"You got it, big guy."

I was pleased to see Max had faxed the guest list for the past three snowboarding parties when I returned to the office. Eliminating duplicate names from one year to the next, there were a mere 252 suspects to clear.

Kelly called around 4:00. "How do you feel about rockin' it again tonight?"

"Babe, you wore me out last night. I had all I could do to drag myself to the office this morning."

"I'm not talking about that," she said. "I got a call from Ellen Varner this afternoon, and she wants to meet at another gig tonight. She thought of something she should have told you from the start."

I still had a headache from the sleeper hold, in spite of the four aspirins I took three hours ago. "I hope you gave her the Alexander Graham Bell lesson plan."

"Ellen's a very visual person. Didn't you see the way she held eye contact with you the whole time you were talking at the show last night? She didn't glance at the stage once while you were speaking," she said.

"She was being polite."

"She's scared, and feeling violated, and very worried about Max. She needs us there tonight, Jason."

I didn't want to appear insensitive, but I also didn't want to tell her about how I got crushed by Jimmy the Human Vise.

"Why don't we get together with them on Saturday night?"

"We're having dinner at your parents' house on Saturday night. Didn't I tell you?" she asked.

"My mother calls you. My client calls you. Maybe I should get a cell phone. Wait a minute – I have one! What's wrong with this picture?"

"Give me a break. I told her we'd be there tonight. The show is at a casino on the outskirts of Oceanside. It's half the distance we traveled last night. Are you going with me or do I have to sit next to one of those hard-body Marines from Camp

Pendleton?" she asked, with just the right touch of tongue-in-cheek.

For the trip to Oceanside I selected a quiet Jack Johnson CD instead of my usual fare, to keep my head from throbbing. She wanted to talk about my resistance to her setting up a get-together with my mother. Kelly's the only non-alcoholic member of a family of five, and is determined to establish and maintain normalcy in her life. I did my best to let her vent quietly while I nursed my aching head.

Ellen greeted Kelly with a hug and gave my forearm a squeeze. If she had given me a neck hug I might have passed out. We were seated at a table in front of the stage and the band girlfriends were at a table to our right. I was glad we were about to hear an emo band instead of hard rock or metal. But the mere thought of amplified music made me flash on the moment my skull connected with the workbench.

"Ellen, is there a place where we can sit down and grab a bite to eat? I'm starving," I lied.

"There's a barbecue on the other side of the poker tables. Let's go," she said, and led the way. Conversation was minimal until we were all seated in front of large plates of gooey beef ribs.

I said "Kelly told me you remembered something that might be significant."

"Before we get into that, did you find out anything about Jimmy Marcello?"

"I found out he does hate Max. He does think Max ruined his life. But he has an alibi for the day of the burglary." I hoped I wouldn't have to elaborate.

Kelly appeared to be formulating a follow-up question, but I stripped off half a rib with my teeth, rendering myself incommunicado. Unfortunately, chewing hurt almost as much as talking.

Ellen said, "When we told you about the dealer who came to our house to assess the collection, what Max didn't tell you is that he was out of town at the time, and I was home alone with the kids. I'm usually not skittish about having workmen around when Max isn't there, but this guy made me feel very uncomfortable."

"What did he do to make you feel that way?" I asked.

"It wasn't anything he said or did. I can't put my finger on it, he just . . ."

"Creeped you out?" Kelly offered.

"I guess so. He looked normal. But I had to get out of there. Max agreed that I could take the kids to Oceanside and start looking for a summer rental."

"When did you leave?" I asked.

"First thing in the morning, the second day he was in town."

"Who let him in the house?" I asked.

"Max gave him a key and the alarm code. He didn't want Graham to think we didn't trust him."

"You barely knew him," Kelly said.

"Max felt that Graham made it possible for us to buy our home by doing a good job selling part of the collection at a time when we only had a few weeks to come up with our down payment. He was also planning on using him to eventually sell off the rest of the collection to finance college for the kids, and our retirement years. I guess he wanted to show faith and confidence in him."

"Did you get the key back and change the code after Graham left?" I asked.

"We got the key back, but Max is superstitious. He had just landed a nice contract with The Tactile Tattoo that included a tour after the CD is released. He was afraid that if he changed the code he would change his luck."

We got up from the table and tossed our bone collection into a trash barrel. "Is it possible Carl actually armed the alarm and Graham turned it off?" I asked.

"Chief Carson says no. The alarm wasn't armed, but Graham couldn't have known that."

"What's Graham's last name?"

"Weston," Ellen replied. "Max has been a wreck ever since this happened. Carl's in community college by choice. He was accepted at USC and wants to go there for his junior and senior years. Next year Kayla will be starting college. It would mean the world to us if you could get the collection back."

Kelly gave Ellen's hand a squeeze and said, "Don't worry, Ellen. If it's possible, Jason will do it."

I loved spending time with Kelly, but there are some things you just shouldn't promise a client.

Chapter 11

I called Detective Darden on Friday morning and introduced myself. "Max Varner hired me to help recover his collection."

"I guess this means I can take a long weekend." Darden's voice was an octave higher than any cop I had ever heard.

"I was hoping we could help each other out."

"Duffy, I have a load of cases and no time to play games with a PI."

"I completely understand. That's where I can help. I'll be spending all of my time on this case. Instead of spending your valuable time chasing down the same leads I just checked out, why not share some information and save some legwork?"

"Because I know how these trades work. I provide all of the information, and you tell your client what I told you, to look like you're actually earning your fee. No thanks."

"What if I could prove to you that I can hold up my end?"

"OK, Duffy. Tell me something I don't know that will actually save me time."

"Earlier this week, I visited the crime scene in Big Bear and found two black ski masks in a tree on an adjacent property. We're not looking for a couple of burglars we're looking for armed robbers. The victims just got lucky that no one was home."

"Those masks were probably left over from one of Varner's ski parties."

"Chief Carson of Big Bear PD said they were brand new and couldn't have been in the tree more than a couple of weeks."

"You showed this to the chief?"

"Was Callison the only dealer contacted?"

Darden replied, "There was another one before Callison - The Concert Collector, in Mission Valley. The perp also tried selling to a private collector in Del Mar since his visit to Callison."

"Did either of them make a buy?"

"No, they didn't. I got a fax out to the dealers, listing the major and more unique items stolen. One of them posted it to an online collectors' newsgroup. So far, all three recognized the collection as stolen."

"Was it just one guy or did both of the perps make contact?" I asked.

"I think the same guy that visited Callison contacted the others. Your information about the ski masks means I'll have to bring Callison back in to look at mugs of robbers."

"Don't bother. He told me he was wearing his reading glasses and just saw a fuzzy image."

"Wonderful. I had him in here for two hours looking at burglars."

"He did ask me to tell you the perp was a smoker. Callison smelled it on him."

"That ought to break the case for us. I have to get back to work, Duffy. Call me if you come up with anything I should know," he said, and hung up.

I gave Jeannine the names Darden had mentioned. She kept walking in and out of my office making minor adjustments to her map. Giving an obsessive-compulsive person that kind of project is like giving an insomniac a hotel room with a leaky faucet.

I spent the remainder of the day calling local dealers, collectors, and eBay middlemen, offering each the same personal appearance deal I offered to Callison. Since most of them were aware of the heist and none of them knew the collection was owned by a professional musician who acquired it first-hand, they were all receptive to my suggestion.

I asked them to play along like they were interested in buying. Then, try to get the perp to bring in the collection, and tell him it would take a couple of days to line up a buyer. I planned to tail the perp home, contact Darden, and retrieve the collection. It was apparent that there was some risk to the shop proprietors, but the potential for major publicity was immense. They all recognized the upside and agreed to cooperate.

I gassed up the RXS and made a rare weekend appearance at my office on Saturday morning. My first order of business was to clean and oil the snub-nose .38 that I usually wear on a belt holster at the small of my back. I felt it was important to get in touch with my confidence and be ready for anything after getting worked over by Jimmy Marcello. I waited for a call from one of the dealers until 3:00 PM, in hopes that the perp would try another drop-in, but it was not to be. The most significant thing I managed to accomplish was to set an appointment for Monday morning with Graham Weston.

At 5:30 PM I picked Kelly up and drove her to my parents' house for whatever she and Mom had been planning. I wondered if we would be celebrating our status as a couple, which was approaching two years, while we slowly made our way through traffic.

It was actually quite an accomplishment, considering that Kelly has been exposed to my father for about a year, and has yet to be grossly offended. In reality, Dad has mellowed considerably since he retired from SDPD four years ago. From the time I was in junior high until Dad's retirement we had a very adversarial relationship. Dad hated the fact that I played in rock & roll bands, even though it financed my education at UCSD. I hated the fact that he managed to insult most of my friends and all of my girlfriends. That is, until I met Kelly Kennedy, my first girlfriend of Irish heritage.

"Happy anniversary!" cried Mom, upon our arrival. I was sure I had guessed correctly. Then she escorted us into the dining room where a huge poster read: *Happy Anniversary Duffy Investigations*. I was stunned. Dad sat under the sign wearing a big smile and drinking Guinness Stout.

We ate barbecued steaks, mashed potatoes, and corn on the cob.

Mom said, "I wanted to invite Jeannine—"

Dad jumped in and added, "But then we'd have to invite

Cory."

Dad was referring to my part-time photographer and stakeout specialist who suffers from Tourette's Syndrome. Not wanting to foul the mood, I let it slide.

Kelly said, "Tell us about your first client, Jason."

"My first client was pretty much like my first hundred clients. Since my office is located on La Jolla Boulevard, I spent most of my time bailing out delinquent children of the rich and famous."

"At least you got a little mileage out of that education of yours," Dad said, referring to my Bachelor's in Psychology and Master's in Counseling.

"I'm sure he uses it all the time," said Mom.

"Oh yeah, I forgot about his staff," Dad said, and I felt my muscles tense.

Kelly gave me a kiss on the cheek. "Be cool," she whispered.

Mom jumped up from the table and exclaimed, "Time for cake and ice cream!"

She jogged into the kitchen and walked out with a cake, inscribed: *Jason, the Best PI in San Diego.*

As we enjoyed Mom's confections, the tension waned. Kelly told us about a field trip that her second grade class took at the end of the school year. Mom told a story about how she helped chaperone an outing at SeaWorld for my sister Lisa's class when she was in second grade.

Just as I was starting to relax and enjoy everyone's company, Dad asked, "So, when are you two getting married?"

Although we had been together for two years, we never actually discussed the subject. After a lifetime of dealing with awkward moments resulting from Dad's inappropriate comments, I was ready to jump down his throat. I was sure it was his way of trying to prod me into marrying a girl of Celtic blood, since his whole social circle was as Irish as Paddy's pig.

My face reddened and my fists clenched. Before I could snap, Kelly said, "You'll be the first to know, Jim." Then, looking at me, she added, "I hate to be a party pooper, but I have to get up first thing in the morning." Turning to Mom, she asked, "Can I give you a hand with the dishes before we leave?"

"I won't hear of it. You two go ahead and get going. I'll take care of the dishes." Then to me she added, "You've done a wonderful job with your business, son. We're very proud of you."

Mom gave us hugs, and Kelly ushered me out the door before I could say a word to Dad.

When we got in the car I said, "Maybe now you'll start to understand the kind of crap he put me through growing up."

"You're right. That was pretty awkward."

Kelly remained silent the rest of the way home. As I was about to exit the freeway to go into my neighborhood, she said, "I want to go home."

My initial reaction was to say it appeared that Dad was getting his way in forcing the issue, but I knew it would only start a fight.

I said, "I can't blame you for not wanting to be around me tonight. Once he gets under my skin, it's hard for me to let it go."

Over the 15 minutes that it took to get to Kelly's condo, it felt like the barometric pressure in the RXS had tripled. It clearly was not a good time to talk about our future, but not talking about it was extremely uncomfortable.

Instead of the usual passionate kiss goodnight, Kelly gave me a quick peck on the cheek, said, "Happy anniversary," and jumped out of the car before I could respond. I felt awful, but had no idea how to make things any better.

Upon arriving home, I got a beer out of the fridge and tried to figure it out. I felt that we had a great relationship and she very well could be the woman I eventually marry. But I'd be damned if I was going to let my father push me into it. In the meantime, Kelly was caught in the middle and I didn't know what to do. I called my friend Justin, a 36-year-old club manager who enjoys a stellar relationship with almost every woman he's ever met. Unfortunately, 11:00 on a Saturday night is not the best time to have a phone conversation with someone who manages a club that features heavy metal rock & roll music. Justin's cell phone was turned off and the person who answered the phone at the club couldn't hear a word I said. I hung up and stared at the phone sitting on my lap. Suddenly it rang, causing me to bolt into an upright position. The phone fell on the living room carpet, and I scrambled to pick it up.

"Hello?"

"Jason, are you all right?" Kelly asked.

"No," I replied, "I've been miserable since I dropped you off."

"Me too. I know your dad made you feel pressured tonight, and instead of talking things out, I made you feel worse."

"Are you kidding? You diffused a major blow-up, and got me out of there before I could say something I'd regret. I didn't even have the good sense to say thank you or tell you how much I love you."

"I love you too, Jason," she replied in a quiet voice.

"You asked me about my first client earlier in the evening and I lied. It wasn't a punk kid with more money than brains. I was hired by a woman to spy on her cheating husband. I've had more of those cases than I'd care to admit. That's why I hired Cory. It had more to do with me not wanting to look through bedroom windows and see marriages go up in smoke, than it had to do with Cory's photography skills."

"Are you concerned that I won't be faithful to you?" she asked.

"No, that's not it. I just want to make sure when I say, 'till death do us part,' that it won't eventually turn into wishful thinking."

"How do we get from here to there?"

"What if we start by having you move in with me?" I asked.

"Wow," she said, more stunned than excited. "I've thought about it, but I didn't see that coming tonight."

"What do you think?"

"I think we should give it a try on one condition," Kelly said.

"What?"

"Never use the excuse that your dad pushed you into it if it doesn't work out."

"It's a deal," I said, and truly hoped I was ready for the commitment.

Chapter 12

Graham Weston's shop is attached to a Hard Rock Café-type restaurant in downtown San Diego called The Stone & Bun Cafe. He operates a modest retail space of about 250 square feet with a separate street entrance. Weston was in the process of trying to make a sale to a teenager when I walked in on Monday morning. The proprietor stood no more than 5'2" and weighed about 110 pounds.

Weston said, "I'll be with you in a minute."

He turned back to the teen, holding an autographed picture in his left hand. "With the kind of numbers his new CD is putting up this year, I'm planning on moving this picture into my *Hall of Fame Probable* category. When that happens, the price will immediately double."

I walked around the shop and tried to find anything that might have come from Max's collection while they haggled. Nothing looked suspicious.

"OK," the teen said. "Ten bucks, right?"

Weston concluded his sale and turned to me. "What can I show you today?"

"Jason Duffy. I'm here to talk with you about Max Varner's collection."

"Oh, yes," he said. "I forgot you were coming."

He must have been sidetracked by the major transaction that just transpired.

"It was a shame what happened to Max and Ellen," I said.

"Max and Ellen!" he exclaimed. "I had big plans for the commission I would've earned on that collection. It was going to be my inroad to the elite collectors. I got robbed too, Mr. Duffy."

"Then I'm sorry for your loss as well, Mr. Weston. I was hoping you could give me an idea of what kind of black market exists for Max's collection."

Weston stared at me for a few seconds before responding. "I'm sure there are numerous collectors who'd love to get their hands on it. But the things that make his collection unique are the same things that would get a collector in a lot of trouble if he displayed it and bragged to his friends."

"So, bragging rights are important in the valuation of collector's items?"

"I'm sure there are collectors who amass collections for other reasons. But most of the people I've met in the business get a great deal of pleasure from games of one-upmanship with other collectors," Weston said.

"If I had just stolen this collection, what would be my best way of cashing in?"

"That depends on how computer savvy you are."

"Let's say I'm your run of the mill thug with just a basic knowledge of email."

Weston replied, "Then you better have a well connected fence. The best way to move the collection would be through eBay. But most crooks get to the sign-up page and figure they'd be making it easy for the cops to trace the stolen merchandise back to them. It's a lot easier to hide the identity of the seller than most people think. That's why I always insist on a face-to-face when making a buy."

"So you don't use eBay yourself?"

"I sell through eBay. I also use it to arrange meetings with SoCal fixed-price sellers who are willing to bring in their items and documentation. But I'd never participate in an auction for a collectible in this field. Letters of authenticity and other forms of documentation are too easy to fake online."

I replied, "Then even if the crooks were knowledgeable of eBay, they might not be able to find a buyer."

"P.T. Barnum said, 'There's a sucker born every minute.' Yes, it's possible that some idiot would shell out the big bucks without personally eyeballing the documentation. But it's not very likely."

"So, what does he do?"

"I'd say his best bet would be to find a crooked dealer with the expertise to recognize the collection as authentic and the contacts to discretely move it directly to one of those rich introverts who doesn't care about bragging rights."

"What if I were to tell you he's already tried this?" I asked.

"I wouldn't be surprised."

"What if I were to tell you he's been contacting dealers and collectors throughout this county?"

"Again, I'm not surprised," he said, looking at his watch.

"What did you tell him when he contacted you?" I asked.

"Who says he contacted me?"

"Are you saying he didn't?"

"No, he didn't. I think it's time for you to leave, Mr. Duffy."

"First, let me see if I've got this straight. You expect me to believe that he skipped your store, even though you advertise that you specialize in rock memorabilia."

"Frankly, I don't care what you believe."

"Then you won't mind when I tell Max that you were either in on the heist or you're trying to play the hero to make sure you get his business if the collection is returned."

"We'll see how pissed he is if I'm the one who gets the collection back," he fumed.

"I think he'll be pissed when the police find your body. It wasn't a single burglar that took the collection. It was two guys who went there in ski masks. We're talking about violent criminals who were willing to shoot anybody who stood in their way." Weston's face drained of color. "When are you meeting them, Graham?"

Weston's mouth opened, but nothing came out.

"Let me help you. I'll tell Max that you stuck your neck out for him, no matter what happens."

"I'm supposed to meet this guy tonight. I told him to come by at 10:30."

"Keep the meeting. Act really interested in the collection, but tell him that you'll need to line up a buyer for a collection of that much value."

"Then what?" he asked.

"Then, I tail him back to his place, have the cops get a search warrant, raid the place, and hopefully, get Max's collection back."

"I was going to pull my piece on him and call the cops," he said.

"I'm afraid if you followed through with your plan you'd be starting a new collection."

"What's that?"

"Mass cards," I replied.

I spent the afternoon going back and forth on the issue of whether or not to involve Detective Darden in my plan. On the one hand, it would be safer if the police were in the picture. On the other hand, a career criminal would case the scene thoroughly before going in. If he sensed the presence of cops, he'd be gone and never get back in touch. More importantly, he'd probably just bring a sample of the collection, as he had done at Callison's. If the cops picked him up, it's unlikely he'd disclose the location of the rest of the collection. Since it was a non-violent crime, he'd shut up, do his time, and hope to emerge from prison with a huge payoff waiting for him. I decided the best bet for recovering the collection was to wait and call Darden after it was located.

Kelly called in the early afternoon. "I just gave notice to my landlord. He said it's OK if I move out at the end of the month."

"Great!" I exclaimed, with as much enthusiasm as I could muster.

"We need to figure out what furniture I'm going to move in and what to do with the rest."

I was in the middle of contingency planning and a bit too distracted for the conversation. I was trying to figure out what to do if both crooks showed up at Weston's in separate vehicles.

"Why don't you make a list of all of your stuff? We can have our Wednesday night date at my place and make all of those decisions." I said, absently.

"You're not having second thoughts, I hope."

"Sorry, hon. I'm in the middle of something right now and it's not a good time. Can we talk about this when we get together?"

"OK, I'll be at your house at 6:00, and I'll bring something to cook," she said.

"Great," I said, realizing that I ended the conversation the same way it began.

I found a parking spot across the street from Weston's store at 10:00 PM and walked into a neighborhood bar a couple of doors down, with a small window facing Weston's street entrance. No problem securing the window table since there were only four patrons and a bartender, all at the bar. I ordered a non-alcoholic beer and watched the street.

Just after 10:30 a gray Ford Explorer drove slowly down the block. A few minutes later it passed the shop in the opposite direction. It made a U-turn at the end of the block and found a parking space just past the shop, facing the opposite direction of the RXS. A man who matched Callison's description emerged from the vehicle, walked to the back of the Explorer, and removed a duffel bag. After he entered the shop, I exited the bar and inspected the Explorer. No one else was inside and no one was sitting in any other vehicles on the block. I walked back to the RXS, drove to the end of the block, did a U-turn, and parked in front of a fire hydrant, four cars behind the Explorer.

At 10:50 the suspect emerged from the shop and placed his duffel bag into the back of the SUV. I started the tail when the SUV reached the middle of the next block. After four blocks he turned right then made his first left. When I rounded the corner I noticed that the suspect increased his speed substantially, and realized I had been made. A red light and heavy traffic on the main thoroughfare enabled me to come within a half block when the light turned green. We weaved through a populated area, and turned into a section comprised of several two-story office buildings that were now closed.

The SUV made a right onto a side street that had a large hedge extending to the intersection, obscuring the Explorer as soon as it went around the corner. When the RSX made the turn, I hit the brakes and cut the wheel hard, as I saw the Explorer thirty yards in front of me in a roadblock position. The suspect was behind the front end and pointing a pistol directly at me. I ducked just as a shot shattered the windshield. I punched the gas pedal and was immediately jarred as the car jumped the curb. I hit the brakes and threw it into park. Staying below dashboard level, I opened the passenger door and crawled out. The RXS was now at enough of an angle to the Explorer that it served as a shield. Pulling the .38 from my holster, I saw the suspect peeking around the back end of the SUV, and fired two rounds at him. One of the shots hit his taillight.

I considered going back into the RXS to retrieve a box of bullets, but the suspect was now on all fours and firing at my feet, under the RXS. So I made a run for a nearby stucco office building that had an exterior staircase with a solid wall supporting the handrail that led to the second floor. I dove behind the wall as one bullet hit it and another sailed over my head and hit the building. Tiny shards of stucco rained down. From a crouching position on the third step, I flung both arms over the wall and fired two rounds at the suspect, who was in pursuit about 20 yards away. As I squeezed off my rounds, the suspect did a belly flop and returned fire.

I quickly dropped down onto the stairs and yelled when I landed on a stone the size of a golf ball. I had two bullets left and could not afford to miss. Lying face up on the stairway, I realized that my pursuer could simply reach his gun over the wall and start shooting randomly. I heard the labored breathing of a heavy smoker rapidly approaching, and realized I had to think fast. I transferred the .38 to my left hand, reached down, found the stone, and flung it sidearm onto the landing at the top of the stairs. I prayed that the gunman would hear the clamor on the next floor over the drone of his respiratory system.

Before I could transfer the gun back into my right hand, the gunman rounded the corner of the stairway, and I fired one round into his chest. Although momentarily stunned, the gunman started aiming his pistol. The word *vest* flashed through my mind. Using both hands, I fired my last round into the gunman's forehead, causing him to fall over backwards, crash into the stucco wall at the base of the stairs, and crumple into a fetal position.

I was pretty shaken. I had never been in a one-on-one gun battle before. The reality that I had just ended the life of another human being hit me instantly. Sleazebag or not, the image of the gunman falling over backwards with a bullet hole in his head, would be with me for the rest of my life.

Feeling an overdose of adrenaline coursing through my arteries, I ran back to the RSX, retrieved my phone, and called Detective Walter Shamansky of SDPD Homicide.

Chapter 13

Tuesday morning I called a mobile auto glass company to have the RXS made roadworthy right away. Thankfully, I found a service that could drive out to the office immediately.

Next I confirmed my lunch date with Detective Shamansky. Because of our relationship from a prior case, I was allowed to go home shortly after the detective arrived at the scene of the shooting. By 10:30 the windshield was replaced, and I was on my way to Metro Police headquarters to file my statement. When I finished, Shamansky and I headed for the detective's favorite restaurant – Larabee's.

The hostess, who bears a strong resemblance to the actress Barbara Billingsley of "Leave It to Beaver" fame, made a huge fuss over the mid-50s, hairless homicide detective. Upon being seated, Shamansky received the visiting celebrity treatment from several of the waitresses. Prior to his promotion to Homicide, Shamansky captured a former partner in the restaurant, who made off with most of the assets and a very attractive waitress. Through some very slick police work, Shamansky not only caught the culprit, but also recovered the assets, enabling the restaurant to stay in business.

After we placed our orders I asked, "What can you tell me about the gunman?"

"Before we go there, how are you doing with that?"

"I'm not really sure if I got completely to sleep last night. Please tell me he was a horrible person."

"Donnie Daniels was a career criminal of the worst kind. His convictions included armed robbery and assault on his pregnant girlfriend. But if that's not enough to get you on better terms with your pillow, he was arrested twice for murder, but wasn't convicted. He was also suspected of several armed robberies, including a convenience store stick-up where a family of four got killed in a car wreck while he was being chased through El Cajon. You should get an award from the commissioner's office."

"Was there any evidence in the Explorer tying him to his accomplice?"

"No. The Explorer was stolen two days ago. There were only two sets of prints and the other one belonged to the owner," Shamansky said.

"What was in his wallet?"

"Strip club memberships, his probation officer's card, and about a hundred dollars. Nothing important."

"How long has he been out of prison?"

"He was paroled four months ago. I put a call in this morning to a guy I know at George Bailey Prison. He's going to check on known associates and get back to me."

Our waitress stopped by the table with a dessert cart and did her presentation. When she finished, Shamansky asked, "At what point did Daniels notice the tail?"

"That's been bothering me. I had two cars between us, medium traffic, and he only made two turns when he took off."

"Do you think it's possible that Graham Weston tipped him off?"

"It doesn't make sense to me." I told him the details of my conversation with Weston earlier in the day. "Why would Daniels contact Callison and the other dealers if he had put something together with Weston before he pulled the job?"

"Maybe Weston wasn't planning on busting Daniels. Maybe he figured he could make more by being his fence," Shamansky said.

"How do we find out?"

"I'll lean on him and see how he reacts," he said. "Care to join me?"

"I wouldn't miss it. I could put Cory on stakeout to take pictures of everybody who goes in and out of his shop."

"Good idea. I'll hold off for a couple of days before dropping in. By the way, I don't think Darden will be joining us. You're on his shit list."

"I was going to call and have him handle the bust. I just needed to make sure Daniels was going to show up, bring Max's property, and follow him to where the rest of it is stashed."

"You could have at least called and given him a heads-up on your plan."

"Darden would have busted Daniels the minute he caught him with a small sample of Max's collection. Chances are, Daniels would have told us he found it, and the rest of the collection would turn into his hope chest for after he got out of jail."

Shamansky knew I was right, but just as I was compelled to act in the best interest of my client, Shamansky couldn't condone any action that would keep a fellow cop from busting a bad guy.

Shamansky said, "Don't expect me to smooth things over with Darden. And, by the way, he just found out you're Jim's son."

"What does that have to do with anything?"

"Ask your father."

Before I could respond, a gorgeous waitress started massaging Shamansky's shoulders. This put him in such a relaxed mood he possibly could have been talked into picking up the check. I decided not to press my luck. Finding out about Donnie Daniels made our pricey lunch worth every penny.

When we got back to Metro, Shamansky gave me a list of Max's collectibles that were recovered from the stolen Explorer.

"Darden wants to hold the items in the property room since there's a second suspect and it could be used as evidence."

"Max is going to be thrilled. Thanks for getting me the list, Walt," I said, sneaking in Shamansky's first name while he was still in his waitress afterglow state.

"Tell your parents I said hello," he commented, and we said goodbye.

I surmised that Shamansky and Dad struck up a casual

friendship when they worked together on my biggest case to date. This was a major departure from Dad's history of socializing exclusively with Irish cops.

I returned to my office and called Max. "I've got some good news. We've recovered a piece of the collection."

"That's great, Jason! When can I get it back?"

"It'll be held by the police until the case is closed. I got a copy of the recovered items and I was hoping we could get together. What's your schedule for tomorrow?"

"We have band practice starting around 4:00 PM."

"How about if I drop by around 1:30?" Max agreed, and gave me directions to their summer rental.

Just before I headed home, Chief Carson called to say he didn't have any luck with the retailers who sold ski masks. Ditto the bartenders and liquor store clerks. He did, however, have a long conversation with the guy who ran me off the road. It turned out that he thought I was a snitch. The chief was currently trying to figure out what crime he committed to spark the paranoia.

Chapter 14

My ride into the office on Wednesday morning was interrupted by Kelly, who called to read me an article in the morning paper entitled: *San Diego PI Kills Career Criminal in Shootout*. It presented me in a positive light however the trend toward sensationalist journalism was not lost on the author.

"Why didn't you tell me about this?" Kelly asked.

"I didn't want you to worry about me."

"We're on the verge of moving in together. It must be a terrible burden, taking a life. If you can't share that with me, I don't know how we're going to communicate as a couple when we're seeing each other half of our waking hours."

Arguing the point looked like a long ugly road to nowhere. "You're right. I've got a lot to learn. I guess I'm lucky to have a teacher moving in."

"Besides talking about my furniture we can talk about this when I come over for dinner tonight."

I worried that I would be starring in one of her chick flicks and was glad that thought wasn't going through my mind during the shootout.

"I'll see you then," I said.

I picked up a half dozen bagels and a tub of cream cheese for the staff meeting on my way to the office. Both of my employees were acting sullen when I arrived. They took the seats in front of my desk as I set out the bagels and opened the cream cheese container.

Although Jeannine suffers from a combination of psychological disorders, depression is not one of them. Besides her immaculate grooming, she usually displays a sunny disposition and an outgoing personality among her small circle of friends. Today she was decidedly glum and distant.

"Let's start with Cory," I said, and noticed Jeannine staring at the wall map. "I want you to stake out the memorabilia shop attached to The Stone & Bun Café. I need a picture of everyone entering and exiting the business. See if you can get a picture of the customers' license plates. There's a parking structure at the end of the block. I'm guessing most of the patrons will use it. Try to arrive early enough to get street parking in between the two buildings."

Cory is rarely quoted due to the volume of inadvertent obscenities resulting from his Tourette's Syndrome. Jeannine and I have learned to filter out the foul language around the office. Unfortunately, it will mean that he'll need to conduct the surveillance from inside his van instead of enjoying the air conditioning and cool drinks from the bar window seat I had used. In his unique vernacular, Cory asked about how to cover the shop entrance inside the café.

"Don't worry about it. Our crook will use the outside entrance to minimize potential witnesses."

Giving Jeannine a bagel normally results in a maddening display of her obsessive-compulsive disorder. She has to cut the bagel exactly in half. This feat takes at least five minutes and involves placing numerous markings around the perimeter, along with exploratory punctures to ensure symmetry around the inner circle. Once the bagel is split, the next phase involves a series of thin cuts to make the surface perfectly flat. Once an acceptable level of flatness is attained, the spreading of the cream cheese goes on for another five minutes. Not only does the amount have to be perfectly symmetrical on both halves, it also has to be line-free and not leak over the side.

Today her bagel sat untouched in the center of her napkin while she continued to stare at the giant map of San Diego County. I looked closely to try to discern what was captivating her attention. All of the pushpins she had used to mark the location of memorabilia dealers were in bright cheerful colors. When my eyes reached the outskirts of downtown, I noticed that she had placed a black pin where the shooting occurred.

"I see you read the morning paper, Jeannine."

Two black streams of mascara ran down her cheeks. She snatched a tissue, stood up, and ran into the restroom while I explained to Cory what was going on. Before Jeannine returned, the phone rang and Cory lightened the mood by asking in his special way, if I wanted him to answer it.

I managed to get one word of my salutation out when I heard my mother exclaim, "Jesus, Mary, and Joseph! You could have been killed!"

When she said this, a thought flashed and I said, "Hang on, Mom." I then yelled, "Cory, hold up!" He stuck his head back into the office. Covering the mouthpiece on the phone I said, "Before you go, let's check the obits and find out when and where Donnie Daniels is being buried." Cory nodded and headed toward his darkroom. Uncovering the receiver I said, "Hi Mom."

"Don't 'Hi Mom' me. I'm having heart palpitations," she said excitedly.

"Then calm down. I wasn't in as much danger as the press made it out to be. You know how they are – anything to sell a few papers."

"I happen to think very highly of our paper," she continued in a strained voice. "I told your father this morning that I wished you were still a rock & roll musician, and for once he didn't argue with me."

"I'm sure Dad has been in his fair share of scary situations."

"Your father had a partner and he called for backup when it got dangerous."

"I've got some good news," I said, hoping to get her blood pressure down. "Kelly and I are taking our relationship to the next level."

"You're getting married?"

"No," I replied. "We're moving in together at the end of the month."

"Your big news is that you're going to live in sin? Are you trying to kill your mother and your father on the same day?"

"I thought you'd be happy for us."

"I am, son. Kelly is a lovely girl. And, I can't say that I

blame you, the way your father forced the issue at dinner. Sometimes that man just doesn't know when to shut his mouth," she said, still sounding like the queen of the espresso machine.

"I've got to get back to work, Mom."

"Before you go, I want you and Kelly to come over for dinner tonight."

"Not tonight."

"I won't take no for an answer. I saw how things ended with you and your father last week. I can't survive another Cold War between the two of you. I'm too old to do that again. You two need to bury the hatchet. Let him tell you a couple of stories about gunfights. It will probably do you both a lot of good," she said, and started showing signs of calming.

"Should I announce our big news?"

"Not unless you want a long lecture on Catholic doctrine, and how you'll go straight to hell if you die while you're living in sin," she said, pointedly.

"It will be our little secret, tonight. But I don't intend to keep it from him for very long."

"I'll look for you around seven," she said, and bid goodbye.

After a mini-therapy session with Jeannine, I got her on the computer to find the funeral info Cory needed to plan his day. I then headed north for my meeting with the Varners.

I arrived just after 1:30 and got hugs from both of them. Apparently, they subscribe to the San Diego paper. I handed Max the list of items recovered from the Explorer and he lit up like the Las Vegas Strip. He brought the list over to Ellen and they read together with unwavering smiles on their faces.

"I don't know how we can thank you, Jason," Max said.

"You put your life on the line for us," Ellen added.

"I realize how important the collection will be for you and your family. I'm glad we got a little bit back, but to find the rest we're going to have to narrow the suspect list dramatically. I'll need your help to do that."

"Anything we can do, just say the word," Max said.

"Tell me about what you found in your lawn and driveway

71

after the burglary."

Ellen replied, "The lawn was littered with autographs. The police took pictures, and then picked them up. Once it was determined that the thieves wore gloves, they gave them back to us."

"Were the autographs all from one file box?"

"Yes," Max said. "They were from this year's collection."

"Did they toss out any other items from the collection?"

"Just the autographs," Max said.

"Were they in alphabetical order?"

"Not in this year's box. I just shove them in during the year, and put them in order after it's over."

"Did it look like the burglars might have dropped the box on the ground, and they were just blown around by the wind?" I asked.

"I'm not sure, but those boxes had strong clasps. I don't think any would pop open if you just dropped 'em from a few feet," Max replied.

I said, "I would imagine if the box accidently spilled, you would have noticed several of the autographs grouped together, and the rest distributed in the direction of the prevailing wind."

Ellen replied, "I didn't see any grouped together."

"Then they probably went through the box page by page until they found what they were looking for."

"What do you think they wanted?" Max asked.

"I don't know yet. But if that's what they were doing it would explain why the pages were separated. Was it a windy day?"

"I don't remember," Max said.

"I'd call it a gentle breeze. The pages moved a little bit while I was standing in the driveway for about 10 minutes, but it wasn't at all gusty that day," Ellen stated.

"How many of the pages in that box were recovered?"

"Thirty-six," Max said.

"How many were in there?"

"Maybe 75," he stated.

"Max, I need you to make a list of every autograph you can

remember putting in that box."

"I'll do my best. What do you think it will tell us?"

"If we're lucky we should narrow our suspect list from over 200 to the 39 names the burglars took with them."

"Smart and brave - Kelly's a lucky girl," Ellen said.

"What were the most recent additions to the collection?"

"Not a whole lot of autographs in the last few weeks. Since I started working for The Tactile Tattoo we've been spending most of our time in the practice room. But before this job I was in the studio for three months and picked up a shitload," he said.

"Max, mind your manners," Ellen said.

"Oops. I should have realized that ex-musician private detectives have fragile sensibilities."

"Don't make fun, Max. Not all musicians cuss like you. Did your band use much foul language, Jason?"

"A shitload."

"See," Max said, "kindred spirits."

Before Ellen could return the volley I asked, "Can you think of anything unusual about those autographs? Maybe an item somebody would want back?"

"I once had a guy give me an autograph on a copy of his divorce papers, but that was a few years ago," he said. "Nothing really stands out."

"Ellen, can you think of anything that might help us here?"

"One of the guys from The Tactile Tattoo gave us an autograph on a napkin from a local Indian casino," she said.

"Who was that?" I asked.

"Chris Barnett, the lead guitarist," she said.

"Don't be stirring things up between me and Chris," Max said.

"They're not exactly on good terms," she said.

"What happened?"

"Back when I first started playing with them, Tony Zembrano, the executive producer of the album, stopped by the practice room to see how things were going. He wasn't happy with the pacing of the song we were playing. He explained to

Chris what he wanted him to try, but Chris wasn't getting it. I worked with Tony before and had a pretty good idea of what he meant. So I used the guitar effect on my keyboards to show Chris. I wasn't trying to show him up."

Ellen added, "Tell him what Tony said."

"He told Chris that they should let me lay down the lead track for that song."

"And Chris took exception," I remarked.

Ellen said, "He started fighting with Max after Tony left."

"He was just blowing off some steam, honey. No big deal. We both took a couple of swings at each other, and it was over in a minute."

"Jake's girlfriend told me that Marni had to jump on Chris's back to get the two of them separated," Ellen said.

"It's called teamwork, babe," he said.

I said, "This means we have a guy on the short list who may have a grudge. I'm convinced that somebody you know is behind this. Why not Chris?"

"We buried the hatchet the next day. Chris isn't a bad guy, he's just passionate about his music. If he wasn't, the album wouldn't have a chance. We're both over it."

"I'll check him out and see if we can eliminate him as a suspect. In the meantime, I'm asking both of you not to discuss what we talked about today with anybody,"

They both agreed, and I promised to keep them apprised of any new developments in the case.

On my way back to La Jolla I called Kelly. "My mother read the paper this morning and totally freaked out."

"Finding out that a loved one was nearly killed will have that effect on you."

"That's why I didn't make a formal announcement yesterday," I replied. "She wants us to come over for dinner tonight so she can recount my fingers and toes."

"What did you tell her?"

"I told her I'd love to, but you were insisting on road-testing the rest of me."

Kelly gave a nervous laugh and said, "You did not."

"OK, I didn't say that. But I did tell her we're moving in together."

"Don't you think that might be a little much for one day?"

"It was the only way I could get her mind off of the shootout."

"How did she react," asked Kelly.

"In a nutshell: We're going to hell; still invited to dinner; don't tell Dad."

"We're going to hell? Does she really believe that?"

"I don't think so. But, she's sure Dad does. I could tell her blood pressure was through the roof. She sounded like she overdosed at Starbucks."

"Poor thing," Kelly said.

I told her I would pick her up at 6:30. We did one of those mushy goodbyes that is best left unsaid.

When we arrived at my parents' house, I was surprised to see Walter Shamansky and a guy I didn't recognize, sitting in the living room drinking beer with Dad. After I shook hands with Shamansky, Dad introduced his friend.

"Kelly and Jason, this is Seamus Fitzpatrick, former bunko detective with San Diego's finest."

"Nice meeting you, Mr. Fitzpatrick," I said, shaking hands.

"Seamus," he said.

Dad said, "Seamus busted a five-city black market ring that specialized in music memorabilia."

"I've been asking dealers for the past week about it, and they've been denying that one exists," I said.

Seamus replied, "Reputation is the lifeblood of the industry. If word gets out that a dealer has questionable ethics, everyone automatically assumes he sells articles with forged signatures. Once that happens, only the most naïve buyer will do business with him. He might as well close up shop immediately."

"So, how do the scammers find buyers?" I inquired.

"The way it usually works is that there are a few auctions each year at major houses like Sotheby's, Christie's, and

75

Julien's. The criminal element keeps tabs on the big spenders. A few of the more sophisticated bad guys get close to the high rollers in hotel bars and when viewing items prior to bidding," Seamus said.

"How do they set up deals with these guys?" asked Shamansky.

Seamus replied, "Here's a good example. I overheard a guy tell a high roller that he was a huge Iggy Pop fan as a kid. He put a collection together once he got out of school and became a stockbroker. But after he heard the scream at the beginning of the song *Loose* in an SUV commercial, he got disillusioned. So he said he was selling the collection and investing in bands that weren't tainted by the almighty dollar."

"Was the guy buying it?" asked Dad.

"Hook, line, and sinker. They set up a meet for the next day. When the bad guy left the bar, I snagged his glass, lifted prints, and ran his sheet. We busted him the next day, and it was info he gave up that led to the five-city ring."

I said, "I'm pretty sure the guys I'm dealing with aren't connected. They immediately started calling legitimate dealers to see if they could pedal their score for top dollar, rather than risk eBay or go through a fence for a fraction of the price. This tells me they're either total amateurs or crooks with no clue on how this niche works."

"Then why go after a score outside their area of expertise?" Shamansky asked.

"Maybe it was a crime of opportunity," said Dad.

"In this case, there was something else going on." I went on to tell them about the autographs strewn around the yard.

While everyone was pondering the implications of this new information, Mom announced that dinner was ready, and we adjourned to the dining room. Out of courtesy to the hostess, we avoided discussing the case over the pot roast. Mom initiated a fun conversation when she asked Shamansky if he was still seeing Svetlana Illich, a strong willed, fortyish Russian woman he met on a recent case. It turns out they had a brief, torrid affair that ended one night when Svetlana emerged from the bathroom in a dominatrix leather teddy, carrying a whip.

Shamansky said, "There's no way I was going to reprise World War II, and let the Russian beat the crap out of the Pole."

Dad brought the men out to the backyard patio for an after dinner beer. "Where do you go from here on the case?"

Shamansky said, "I'm going to check out known associates of the deceased. I've got a friend at George Bailey Prison where Daniels spent most of the last five years."

"Good idea, Walt. I've always felt that our corrections system has gone from being punitive to being one big networking opportunity," Dad said.

"In Bunko, we call it Criminal Club Med," said Seamus. "It's a place where unsuccessful criminals can go to improve their skills and meet people who can help them go on to bigger and more profitable crimes."

"Exactly," said Shamansky. Then he asked, "So Jason, what are you going to do to keep the accomplice from going underground?"

"I'm sure there's a connection to a musician. Max was in the process of collecting autographs from The Tactile Tattoo just before the heist. The collection could have gone anywhere after it was stolen, but it ended up here. I don't think any of us believes in coincidences. I'm going to start asking some questions and see who gets nervous."

Dad said, "If you need any help, just ask."

Mom popped her head out the back door. "Jason, can you come in and spend a few minutes with your mother?"

"You better get in there," said Dad. "She's been a wreck ever since she read the morning paper."

Kelly was nowhere to be seen when I entered the kitchen. Maybe my mother had her saying a rosary to get a head start on penance for living in sin. Mom tapped the kitchen table and I sat. She lifted a heavy cardboard box off of the countertop and placed it in front of me. I recognized the rollerblades box as the home of my music memorabilia collection.

"Wow! I haven't seen this in years!" Inside the box were concert ticket stubs from numerous shows, plus several souvenirs.

"I thought you might want to have these because of the case you're working on, and with you and Kelly getting serious, who knows. Maybe someday you'll have your own son to pass it along to," Mom said with moist eyes.

I could tell by looking at her that it had been a very stressful day. "This is great, Mom. You've taken excellent care of it."

Mom started crying. "I hate to see you in so much danger."

"I'm getting to be friends with Shamansky and some other guys on the force. I'll give them a call next time I get into a questionable situation," I said with the best of intentions.

I was evasive on the drive home when Kelly asked about my conversation with my mother. I showed her my collection, and she responded with a look that told me she didn't appreciate my abridged edition of the truth.

Chapter 15

Leandra purchased a newspaper and walked to Delucci's Italian Restaurant at the end of the block for a quiet lunch late Wednesday morning. She placed her order and casually read her way through the first few pages. Just as her food arrived, she saw the article about the shootout and realized that it was her brother's prison buddy who had been killed. Once again she experienced her elm tree feeling, and couldn't put a fork to her salad. The shadow that her tresses cast on the newspaper reminded her of the stand of elms turned upside down.

She called her brother and they agreed to meet at home right after work. While they kept their conversation brief, she could tell by the sound of his voice that he knew what had happened to his friend.

It didn't take Poppy long to know that something was wrong. "Don't tell me one of our customers gave you the summer flu."

"I'm OK, Poppy," she said.

"You've been staring off into space for the last half hour. Do you want me to call Ginger and see if she can cover for you?"

"No. I swear I'll be fine." She felt compelled to elaborate. "My brother is back living at home, and it's causing a few problems. I'm sorry if I've been distracted. I'll pay closer attention to what I'm doing."

Leandra arrived home at 6:30, prepared to grill John on what he and Donnie had done to sell the collection since the burglary. But John was not around. In fact, he didn't arrive until nearly 9:00.

She used that time to search the apartment and garage for the remainder of the collection. If she had located it, she planned to put everything in trash bags and drop them into the Dumpster of a business down the street from the pharmacy. But the collection was nowhere to be found.

When he walked in, Leandra asked hotly, "Where have you been? We agreed to meet right after work."

"I've been working on a solution for our little problem. Where's Mom?"

"She passed out around 7:00. What kind of solution?"

"The permanent kind," John said, solemnly. "The PI that killed Donnie has been all over Southern California making it impossible to sell the collection."

"Where is it now?"

"Why?"

"Because now that a dead body is involved, we need to get rid of it before it gets traced back to us."

"Are you crazy? It's worth over two million bucks. That kind of money could set us up for life."

Leandra moved closer to him and sniffed. "Have you been drinking?"

"I told you, I've been working on fixing our problem. I met a guy in a bar."

"Great," she said. "Now a bar full of people knows about it."

"Give me a little more credit than that. We sat in a booth away from everybody else. I know a bit more about this sort of thing than you do."

"What sort of thing?"

"This Jason Duffy, the PI that shot Donnie; he's got to go," John said.

"Are you out of your mind?"

"Think about it. This guy isn't going to let up. The cops have better things to do than look for some autographed music shit. But this Duffy is on it full-time."

"So what! If we take that collection and pack it in trash bags, we could put the whole thing behind us, and never have to give it a second thought," she said.

"Maybe you wouldn't give it a second thought with your

Rock Star boyfriend. But what do you think my chances are with a felony conviction and a prison record?"

"I thought you were doing this because you wanted to be the big brother I needed in high school."

"I suppose you're going to take care of your convict brother once your boyfriend is on MTV."

"John, I don't know what the future holds for any of us. Yesterday, I thought that I did, but now I'm sure that I don't. I believed that you were interested in making us a family again."

"I do want that, Leandra, but you're just going to have to trust me."

"Trust you? I trusted you when you recommended the pseudoephedrine deal. Now I'm part of a drug felony. I trusted you when you said we should steal the collection. Now I'm an accessory to burglary. Tonight you involved me in a conspiracy to commit murder. John, you've been home for three months and my life is falling apart." She covered her face with her palms and sobbed.

"I'm sorry, sis. I never meant to bring this on you. But I'm afraid we're beyond the point of no return with this Jason Duffy guy. After I read the paper, I did an Internet search and read quotes about him from the cops, a hot shot lawyer, and a major real estate developer. All of them talked about how smart he is and how he can figure things out from just a few little clues. Do you really want that guy coming after us 24/7 until he puts us away?"

Leandra's sobbing stopped and she placed her hands in her lap. "I don't think of myself as the kind of person who could get involved in murder."

"Me either. But everyone has a survival instinct. Mine tells me it's us or him."

"What do I have to do?" she asked.

Chapter 16

Thursday morning was worse than Wednesday. The office phones sounded like a PBS fundraiser in the middle of a Rolling Stones concert broadcast. I heard from people I barely knew in high school and at UCSD. The smell of death brought a morbid celebrity that attracted an unusual demographic. I was about to tell Jeannine to let the calls go to voice mail while we took our lunch break, when a young woman called and said she had information about the collection.

"This is Jason Duffy."

"I don't want to give you my name, but my boyfriend has the collection that you've been looking for," Leandra said.

When I was in college, my mother talked me into attending one of our Irish cop backyard barbecues. The main topic of conversation that day was false confessions. For over two hours I listened to one story after another about people who confessed to crimes they didn't commit. Many involved scorned lovers who reported the ones who jilted them or otherwise did them wrong. I was ready for this to be a very brief conversation, especially after the cauliflower ear I had developed spending my entire morning on the phone.

"I see. What can you tell me that wasn't in the papers to assure me I'm not wasting my time?"

"There were two people who did the burglary: my boyfriend and his friend, Donnie."

"Thanks for the call, Miss. I'm sure you and your boyfriend will work it out," I said, preparing to hang up.

"Wait!" she exclaimed. "They didn't take all of the autograph boxes in the basement. They only took the autographed pictures and this year's autographs without photos."

It's possible that the Big Bear paper mentioned boxes left behind in a follow-up to the story I read, but I was certain there was no mention anywhere about this year's autographs.

"OK, you've got my attention," I said, hoping she would reveal more if she thought I was only partially convinced.

"He's really not a bad guy. He was never in any trouble before he met Donnie. Now, without Donnie, he knows he's in over his head, but he's planning on taking the collection to the East Coast where he thinks the heat is off," she said. "I'm afraid he's going to get caught or killed in a rip-off."

"Where do I come in?"

"At first I thought about just throwing it all away. But I was afraid that you and the cops would keep looking until you found him. Then I thought about giving it to the cops. But they're looking for a bust, and would probably end up arresting me to get to my boyfriend," Leandra said.

"So, why me?"

"Because you were hired to find the collection, not to make a bust. I figure you got enough justice by killing Donnie, and wouldn't need to help arrest a kid who fell in with the wrong person."

"How do you suggest we do this?"

Leandra replied, "I've given it a lot of thought, and what I want to do is meet you someplace public, but not too public. I want to be able to walk by and check things out without you knowing it's me. But I don't want so many people that a cop could blend into the crowd."

"OK, I can understand that."

"I've put the whole collection in trash bags. I'll drop them off next to a Dumpster near the place where we meet. When I'm convinced that the cops aren't in the neighborhood, I'll walk up to you and tell you where to pick up the collection."

"That seems reasonable to me. Where and when do you want to meet?"

Leandra gave me an address in Hillcrest and I gave her my cell phone number. The meet was set for 8:45 PM.

I was elated that this gruesome case that forced me to take a life was finally coming to a conclusion. I reflected briefly on my promise to my mother that I would let the police be my backup in the future. However, I also knew that this young woman was right. The top priority of the cops would be to secure the bust, and that would mean a heavy police presence to cover all of the Dumpsters in the area. I got the impression she was very bright, and concluded that she might easily be spooked, even if the cops were reasonably well disguised.

When I emerged from my office, I found a note from Jeannine stating that she had a shopping emergency, and would have to take a rain check on lunch. Stood up for a blue light special – how degrading.

I called Cory, hoping I might learn the identity of the mysterious caller from the funeral photos. Unfortunately, the only attendees at the service were Donnie's parents and an older brother.

I drove to the take-out window of a nearby fast food restaurant and got stuck behind five vehicles in line. While I waited, I moved the box holding my memorabilia collection onto the passenger seat and began sifting through childhood treasures.

The ticket stubs led me on a journey back in time. So many vivid memories were sparked by those cardstock rectangles: My first date, my first kiss, my first beer, bonding with my first band. I resolved on the spot to buy a scrapbook.

As I moved to within one car of the take-out window, the Neil Young classic *Heart of Gold* played on the radio. I reached into the near corner of the skate box and found my Marine Band harmonica. Although I hadn't played the song in 10 years, the notes came back instantly. The girl behind the cash register patiently waited for my solo to end before conveying my total with an amused look on her face. I stuck the harmonica in my shirt pocket and reached for my wallet.

The minute I paid for the food my cell phone rang. It was Derek, the drummer from my old band, calling to talk about the shootout. Maybe if I wrote a letter covering the FAQ on the incident, and emailed it to everyone on my Christmas card list, I could actually get some work done.

Leandra went to Poppy in the middle of the afternoon and told him she wasn't feeling well. He called Ginger, who agreed to come in immediately. A half hour later she went home to tell John she wanted him to call off the hit. When she arrived, her mother was two-thirds of the way through a bottle of vodka, and giving John a hard time.

"When are you going to start pulling your weight around here?" she slurred.

"It's tough out there for a guy with a record," John said. "I do bodywork at the garage whenever they call me."

Looking at Leandra she said, "You don't see Leandra laying around here watching television all day. She's going to make something of her life." Mrs. Lundquist gave her a loopy smile and forgot that she was in the middle of chewing out her son.

Leandra jumped in, "Thanks, Mom. Why don't I make you a nice gimlet and get you settled in before your soap comes on?"

"You're such a dear." She slipped into a compliant mood and allowed her daughter to guide her to the fainting couch in front of the TV.

While Leandra prepared the drink, she said to John, "We've got to call this thing off. I just can't go along with it."

"I thought we went through this last night," he said. "Did you make the call?"

"I did."

Mrs. Lundquist called, "Where's my drink, Leandra?"

She dutifully served it and returned to the kitchen.

"Is he expecting you at the time and place we agreed on?" asked John.

"I've got a really bad feeling about this. I just know we're going to get caught."

"We're not going to get caught because we're not going to be there. Maybe it will help if I tell you some things about the guy who will be meeting Mr. Duffy tonight. His father is a Mexican citizen and his mother is a Mexican American. He grew up on the streets of Tijuana and, as a teenager, ran drugs across the border using the back trails where he learned how to recognize dangerous situations to avoid the Border Patrol.

"When he was 16, a buyer tried ripping him off for a good-sized order. Luis pulled out a little .25 caliber handgun that was so small it was almost completely concealed by the palm of his hand, and he shot that rip-off artist right in the heart. After that, the cartel promoted him to enforcer and it's said he's killed over twenty men without getting caught."

"I thought you said that you met him in prison."

"I did," he said. "He was in for a bar fight in National City, where he ruptured the spleen and broke the jaw of the bouncer. While Luis was finishing him off, one of the bartenders snuck up behind him and broke a Frangelica bottle over his head, knocking him out till the cops got there."

"Ouch."

"I understand that as of last month, the bartender is no longer among the breathing," John said.

"What are you doing being buddies with a guy like that?"

"You used to watch those reality shows. I had to form alliances if I wanted to stay alive without being somebody's bitch."

"So, Luis provided protection for you. What did you do for him?"

"I utilized my natural brilliance to join the ranks of the jailhouse lawyers. It wasn't just Luis and me against everybody else. There were about 20 of us that looked out for each other. Luis was definitely the baddest of the bunch."

"What about Donnie?" she asked

"I asked Donnie to help me because he was always very loyal. I'm sure that if Donnie was arrested instead of killed, he never would have given me up to cut a deal."

"In the newspaper article, the PI said that Donnie swung his car around and started shooting at him without provocation. Why would he do that?"

"Donnie grew up dirt poor in a well-off neighborhood, like us. The other kids made fun of him, and he hated them. He started ripping off custom homes when he got into high school. Besides just stealing whatever he could carry, Donnie also took a great deal of pleasure in vandalizing the shit out of those rich people's houses. After he got busted, he found out that one of his victims was a drug dealer who plays rough. Just before he was released, he got a *Congratulations* card that said, 'I can't wait till you get out.' Inside was a picture that, to the guards in the mailroom, looked like a kid's drawing. But actually, it was exactly what Donnie had spray-painted on the guy's walls. The only difference is, the guy used a lot of red crayon. Donnie got the message. I'm sure he thought the PI was a hitman, hired by the dealer."

"Then why does the PI have to die? I might understand if the guy did something to deserve it. But all he did was act in self defense over a case of mistaken identity."

"Donnie tried to kill him. There's nobody in the world more determined to finding Donnie's accomplices and putting them in jail than Jason Duffy. Now that Donnie's death is tied to the crime, there'll be no sweet deals with the DA. The stakes got raised to a whole new level," John said.

"Isn't there another way, John?"

"It's got to be done, and Luis is the best guy to do it. Let him do his job and we can go on with our lives without worrying about Duffy showing up on our doorstep."

"I hope you're right," she said.

Mrs. Lundquist called, "Leandra, be a dear and bring me another one."

"I just hope my conscience doesn't make me turn out like Mom," Leandra said, taking a swig from the vodka bottle.

Chapter 17

By 7:00 PM I couldn't wait around any longer. I drove to the rendezvous site and took a walking tour of the immediate area. There was light foot traffic on the block where we were to meet. The address belonged to an antique store that closed at 6:00. On the far end of the block was a moderately priced restaurant that had a window facing the street, but was not large enough to offer a view of the antique store. I stood in front of the window, trying to give the impression that I was looking at the menu taped to the lower left corner. The bar and tables were about half full. The only other open business between the restaurant and the antique store was a computer repair shop that would be closing at 8:00.

I crossed the street and noted a block full of small businesses that supported the numerous office buildings in the vicinity. Street traffic was still fairly heavy as the more ambitious business people were finally calling it quits for the weekend.

I walked a pattern away from the antique store. When I approached alleys where Dumpsters could be located, I slowed my pace and glanced quickly, without being conspicuous. I was concerned about the number of people who were in the alleyways. I spotted at least ten homeless men, four teenagers smoking a crack pipe, a trio of gangsters, and a hooker with her trick emerging from behind the Dumpster of love.

I began to worry that the woman who called would be unable to find a secluded place to stash the collection. I also worried that she would be seen doing it, and the collection would be gone when I arrived to retrieve it.

By 8:30 darkness had crept in. Even though it was August, an ocean breeze left a chill in the air. Most people on the East Coast don't understand this phenomenon. That's because the

Gulf Stream brings warm water up the coastline and, as a result, the air stays warm after the sun goes down. On the West Coast, cool water flows down the coastline from Alaska, causing the opposite effect. Five minutes before our rendezvous time, I returned to the Acura and put on a light jacket. I spotted a young woman a block away, heading toward the antique store. After zipping my jacket, I crossed the street, which was now much quieter than the previous hour. I walked up to the display window of the antique store and glanced at an old-fashioned spinning wheel in the middle of several less interesting pieces. I looked back just in time to see her turn right onto the intersecting street. I wondered if it could have been the girlfriend.

Over the next fifteen minutes I counted five people pass by: four males and a fifty-something woman. In those fifteen minutes, it had grown quite dark. The streetlights were on, but the antique store was about midway between the lampposts, and made me appear to be lurking in the shadows. Two young women crossed the street when they got to about 50 feet from where I was loitering.

While I focused on how suspicious I looked, a Hispanic man who appeared to be homeless, stopped when he got in front of me.

"I haven't eaten all day. Can you spare a buck?"

I was concerned that the young woman would see two people instead of one, and get scared off.

"Sure," I replied, and reached for the wallet in my back pocket.

When I did this, the Hispanic man extended his hand and I assumed he was reaching for the handout. But when I looked, his palm was down, rather than in the usual palm-up position. Instead of the hand stopping at the edge of my comfort zone, it kept extending toward my chest.

Suddenly, I saw a flash of fire come out of the hand and heard the unmistakable sound of a gunshot. It felt like a weightlifter with very large knuckles had punched me in the chest with all of his might. I clutched at where I had been struck and fell backwards, banging my head on the brick wall of the antique store. At that point I lost consciousness.

When I awoke, I was lying on the sidewalk with two paramedics standing over me. I reached for my chest, and one of the paramedics grabbed my forearm and returned it to my side.

"No touching," he said.

I had a headache that would make my all-time worst hangover seem like a minor inconvenience. I started reaching for my head, and again was restrained.

"We need to tape him to a board," the other paramedic said.

"What happened?" I asked, and realized that talking made his head throb.

"Don't talk," said the first paramedic. "Somebody shot you in the chest with a small caliber gun. But the harmonica you had in your shirt pocket slowed the bullet down to where it barely broke the skin. You took a worse hit bouncing your head off of that wall."

Taped to an immobilizer, I was transported to the ER of the nearest hospital. Upon arrival, I was surprised to find my wallet still in my back pocket. The pain meds had kicked in by that point, and I was able to tolerate the bright lights of the ER.

A hospital administrator asked, "Who do you want me to call?"

"Detective Walter Shamansky, SDPD Metro," I replied, and closed my eyes.

Over the next 90 minutes I struggled to focus on what had happened. Besides dulling the pain, the drugs also fuzzed my ability to instantly recall the details. I hoped I could pick the assailant out of a mug book, but I was doubtful.

When Shamansky arrived he bellowed, "What the hell happened to you?"

"You need to turn your volume way down or my skull is going to split right down the middle."

"I got a concussion once playing high school football. Say no more," Shamansky said, quietly.

"Did you talk to the doctor yet?"

"Your nurse told me somebody tried shooting you in the chest, and you have a nasty concussion, but that you're going to be all right. What happened?"

I described what I remembered.

Shamansky chided, "I hate to say it, but that's what you get for lying to your mother. Just last night you told her you'd get San Diego's finest involved in anything dangerous."

"Let's do the *I told you so* thing another time." I cupped my hand over the right side of my head. "I'm barely holding on to a fading memory of the gunman and I want to give you my best description before it goes away entirely."

Shamansky pulled a pad and pen out of his pocket and said, "Let 'er rip, buddy."

"He looked about 5'9" but he could be taller. I think he stooped a little, trying to make himself look homeless. The clothes were crummy, but I can't remember details."

"Don't strain yourself on that one, Jason. I'm sure he's changed by now. Tell me about his face."

"He was Hispanic, and had a very square jaw. He reminded me of one of the ape dudes from Planet of the Apes."

Shamansky laughed, "Do you think I should put out an APB on an ape dude?"

"I meant his beard and haircut reminded me of the ape-men in the movie."

"I understand," he said. "I was just messin' with you for shining on your mom. Do you remember any scars, tattoos, or piercings?"

"There was something on his arm. It's pretty fuzzy. I can't quite bring it to mind. Do you think I might be able to remember it when the drugs wear off?"

"No way," Shamansky said. "You're going to be in a world of hurt. You'll be lucky if you can think of a good excuse why you didn't call Kelly to be at your side in your time of need."

"I don't want Kelly or my parents hearing about this until I'm good and ready to tell them," I said at a volume that caused a sharp pain to follow.

Shamansky read my expression and said, "Back to the

tattoo. Was it a name, a face, a shape?"

I closed my eyes for a minute. "This is going to sound weird. I have no idea of what it was, but I sort of remember thinking it didn't look very professional."

"Sounds to me like a prison tat. Donnie Daniels just got out a few months ago. I wouldn't be at all surprised if they were in the same jailhouse gang together. You done good, Jason. If you're up to it on Monday, we can take a little road trip to George Bailey prison. Now get some sleep, and call me tomorrow."

Chapter 18

I was discharged from the hospital at 11:30 Saturday morning. My head still felt as if an amplifier had fallen on it, so I stopped at my neighborhood pharmacy and filled a pain med prescription. I also purchased ibuprofen in hopes of switching to something less mind-numbing as soon as possible.

I called Kelly shortly after returning home.

"Where have you been?" she asked, excitedly.

"I was on a stakeout. What a pain," I said, hoping I wasn't technically lying.

"After what happened earlier this week, I can't believe you'd completely ignore me for two days."

The anger in her voice was unmistakable. My exposure to Kelly's temper had been limited to hearing one side of her phone conversations with her family, until now. I definitely wasn't feeling well enough to argue, but wanted to nip the temper display immediately.

"Is this a preview of what I can expect when you move in?"

Kelly was silent for a few moments. "You know I'm not a nagging control freak. Just, please keep me in the loop if you go incommunicado again."

"Yes, dear," I replied in a patronizing tone, hoping she wouldn't sense something was amiss.

"Is something wrong?"

"I woke up with one of the worst headaches I've ever had."

"Awww, poor dear," she fawned. "Are we still on for our date tonight?"

"How about if we rent a couple of movies and have a quiet dinner at home?"

"I'll tell you what. Since you're hurting, I'll stop by the market for a couple of steaks. I'll also go to the movie rental place by your house, OK?"

What a girlfriend. "You're the best, Kelly. Just one thing."

"I know, no chick flicks. Feel free to call in the order yourself."

"Why don't we do this? I'll pick one and call it in, and you pick the other. Does that work for you?" I asked.

"Sure," she replied. "Let's see if I've got this straight. I'll do the shopping, the cooking, and the cleanup. Afterwards, we watch your movie. Then, you fall asleep on the couch while I watch my movie."

"That sounds good to me."

"So that means I can rent a chick flick since you'll be asleep, right?"

"What if my headache keeps me awake"

"You always said chick flicks could put coke-heads to sleep. Here's your chance to prove you were right," she said.

"OK, get what you want. Just don't get anything too hot because *I've got a headache!*" I exclaimed and hung up. I immediately wished I hadn't yelled.

I took two of the Tylenol with codeine that my doctor prescribed, and fell asleep within a half hour. It was a fitful sleep, filled with one nightmare after another. In each, I was under attack by unknown assailants. Kelly was by my side in every one.

When I awoke, I couldn't shake the feeling that my subconscious was telling me how much I'd be endangering Kelly if we proceeded with our plan to move in together. I spent an hour trying to rationalize that many cops lead relatively normal family lives.

But then I recalled a kitchen conversation I overheard at one of the Irish cop backyard barbecues. Mary Sullivan, whose husband was partners with one of Dad's best friends, told Mom and several other women that cops had a higher divorce rate than any other profession. She also talked about their high suicide rate. I was 10 years old at the time, and stood frozen on the other side of the entrance to the kitchen. I had just come in for a soda, and came away with the same worrisome feeling I was experiencing today.

I checked the front of my prescription bottle and saw that the meds started wearing off in four to six hours. I was still tired, but forced myself to stay awake. If Kelly walked in with a horror movie I'd send her home.

At 6:15 Kelly called from the movie rental store. "I thought you were going to call in a selection."

"I've been asleep for most of the afternoon."

"That must have been one long stakeout. How's your headache?"

"A little better, but still there."

"Do you have a movie in mind?"

"You know what I like," I replied. "Maybe we should go for more of a mystery instead of a loud action flick."

"I'll be there in about 20 minutes," she said, and hung up.

I felt horrible. My skull was pounding and my brain was saying I was putting this wonderful woman directly in harm's way. I popped a couple of ibuprofen tablets, and flushed the Tylenol with codeine down the porcelain fixture.

I looked in the bathroom mirror and noticed a 3"x 3" gauze bandage taped to the back of my head. I realized that there was a fair amount of caked blood in my hair when I started removing the bandage. A year ago Kelly said my hair resembled Johnny Depp's. Today I had Halloween hair. I turned on the shower, walked to the living room, unlocked the front door, and returned for a much-needed cleansing.

Unfortunately, the ibuprofen hadn't yet worked its magic by the time I washed the area around the wound. As I rinsed, I had a little daymare, imagining that I would emerge from the bathroom and find my assailant holding a gun to Kelly's heart.

I walked out of the bathroom just as Kelly was walking in. "You look awful."

"Geez, I just took a shower. This is as good as it gets."

"Do you want to eat first, or watch a movie?"

"I'm not very hungry yet."

"We could just chat for a while," she offered.

"What movies did you rent?"

"Thanks a lot," she said, feigning insult while handing me

95

her selections.

I read the blurb on the back of the packaging. Ugh! A couple of snoozers. "All we've talked about today is me. Tell me what you've been up to."

We spent the next twenty minutes in the kitchen while Kelly prepared a pasta salad for later. She was volunteering at Children's Hospital for the summer, and told me about a seven-year-old cancer patient she had been teaching to read. A hospital social worker said that her efforts added a level of normalcy to a family whose lives had been turned upside down. When the girl was diagnosed, the mother had been unable to spend more than a few minutes at her bedside without breaking down. But as she saw her daughter work on her reading skills, the mom began to participate in the process, and dealt with her grief.

All I could think about was how many lives she touched as a teacher, a volunteer, and in her everyday existence. I wondered if I was about to deny the world an exceptional human being for my own selfish needs.

"Are you sure you're ready to move in with me?" I asked.

"What?" she asked. Her eyes narrowed as her eyebrows drew closer together.

"I can't help but feel like my father pushed us into it."

"Jason, we've been dating for two years. We're not exactly rushing into this like a couple of impulsive teenagers."

"I know, but look at what happened with my parents. They were perfectly happy until I asked for an electric guitar when I hit my teens. After that, the Civil War was on at the Duffy household until I moved out six years later. Who's to say something similar won't happen to us?"

"Nobody can look into the future, Jason. But we can't allow it to make us become victims of paralysis by analysis. Sometimes you've got to let your feelings guide you in matters of the heart."

"You're right. But I'm feeling like it's not the right time for this move," I said, wishing I was anywhere but in the middle of this conversation.

"I don't believe you," Kelly said hotly. "I've given notice at my condo. The owner tore up my sublease and put a new agreement together with somebody else on Thursday. Do you think I should become homeless because you're having second thoughts?"

"Of course not," I replied. "Don't you have a girlfriend who might be looking for a roommate?"

"Maybe I could move back in with my family," she said, knowing that I had heard countless tales of her dysfunctional alcoholic kin.

"Maybe you could stay with my family while we sort things out," I offered. "They love you."

Kelly was on the verge of tears. She grabbed her purse and headed for the door.

"Too bad their son doesn't feel the same way!" She slammed the door.

My instincts told me to go after her, but his brain said to let her go until the case was over. My head thumped like a bass drum, and I felt like a total schmuck. Whoever sang "Love Hurts" knew what he was talking about.

The following morning, Leandra finished going through the Sunday edition of the Union-Tribune for the third time. There was no mention of a homicide involving Jason Duffy. No mention of him whatsoever. Hoping that his wallet was stolen, Leandra poured over all of the police reports, and didn't see any crimes of violence listed for Hillcrest. She couldn't wait any longer, and shook her sleeping brother's shoulder.

"John, wake up!"

He cleared his throat and asked, "What do you want?"

"Another one of your jailhouse buddies screwed up," she said, holding out the newspaper.

John snatched it out of her hand and started scanning. "Where?"

"Nowhere," she replied. "Not a word. No Jason Duffy, no homicide, not even an assault reported in the neighborhood in yesterday or today's papers. It looks like one of them didn't show up."

"You went through the whole paper?"

"Three times," Leandra replied. "I'll bet your buddy used the money you gave him to get loaded and forgot all about it, or just blew it off."

"Luis is a pro. He'd never do that. He relies on word of mouth for his business. If something like that were to get out, he'd have to go back to running drugs through sagebrush to pay the bills. I really don't think so."

"Why don't you give him a call and see what you can find out?"

John was perturbed by his sister's accusations. He took the phone into the bathroom and emerged five minutes later.

"He said he shot him directly in the heart from a distance of about two feet. There's no way he could have survived."

"Then why wasn't there anything about it in the paper?"

"Sometimes cops have their reasons for keeping a lid on things. Personally, I believe Luis did what he said he did. But if you don't trust him, you're welcome to go down to Duffy's agency on Monday and see for yourself."

At 9:30 the following morning, Leandra said she needed a break and walked to the pay phone at the end of the block. She called Duffy Investigations, and hung up when Jason's familiar voice came on the line.

Chapter 19

Shamansky arrived at my office on Monday and was greeted by Jeannine.

"Remember me?" he asked.

"The finest of San Diego's finest. To what do we owe the pleasure, Detective Shamansky?"

"I'm taking your boss on a road trip," he replied. "If you want to accompany us, I have no objections."

Hearing this exchange, I appeared in my interior office doorway. "The detective can't resist a pretty face."

"Duffy, aren't you Johnny on the spot this morning. I don't think your receptionist had the time to properly receive me just yet."

"Jeannine's my assistant, not a receptionist. I think she's caught as much of your act as she needs to this morning. Ready to go?"

"Can I have a word with you in your office first?"

I did an about-face, and Shamansky closed the door. "I was serious about inviting Jeannine to come along."

"To a maximum security prison? Has the debonair detective been getting shut out lately?"

"Think about it, Duffy. It's obvious that somebody wants you dead. You're not apt to fall for another set-up. So, what are the perp's alternatives if he's intent on finishing the job?"

I took a deep breath and blew it out. "You're right. This could be a dangerous place till that guy gets taken out of circulation. I'll have her work from home till then."

"She's your assistant. Why not let her assist?"

"Let me ask you this, Shamansky. What do you think would be more dangerous – Jeannine operating a laptop on her kitchen table, or having her ride in a car at 70 miles per hour while the driver tries to sneak peeks at her legs?"

"Damn it, Duffy! Didn't your dad ever teach you how to reciprocate on a favor? Not only am I taking you along with me today, but I also managed to keep your second near-death experience out of the papers. Doesn't that count for anything?"

"All right, she can come along on one condition."

"Name it," Shamansky said.

"That she sits in the back seat, and you only look in the rearview mirror for brief, traffic safety reasons."

"I hate to nit-pick, but that's two conditions," Shamansky replied.

"Can you, in the immortal words of Jim Morrison, *Keep your eyes on the road, your hands upon the wheel*?"

"I'll be the safest driver on the road," he said, holding his right hand up in the swearing-in position.

"You do know she's going steady with my friend Michael Marinangeli, from Doberman's Stub."

"Just because you're on a diet doesn't mean you can't look at the menu. Let's get out of here. It's a long drive to the border."

Jeannine was delighted to be going on the roadie. She put a sign on the front door and walked into the restroom.

I said, "I think the girl who set me up called back this morning to see if I was still breathing. She hung up as soon as I answered, but Jeannine said it was a young woman who asked for me."

"Any other reason that you think it was her?"

"I heard the same street noise in the background. It was definitely her."

"It certainly makes sense. She's probably been scouring the news and obits."

I was sure I'd told Shamansky about Jeannine's idiosyncrasies on the case we worked last year. He knew she and Cory were both clients of mine during the two years after college when I worked as a counselor at an outpatient county mental health clinic. But Jeannine's beauty has caused many an admirer of the female form to turn a blind eye to her obsessions and compulsions. It didn't take long to put Shamansky to the test. First, he made the mistake of driving a four-year-old Crown Victoria from the motor pool that had seen more than its fair share of action. Shamansky had the windows down halfway and Jeannine immediately asked him to put them up because the wind was messing her hair. This was a reasonable request. Since the air conditioning appeared to be in working order, Shamansky was glad to do it for her.

"Detective Shamansky," she said in her lilting voice.

"Call me Walter."

"Walter, your window didn't go up all the way."

Sure enough, the rubber stripping around the window had been pulled away, and the wind caused a constant noise. Most people would tune it out, but I knew it would become the focus of Jeannine's world. Shamansky put his palm on the glass and shoved upward. That did the trick for about a mile, until it slipped back down. We were on the freeway by that point.

"Walter, it's down again," she said.

Shamansky repeated this scenario at least five times, then suddenly exited the freeway and pulled into a hardware store parking lot. Five minutes later he returned with God's gift to man – duct tape. In a couple of minutes the car was air tight and on the road again. We were in a section of heavy traffic, and it took about 10 minutes to work our way from the entrance ramp to the fast lane. We went from five miles per hour to 50.

No sooner did we reach maximum velocity when Jeannine said, "Walter, I've got to use the little girl's room."

"What!" Shamansky retorted, starting to lose his cool.

"She's got to pee," I said with upturned palms.

"Didn't you just go before we got started?"

Jeannine unlatched her seat belt, sat forward, and whispered in my ear. "I couldn't go then."

Shamansky looked at me as she buckled up. "Let's just find a place to pull over," I said.

Shamansky looked annoyed, but made his way out of the fast lane and back across three lanes to the next exit. Unfortunately, there were no gas stations or fast food places in the immediate vicinity. We drove about a mile into a seedy neighborhood. Eventually, we found a gas station, and Jeannine emerged from the office carrying a key attached to a small steering wheel. She was in and out of the restroom in five seconds. She returned the key to the office, and got back in the Crown Vic.

"What's wrong?" I asked.

"It was the most disgusting bathroom I've ever seen in my life."

"This isn't La Jolla, Jeannine. All of the public restrooms in this neighborhood are going to be dirty," Shamansky said.

"I'm feeling very uncomfortable," she said.

"Let's go back to the freeway and see if we can find a better place," I suggested.

"I can't wait," she cried.

I spotted a run-down park at the end of the block, and pointed it out to Shamansky. He let us out of the car and I found a patch of bushes that provided adequate privacy for Jeannine, while I stood guard.

When she finished, I heard, "Pssst! Pssst! Jason." I turned around, and she whispered loudly, "I need toilet paper."

"Can't you use a leaf or something?" I asked.

She made a noise that sounded like a whimpering puppy, so I made Shamansky go back to the gas station. I could see him from where I stood in the park. After arguing with the cashier, I saw him pull out his badge and eventually go trudging off with steering wheel in hand. The pit stop took at least 30 minutes.

Jeannine's foibles caused several more Maalox moments for Shamansky. At one point he picked up the duct tape, looked at me, then at Jeannine.

"You insisted," I said, and Shamansky dropped the duct tape back down on the console.

We arrived at George Bailey Prison at 2:15. Jeannine agreed to stay in the vehicle and work on the laptop to avoid causing a prison riot.

We entered the guardhouse at the main gate, where Shamansky showed his credentials, and the guard confirmed our appointment. After checking our weapons, we were directed to a waiting area. Ten minutes later, a guard in his mid-twenties escorted us to "C" Block, where Donnie Daniels resided prior to his discharge. Shamansky's friend arranged for us to meet Jamal Tucker, a large, muscular guard in his mid-thirties. He was seated behind a desk at the end of a long hall with two tiers of cells on either side. We could hear a few televisions and radios coming through the cell doors. We could also see a dayroom with about seven inmates watching a soap opera. One of the inmates slowly pushed a broom around the commons area.

"Have a seat, gentlemen," Tucker said, nodding at the two folding chairs in front of his desk. "What can I do for you today?"

"I don't know how much Tolliver told you, but one of your recent grads, Donnie Daniels, tried to ambush Duffy, here," Shamansky said.

Tucker flashed his teeth and said, "I heard that you did your part to help reduce our recidivism rate."

"What can you tell us about Daniels?" I asked.

"Just another uneducated loser. He was pretty quiet, and seemed to get along with the other inmates. I didn't have any trouble from him, which is not unusual when a guy is pretty close to getting out."

"Who did he hang with?" Shamansky asked.

"Do you mean guys that are still here, or guys that have already been released?"

"Out," Shamansky said.

"Frank Carpinski and Rovie Citron are the only two that come to mind."

"Were they good friends?" I asked.

"I don't think Donnie was anybody's bitch, if that's where you're going."

"I'm looking for somebody he might have helped on a burglary after he got out."

"Neither of those guys did a burglary bit. Carpinski was in for assault and Citron was a drug dealer."

"What else can you tell us about Daniels?" Shamansky

asked.

"Like I said, he was doing short time, so he kept his nose clean. He hung out with other guys in the same boat. They talked tough, acted tough, but I could tell they weren't looking for trouble," Tucker said.

"Anything else?" asked Shamansky.

"Sorry I couldn't be more help."

"Did he see his counselor at the clinic?" I asked.

"Sure. He had to get things lined up for when he got out."

"Do you know which counselor he saw?"

"We go by last name initial. That would be Ray Harmon," he said.

"Any chance you could get us in to see Ray today?"

"Those guys keep pretty tight schedules."

Shamansky said, "We drove all the way down here, Tucker. We need more than a good citizenship merit badge to take back with us."

Tucker stood up. "I'll see what I can do."

He walked to the glass booth behind his desk and his partner buzzed him in. He spent a couple of minutes on one call, then made another. He also spent a few minutes telling his partner what was going on.

When he emerged from the booth he said, "Harman can give you five minutes. A guard will be by soon to escort you over there."

He walked back into the booth, appearing miffed at Shamansky's comment.

"I hope the trustees out mowing the lawn aren't hitting on Jeannine," I said.

"She's probably pointing out blades of grass that they missed," Shamansky replied.

A couple of minutes later, the guard that had escorted us to "C" Block led us to the counseling clinic. We entered a cinderblock building and stated our business to a no-nonsense receptionist. After a quick call to Ray Harmon, she directed the guard to take us to his office. We walked down a flight of stairs to a long row of glassed offices on both sides of a narrow

104

hallway.

Ray Harmon was in his late thirties and wore a bushy mustache. He introduced himself, and directed us to chairs across from his desk.

"I only have a few minutes."

"Then we'll get straight to the point," I said. "I shot and killed Donnie Daniels last week. On Saturday, one of his buddies tried to return the favor. We need to find out who he hung with that might be responsible, and we didn't get much from his guard on "C" Block."

"He was only on "C" Block the last four months. All of his buddies were on "B" Block."

"Do you know his associates?" Shamansky asked.

"Offhand, no," he replied. "It's possible there could be a reference or two in my notes, but that falls under some complex confidentiality rules."

"I was a counselor at County Mental Health for two years, Ray. There's got to be some kind of workaround you could suggest."

Ray turned his head sideways, and looked at his watch. "The "B" Block guards usually go to a cop bar called Hanrahan's at "F" Street and Broadway in Chula Vista. The shift change happens in ten minutes. Look for Hawaiian shirts and guard pants."

Ray stood up and extended his hand.

"Thanks, Ray. We got more done in three minutes with you than we did all day," I said.

"Glad to help out. If you can make your way back upstairs, Margaret will call your escort," he said and herded us out the door.

When we returned to the parking lot, two guards were hanging on the side of the Crown Vic chatting up Jeannine.

"Don't you men have a shift change to get to?" asked Shamansky.

"Yes sir," replied one of the guards, and they left immediately.

Jeannine brought up an Internet map and directed us to

Hanrahan's. "You're not going to make me wait in the car again, are you?"

"Not a chance," Shamansky said. "You're going to be the hot ticket in this joint. We should have no problem getting a sit-down with the guardians of "B" Block with you at our side." He then briefed Jeannine on the plan.

The three of us walked into the bar and let our eyes adjust to the dark.

"Too bad Dad isn't here," I said to Shamansky. "I think he has a discount card for all Irish cop bars in California."

There were only a half dozen people at the bar, and none of the tables were occupied. Seated in the middle of the bar were two guys with close-cropped hair, wearing Hawaiian shirts. From the entrance we couldn't tell if their pants had the telltale racing stripe, but I was fairly certain those were the guys we were seeking.

We sat at a table directly behind the guards, figured out our drink orders, and sent Jeannine up to the bar. Five minutes later, she brought the guards back to the table.

"Have a seat guys," Shamansky said. "We just spent the afternoon at George Bailey talking to guys wearing your same style of pants. I'm Walter Shamansky, SDPD, this is Jason Duffy, SDPI, and I see you've already met Jason's assistant, Jeannine."

"We just got off duty. Time to relax," said the taller and older of the two.

Shamansky said, "Jason, here, shot and killed Donnie Daniels last week."

"This could be interesting," said the shorter one. "Did you say you were buying?"

"No problem," I said.

"I'm Reggie Burton and this is Darnel Akers," said the older guy. "Not that we aren't naturally trusting souls, but I want to see a shield before we make ourselves comfortable."

Shamansky handed over his badge and Reggie gave it a close inspection.

"Was Donnie ever under your supervision?" I asked.

"Oh yeah. We supervise "B" Block. Donnie was with us for at least two years," said Reggie.

Jeannine delivered the drinks and pulled up a chair between the two guards. "I feel so safe sitting with you guys."

"What can you tell us about Daniels?" Shamansky asked.

"He was a follower. I read his jacket. He was in for armed robbery, but he wasn't the kind of guy that would start trouble," said Reggie.

"But if anybody got on him or one of his little clique – look out," Darnel said to Jeannine with enthusiasm.

I said, "We think he pulled a job with somebody from his clique. Can you give us some names of guys who were released this year that might team up with him on the outside?"

"Yes and no," said Reggie. "You've got to understand prison cliques to know what I'm talking about."

"What do you mean, Reggie?" asked Jeannine.

Reggie smiled and said to her, "It ain't high school. The inmates get into these loose associations to keep from getting assaulted, or made to be somebody's bitch. But guys move in and out of cliques on a pretty regular basis."

"How come?" she asked.

"Because most of these cliques are like playing King of the Mountain. They fight over the pecking order all the time. In some prisons you have these groups set up along racial lines, some are dictated by gang affiliation, but at Bailey it's a matter of cutting your best deal," Reggie said.

"Who was he tight with that got released this year?" Shamansky asked.

"Do ya mean a guy with the balls to commit murder?" asked Darnel, trying to get Jeannine's attention.

"That would be a good place to start," replied Shamansky.

"Luis Hernandez," stated Reggie, beating Darnel to the punch. "He was the enforcer for his group. Nobody messed with Luis."

Darnel added, "He was supposed to be the hitman for a drug cartel. They called him *The Heartbreaker* because he claimed he shot most of his victims in the heart."

Shamansky exclaimed, "Bingo! That's the guy."

Over the next ten minutes the guards gave a few details and repeated some prison gossip. The most relevant being that Luis was released to San Diego four months ago, and that he was known for using a small caliber handgun that fit into his palm.

When we got back into the Crown Vic, Shamansky called Metro Division and started giving orders on what info he needed by the time he returned.

"I was beginning to think this trip was a total waste of time," Shamansky said. "By the way, thanks Jeannine. I don't think we would have gotten half of that information without your help."

"I wish you would have told me about nearly getting killed again, Jason."

"You seemed so shaken up by the Donnie Daniels shootout that I didn't want you to worry."

"I can understand why you would keep that from your mother, but I'm your assistant. How can I help you solve the case if I don't know what's going on?"

"I'm sorry, Jeannine. After seeing how well you did today, I'll be sure to keep you current in the future. But until Luis Hernandez is behind bars, we'll be taking lots of extra precautions at work."

"Are you going to rehire Delbert Henson to guard the office again?" she asked.

"I sure hope not. Please tell me you don't want Delbert back," I pleaded.

"We don't need Delbert. But you must admit, we didn't have any more trouble at the office once Delbert started temping as a security guard."

"We also didn't have any earthquakes, tidal waves, or riots," I replied.

"What did Delbert have to do with any of that?" she asked.

Shamansky replied, "About as much as Delbert had to do with keeping the office safe."

I added, "Just think of how much time you'll save, not having to pick cookie crumbs out of the carpet."

I was referring to Delbert's habit of stuffing his mouth full of Oreo's while attempting to carry on a conversation. Jeannine winced and lightly brushed at her hair with her hand.

During the ride back to San Diego, I contemplated the mess I made of my relationship with Kelly, and couldn't come up with a viable plan to straighten things out. I briefly considered calling on one of my former mental health coworkers to talk it out, but recalled that most of them had worse domestic problems than my own. I decided to follow up with the guy who knows more about women than anyone I've ever met.

Shamansky dropped us off at Jeannine's apartment, one block from the office. After making sure she was safely inside, I walked to my office and called Justin Emerson.

"Sorry I didn't get back to you sooner, Jason, I've been short-handed. What's going on?"

"I need some sage advice from the guru of women."

"I'm afraid we only have a few minutes before the band cranks up."

"It's not even eight o'clock, and it's Monday night," I replied.

"The owner thinks we can get a crowd after Monday Night Football if we establish ourselves as a happening place before the season starts. He thinks if we get the women out dancing at 8:00, the men will roll in after the game finishes around 9:00."

"Does that mean the owner thinks women come to clubs in hopes of meeting drunk guys who are amped-up on sports?"

"I'm sure he's looking at it from the drunk-guy's perspective," Justin observed.

"That's what I'm calling about, Justin. You understand women better than any guy I've ever met. Is there any way you can meet me for lunch tomorrow?"

"C'mon, Jason. It can't be that bad."

"I asked Kelly to move in with me. Then, after she gave up the sublease on her condo, I backed out."

"You *are* screwed, my friend. OK, I guess that does constitute an emergency."

"How about a o'clock lunch at *World Famous?* My treat."

The band started to roar. "OK. Gotta run. I'll see you then," he said, and hung up.

Chapter 20

My cell phone rang as I was about to step into the shower on Tuesday morning. Shamansky said, "I have an address in Encanto for Luis Hernandez, and I'm promised a warrant at nine o'clock."

"Where can I meet up with you?"

"No can do," he replied.

"Why not?"

"Because I need you to pick him out of a line-up after he's in custody. Since there were no other witnesses, it would be your word against his. If you get a look at him before the line-up, your testimony won't hold up in court."

"Damn!"

Shamansky concluded the conversation by saying, "Go to your office and stay by the phone. I'll call when we have him."

The morning moved in slow motion. Jeannine and I spent most of our time making calls and sending emails to memorabilia dealers across the country. I postponed my luncheon with Justin until tomorrow.

I met with Cory to find out what Chris Barnett had been up to. Cory indicated that he's enjoying this assignment because of the amount of time Barnett spends at the area casinos. Last night Cory won $60 playing slot machines while observing Barnett playing Pai Gow. Barnett also has an affinity for playing Texas Hold 'Em at a card room near the band's practice facility.

"Does he bring his girlfriend along for good luck?" I asked.

Cory hadn't seen her. He also was not accompanied by any of his band mates.

Noon came and went without a word from Shamansky. I called area dealers to see if I could sense a contact not being reported. But all I got were questions about the owner of the collection, and requests to handle the sale if it's ever recovered.

Shamansky called at 2:00 PM. "He got spooked."

"What happened?"

"When I returned to Metro yesterday, the captain authorized putting a tail on him. I got a call from the tail around midnight that he was outside Hernandez's apartment and could see him through the window. He stayed there all night and all morning. I got a warrant, coordinated with SWAT, and raided the apartment at 11:45. But Hernandez pulled a disappearing act."

"Is there a back door?"

"No, but there's a fire escape. The window next to it was wide open and the ladder was fully extended."

"Any sign of the collection?"

"Nothing."

"How did he know you were coming?"

"I Star-69'ed his phone, and guess who answered?"

"I give up."

"George Bailey Prison. I'm guessing that somebody on "B" Block overheard our drinking buddies talking this morning," Shamansky said.

John Lundquist walked into his sister's place of business. "We need to talk right now. Can you take a break?"

Leandra got permission from Poppy and they walked out to the parking lot.

"What's so important?"

"The cops showed up at George Bailey yesterday, and raided Luis's apartment this morning."

"Are you sure he's not wanted for another crime?"

"Duffy was at the prison, too," he said. "Luis had to bail at the last minute. Now he's stuck with no place to live, no money, and he's in violation of his parole. He needs some coin to chill for a while."

"He wants money from us? We already paid him. He should be giving us a refund for screwing up. Tell him to sneak back across the border if he's scared."

"We're his bargaining chip with the cops if he gets picked

up. Duffy's going to be a bigger threat than ever right now. We need Luis to finish the job."

Leandra took a deep breath, put her head down, and took a few steps away from her brother. She needed time to think. If everything went down the way John had described it, she could definitely see the need to dip into her savings to keep Luis safely hidden until he could finish the job. On the other hand, she wouldn't put it past her brother to make up a story to get money to travel to the East Coast, sell the collection, and live happily ever after.

"I'll give him some money on the condition that I hand it to him personally, and get his commitment on what he's going to do to fix this situation."

"That's stupid! Right now you have complete deniability on everything. I'm the only one who knows you're involved. If you meet with Luis, your deniability goes right out the window."

"Then I'll talk with him on the phone. But if I don't care for what I hear, he shouldn't expect any money," Leandra said.

"Are you kidding? Nobody gives Luis Hernandez an ultimatum."

"Excuse me if I'm less than impressed with his professionalism. The guy he supposedly blasted in the chest sounded perfectly fine to me."

"The call can't be from home or your cell phone."

"Walk down to the end of the block and get the number off of the pay phone next to the check-cashing place. I have to be here to open up tomorrow at 8:30. Tell him to call me at 8:15, and make sure he doesn't keep me waiting," she said, and walked back into the pharmacy.

The following morning, Leandra bought a paper from the machine next to the pay phone. It rang at exactly 8:15. She was determined to come across as a tough, no-nonsense woman.

"What happened?" she asked.

"Is this John's sister?"

"No, I'm the phone booth receptionist. How can somebody

be shot in the chest one day and be perfectly fine the next?"

"That's what I keep asking myself. I followed him for 15 minutes before the hit, and was 20 feet away when he put on his jacket. I got a close look at his back when he bent down to get it out of his car, and he definitely wasn't wearing a Kevlar vest. I saw the hole in his jacket after I pulled the trigger."

"Then how did he survive?"

"I don't know. Maybe he has a pacemaker," Luis said.

"Can he identify you?"

"I stood in front of him and pulled the trigger. What do you think?"

"You need to finish the job if you want to stay out of prison."

"It's gonna be a real tricky job," he said. "I went by his office yesterday afternoon. He has these huge bushes out front that would be a perfect place for a hit. I picked out my spot and got halfway across the street when I saw the bush move. An undercover cop was keeping an eye on the entrance. I went around back and saw a gardener that didn't look like a gardener, if you know what I mean."

"So, what are you going to do?" she asked.

"First, I need to find a place to hide out, where the cops won't come looking for me. That means no relatives or friends, and that costs money."

"How long will it take you to finish the job, and how much do you need till that happens?" she asked, in her tough-girl persona.

"They won't keep the stakeout going for more than a couple weeks. I should be able to hit him then. I'd say two grand should tide me over."

"I'll give $700 to John at lunchtime," she said, and hung up.

Chapter 21

Shamansky called on Wednesday morning to say the APB on Luis Hernandez had turned up nothing.

"Thanks for the bodyguards, but I think I can take care of myself," I said.

"They're not for you, Mr. Presumptuous. I'm keeping an eye on Jeannine."

"Tell them they can take a half-day off. I'm leaving for a long lunch at 11:30 and I'm dropping Jeannine off at her apartment beforehand."

"What time will you be getting back to your place?"

"I thought you were guarding Jeannine."

"If you don't tell me, you're going to be responsible for a couple of very bored cops wondering why they're wasting their time."

"I'm gonna take a ride up to Oceanside and try dropping in on Max's band mates later in the afternoon. If they're not at home, I'll be back around seven. If they are, it'll be closer to eight."

"Any chance Hernandez could be watching the Oceanside place?" he asked.

"I seriously doubt it. I'll give you a call when I'm heading home."

Shamansky approved the plan.

Twenty minutes before it was time to leave, I got up from my desk and started pacing through the office suite. Jeannine has seen me do this several times, so she continued working without interrupting my thought process.

I hadn't been in touch with Kelly since Saturday and felt the need to address date night, but didn't want to have a conversation until after my meeting with Justin. I picked up the phone and made the call. Fortunately, I reached her voice mail and left a message that I'd be tied up until tonight, but wanted to get together later if she was willing. By that point I hoped to have a plan for salvaging our relationship.

When I got to Oceanside, I stopped by the Varner's to follow up with Ellen on a request. "Did you put together the list that I asked for?"

"We did," she said. "Come in while I get it."

I walked into the modest living room and watched Ellen remove a page from behind a magnet on the refrigerator. It was hand printed and well organized.

Ellen said, "The first column is Max's best recollection of the autographs he collected so far this year. The second column is the autographs found in the lawn."

"What about these last three columns?"

"The first one lists the guys in Dicey Dreams. They were invited to the party, but have been on a European tour all summer. The second column lists guys Max met in the studio, who have no idea where we live. The last column lists the musicians he met in clubs that he didn't invite to our party, and also don't know we live in Big Bear."

"That narrows it down to the four members of The Tactile Tattoo, plus Pedgy," I said.

"Max has been good friends with Pedgy for years. In fact, he's Carl's godfather. The only reason he's on the list is because Max had him autograph a page he ripped out of a trade magazine that mentioned Pedgy's work with another band," she said. "It's hard to believe one of the band members could have stolen from us."

I didn't want to debate my theory, so I emphasized the need for Max not to mention it to anyone, and headed off to the restaurant.

I had the distinct impression that relationship advice would not come cheap today. Justin had a morning golf date at The Four Seasons in Carlsbad, just south of Oceanside. The plan was for us to meet at the bar and eat at the resort. As I walked through the pro shop and glanced at the prices, I got a severe cramp in my wallet.

Justin was seated at a table in the bar with the rest of his foursome, and introduced me. "I was telling Danny about the night you played with Doberman's Stub, and your credits on the *Cain & Abel* CD."

Danny said, "I've been a rock fan since I was a kid. That's how I got to know Justin. It's really a pleasure meeting you."

Justin said, "Danny's a developer. Believe it or not, this place is his hangout."

"Only during the day," Danny said. "At night it's a little too tame for my taste. Justin tells me you're up here to get some advice from the master. You definitely came to the right guy. If it wasn't for Justin I never would have made it through my first year of marriage," turning to Justin he added, "both times."

"Number two is going much better," Justin commented.

Danny said, "That's right. So, I told the maitre d' to put your lunch on my tab today. It's the least I can do."

"I appreciate the offer Danny, but it's my problem, so it'll be my treat."

Danny replied, "You're just starting your tab today. I'm in arrears to this guy. I'm hoping to close a shopping center deal later this afternoon. Buying lunch for a buddy and a rock musician would be good luck for me."

Justin said, "You don't want to be held responsible if Danny's deal falls through."

We spent another 20 minutes in the bar while scores were tabulated and side bets were paid. I accompanied the guys to the locker room where they changed out of their golfing attire. As Justin and I were leaving, one locker room attendant was running a lint brush over Danny's suit while another shined his shoes.

I let out an audible sigh the minute we were seated in the dining room.

Justin said, "I normally wouldn't have gone along with Danny's offer, but he insisted that I cancel my tee time at Balboa and drive all the way up here. So, what the hell. Let's pig out. The better the lunch, the better the luck."

"OK, I'm gonna need some serious comfort food when I get my problems out on the table."

"Sometimes these domestic things have a way of sorting themselves out. Are you and Kelly in better shape than when we talked?"

"I haven't spoken with her since then. But I did leave a message before coming here that I wanted to get together tonight."

"So, you think your old buddy will impart some wisdom that will allow you to have your beer and drink it, too?"

"Great idea! Let's order a couple of brews before we start working on the big fix."

Justin flagged a waiter, and we kept the conversation light while our order was processed in record time.

After the first sip, I asked, "Have you given any thought to my problem?"

"You've dug yourself into a pretty deep hole this time, buddy, especially if you still aren't willing to tell her why you pulled a 180 on her."

"What do you think she'd say if I told her I had a drug cartel hitman stick a gun in my chest and pull the trigger?"

"I know exactly what she'd say. She'd tell you to get out of the business and into something safe, like going back to being a counselor."

"You're reading my mind, Justin."

"That's why you'd never phrase it that way. Women have a tremendous capacity for understanding, compassion, and sympathy. But they also feel that if a loved one presents them with a problem, they have an obligation to help fix it. You just have to learn how not to force them into that role."

"What can I say to get her to put off the move without telling her what's going on, or having her hate me?"

"Start off by telling her you haven't been completely honest with her about why you don't want her to move in just yet. She's figured that one out by now, and by stating it from the top, you can go a long way toward reestablishing your credibility."

"I love it. Then what?"

"Tell her that killing that bad guy had a profound impact on you. Tell her you hadn't been sleeping, and you weren't thinking straight when you totally flubbed things on Saturday night."

"I had several dreams about the two of us being ambushed by more killers."

"That's good. It gets to the heart of why you acted the way you did. But I wouldn't get into describing any of the dreams in detail."

"Good idea."

"Tell her you're really conflicted because, as a PI, you've found your true calling in life. But life wouldn't be worth living if anything happened to her."

I was about to reply when our lunch was presented. A flock of waiters descended on our table with the efficiency of a NASCAR pit crew and the panache of a group of magicians. After giving a thumbs-up to the headwaiter, the flock disbursed.

"Once you've reassured her that you love her, and that you're committed to your job, tell her that the guy you shot was a violent ex-con who's working with other ex-cons. Tell her you just need to tie up this case before you make the big move."

"What if she says that there will always be bad guys out there?"

"Let her know that once the case is over you'll take precautions to keep both of you safe. Tell her you'll put in a security system; that you'll buy body armor; and that you'll buy her a puppy that will grow up to be a wonderful guard dog."

"A puppy?" I asked.

"The puppy will be the dealmaker. Not only does she get to feel safer, you'll be showing your willingness to make a long-term commitment. And, she also gets to check you out as *daddy material*. Trust me," Justin said with a broad smile.

Over the rest of our leisurely lunch we talked about old

friends, Justin's current girlfriend, and his present employer. I was able to relax and enjoy my friend's company, knowing that I had a game plan that couldn't miss.

At the beginning of the day I assigned Cory to keep an eye on The Tactile Tattoo's practice facility, and photograph all visitors. When my late lunch was over, I drove to the practice facility lot and parked next to Cory's van. It was almost 5:00 PM and, according to Max, the session should be breaking up any minute. Cory said that during a smoke break he heard Barnett ask Thompson if he was up for a spaghetti dinner at home after practice. Thompson told him he'd stop at the store to pick up tomato sauce.

"Do they live together?" I asked. Cory nodded and said that Jake also shared an apartment with them.

I showed up at the apartment an hour later with a 12 pack of Heineken. Barnett answered the door.

"Who are you?"

"My name is Jason Duffy. I'm a private investigator, hired by Max Varner to find his memorabilia collection. I'm going to be talking to everybody he's worked with this year. Can you spare a few minutes?"

"We're in the middle of making dinner," Barnett said.

"That should make it cocktail hour," I said, holding up the twelve-pack. "I brought along the beer."

"In that case, come on in," Barnett said, "but just for drinks. We didn't buy enough for an extra guest."

"Not a problem," I said, and entered the apartment.

It was a ground floor shoebox-shaped abode that appeared to be built in the '60's. I was shown to a couch at the far end of the living room. Just beyond the couch was a small dining area, one step down and separated from the living room by a wrought iron railing. The dining room held an old maple table and six chairs. Across from the dining room was a galley kitchen.

"C'mon out for a minute, guys," said Barnett.

Two men in their early 20s walked out of the kitchen, and into the living room. "Guys, this is a private eye Max Varner hired to help find his collection," Barnett said.

Extending my hand I said, "Jason Duffy."

"Garvey Thompson," replied the taller of the two.

"Jake Fuller," said the other. Eyeing the beer he asked, "Is that for us?"

"Absolutely," I replied. "Help yourselves." When everyone had a beer I asked, "How did your session go today?"

"It's all finishing touches at this point," said Thompson. "We go into the studio to lay down the tracks on Monday."

"Max told me your instrumentation is terrific, that your singer has a solid four octave range, and that the lead guitarist does an amazing transition from the pentatonic to the diatonic scale on the first cut," I said.

Barnett said, "It sounds like you have a bit of a musical background yourself."

"Did you ever hear of a club band called Tsunami Rush?" I asked. All three looked at each other and shook their heads. "We broke up four years ago."

"We were in high school, dude. I guess you were before our time," said Fuller.

"I played rhythm guitar on one of the tracks from the last Doberman's Stub CD," I noted.

"Awesome!" exclaimed Thompson. "How did you land that gig?"

"I got to know them while I was working on Terry Tucker's murder case."

"Why are you meeting with the musicians Max worked with?" asked Barnett.

"I don't know if Max said anything, but one of the thieves tried selling part of the collection. I ended up in a gunfight with him, and he was killed. Before he died, he said something that directly linked him to a musician."

I hoped my fabrication would stir things up.

"What did he say?" asked Barnett.

"I'm afraid the homicide detective in charge of the case won't let me tell anyone - not even Max. But it left absolutely no doubt that one of the musicians Max worked with this year was in on it."

"Wow," said bassist, Jake Fuller.

Barnett asked, "So, what are we supposed to do now? Convince you that it wasn't us?" He drained the last of his beer and cracked another.

"My job, at this point, is to eliminate suspects. Getting to know the people in your band will help me to do that."

"We've got spaghetti on the stove. What do you want to know?" Barnett asked.

"Do what you need to do. I'll be out of here before you sit down at the table."

"C'mon guys, I'm starved," Barnett said.

They walked into the kitchen that was within earshot, but out of my sight line.

"First of all, did any of you see or hear anything suspicious?"

All three gave a negative response.

"Do any of you know any former inmates from George Bailey Prison?"

Fuller popped out of the kitchen with three plates and three glasses. He shook his head while he set the table. The others said no.

I heard the spaghetti being poured into the colander and knew I didn't have much more time. I decided to take a chance.

"I wasn't totally honest with you earlier. You see Max's collection wasn't stolen because of its value on the open market. The thieves were looking for a specific autograph from somebody in your band."

Barnett seemed annoyed and asked, "How do you know that?"

"Because they went through a file of Max's most recent autographs in his driveway, and tossed the ones they didn't care about in the yard."

"How many suspects does that leave you to check out?" Barnett asked, as he and Fuller returned to the kitchen.

"Just you three, Marni, and Pedgy," I said.

A piece of silverware bounced off of a tile countertop and

onto the floor. I jumped off of the couch and leaned over the wrought iron railing to see into the kitchen. The three of them were standing there with nothing in their hands.

"Who dropped the fork?" I asked.

"I think you just wore out your welcome," Barnett said, angrily.

"If whoever dropped it wasn't involved in the burglary, he has nothing to worry about."

"Get the fuck out of here before I throw you out!" Barnett yelled.

"OK, I'm leaving." I backed into the living room and made my way toward the door. "Thanks for narrowing it down from five to three."

I closed the screen door just as a full bottle of Heineken smashed into the wall next to me.

Before I could even think about my next move with the boys in the band, I had to face something that could have a much more profound effect on the rest of my life – Kelly. I planned to call and hopefully see her immediately after leaving the boy's apartment. But after ending our meeting on such a sour note, I felt I had better go directly to Marni's house. She probably wouldn't be receptive to a chat tomorrow.

I reached the Hawley homestead in about 15 minutes. The house was easily over 4000 square feet and had an excellent view of the Pacific. After listening to the stately chime of the doorbell, I was greeted by a guy in his mid-twenties, sporting an upscale surfer look.

He said, "I know you, dude."

I replied, "I don't think we've met."

"The Terry Tucker murder. Your picture was in the paper."

"You're right. I'm Jason Duffy."

"What was it like being on stage with Doberman's Stub?"

I replied, "It was awesome, dude. Hey, is your sister around?"

"I didn't think you came to see me."

"Are you her brother?"

"One of four," he replied.

"One more and you'd have a basketball team," I said, noting that the brother was taller than the average surfboard.

"Are you kidding? Marni is an awesome point guard. We used to kick ass in this neighborhood back in the day. She's in the garage, c'mon."

He led me through a beautiful living room and kitchen, into a four car garage. The brother nodded at the lower half of a body working under the hood of a classic Camero. "Mar, you've got a visitor," he called, then backed into the kitchen and closed the door.

A blond ponytail, sticking out of the back of a Chevy baseball cap, whirled as Marni spun toward me. "I've seen you with Ellen Varner at a couple of our shows. You brought the girl with the chestnut hair and green eyes."

"That's me. I'm Jason Duffy. Max hired me to help find his collection. I'm talking with musicians who gave him an autograph this year, and also got invited to his annual snowboarding party. Do you have a few minutes?"

"Can we talk while I finish changing my points and plugs?"

"No problem," I replied.

I asked a few easy questions about what kind of paper she signed for Max and how he conveyed his Big Bear address.

After answering she asked, "Can you hand me the timing light and go start her up?" I stepped over a hose running from the tailpipe out a side entrance to the yard, and cranked the engine. After a few minutes she yelled, "OK, shut her down."

I walked to the front of the car. "This is a beautiful house. I don't suppose your other band mates had it quite this good when they were still living at home."

"Did you get that from our blue collar songs or from their apartment on the wrong side of Interstate 5?"

"I know how tough it is being in a band these days. I played the local circuit for 10 years," I said.

"Let's cut the rapport building and get down to why you're really here." Marni's expression was now serious and her tone lost its lilting quality.

I told her about the autographs and how I had narrowed his suspect list down to the members of The Tactile Tattoo, plus Pedgy.

Instead of demonstrating a temper, as I had anticipated, Marni asked, "Did you consider the possibility that the burglars could have been looking for something else, and quit throwing autographs around when the box was empty enough for them to realize it wasn't there?"

"There were several boxes taken. But this year's autograph box was the only one that was rifled."

"Maybe they noticed something a lot more valuable that was breakable, and didn't want to see it get squished. So they made room in the box by dumping some autographs, and tossed it inside," Marni said.

"The wind distributed them as if they were removed and released one at a time."

"All I'm saying is that there could be other reasons the autographs were blowing around the yard that have nothing to do with my band." Marni slammed the hood of the Camero. "Don't jump to conclusions." She held up her greasy fingers. "Now if you'll excuse me I'm going to take a shower."

As expected, Justin provided an insight into the female perspective that escapes most men. I mentally replayed much of our luncheon conversation, and called Kelly from the road.

"We need to talk," I said.

"That's what your message said," she replied.

"Can I come over?"

"With my décor of half-packed boxes, there isn't anywhere to sit."

"We can walk down to the park near your house."

"It's almost dark. Were you thinking of the homeless section or the junkie section?" This was not going well.

"You name it, that's where we'll go. I just want to try to work this out."

"If you're so anxious to work it out, why did you wait until today to call?"

I hoped that if I was forced to play the sympathy card, it would be much farther along in this process. But I sensed that I wouldn't get the chance if I didn't go into survival mode immediately.

"I never killed anyone before. I guess I didn't realize there was a time limit for getting my head on straight."

After a brief pause she replied, "We can go over to your house." Kelly hung up without waiting for a response.

When I arrived at her condo, she was standing in front with her arms folded, wearing the least sexy outfit ever made. I wondered if she bought it for this occasion. The only practical function for that outfit would involve the treatment of men who overdose on erectile dysfunction drugs.

We were in Southern California in August, but the trip to my place was frostier than Manitoba in January. When we arrived, rather than sit with me on the couch, which is our customary routine, Kelly sat in a chair. I wondered if she had unfolded her arms at any time since I picked her up. I reminded myself that I was operating on the sage advice of Justin, the oracle of male/female relationships. Why didn't I feel more self-assured?

"Let me start off by saying that I wasn't completely honest when I told you I don't want you to move in immediately. I realize that the guy I shot was a very bad guy, but it had a profound effect on me. When I saw you on Saturday, I hadn't been sleeping, and when I did doze off, all I could dream about was being attacked again, while I was with you."

"As long as you work in a criminal justice job, there will always be the possibility that a bad guy will come after you. Cops and their wives deal with it on a daily basis."

"I know, but being a PI is a little different. Bad guys can't look cops up in the Yellow Pages and know where they're going to be a good part of every day."

"Then why do you do it?"

"It wasn't until I became a PI that I truly found my calling in life. But life wouldn't be worth living if anything happened to you," I said, thoroughly expecting to close the gap between the chair and the couch.

"Where did you get that line, the Classic Movie Channel?" she asked.

"I don't care if you think you heard it before. I'm crazy about you, Kelly."

"Well you have a bizarre way of showing it; turning me into a homeless person."

"The guy that I shot, Donnie Daniels, was recently released from prison. I know that he was working with at least one other violent criminal that he met in jail, and there could be others. Daniels wasn't cornered. He led me on a chase until he got to a place where he figured he could ambush and kill me. Murder is not a last resort for these guys. I just need to tie this case up before I can welcome you into my home without being worried out of my mind."

"There's going to be a certain amount of danger with all of the cases you take on. I can't be expected to go away every time you get uncomfortable."

"When this case is over, I plan on taking some precautions that should make us both feel safe," I said.

"Such as?"

"I'll have a security system installed that's hooked up to a live response team."

"Can't that be done in just a few days?" she asked.

"I don't know. I imagine they come out to the house first and give us a quote. If we go for it, we'd probably get put on a list for installation. Then, when our name rolls around on the list, the job gets done. I have no idea how long that takes."

"I'll bet that if I pick up the phone tomorrow, call the first place I find in the Yellow Pages and say, 'I have two bids on a security system from other companies, but they can't do the job fast enough for me. How soon can you have one completely installed?' they'd tell me three or four days, tops."

"A security system was only one of the things I was thinking about to protect you. I also think we should get a puppy that will grow up to be a guard dog," I said, hoping the prospects of a fuzzy-faced, tail-wagging cutie would at least get her arms uncrossed.

She let out a controlled scream. "You make no sense at all! First you want to protect me, then you want to give me a puppy that will have to be walked and trained. It'll take at least a year before the puppy is big enough to offer any type of protection? What am I supposed to do in the meantime, live with your parents?"

The plan sounded so much better at The Four Seasons. I said, "I was just trying to—"

"I know exactly what you were trying to do – throw me a bone to keep me quiet until you solve your case. Well, it's not going to work! We're either in this together or we're going it alone. I can't be pushed aside because you think I'm a burden. There will always be dangerous cases. I have no intention of hiding out with a girlfriend every time you worry about me. I've got news for you, Jason. I worry about you all of the time. Deal with it!"

I had never seen Kelly so feisty. I briefly considered going for full disclosure by telling her about my harmonica with the .25 caliber hole, but quickly realized that would only compound the problem.

"I want to be able to offer you a semblance of normalcy. It isn't usually this dangerous. Things are happening quickly. As of today, I've got it down to three suspects. But right now there's a killer running around who knows I can have him put back in prison with a simple identification. He's going to do whatever he can to keep that from happening. I can't see us unpacking a U-Haul, wondering if we're in his gun sights."

"Then there's only one thing we can do," she said.

I asked, "What's that?"

"Get your father to ride shotgun on the U-Haul," she said, and smiled for the first time since I picked her up.

"Very funny."

"Then let me be serious, because I've had a lot of time to think about it since last Saturday. Somehow you have this idea that I'm some frail female who needs to be protected and provided with a safe environment. I can see how you might

128

make that assumption if we had just met, but we've been going out for two years. I told you about growing up in a house with alcoholic parents and older brothers. Sometimes it was hell. Sometimes I felt like Marilyn Munster, the only normal one in an otherwise crazy house. But that kind of extreme environment made me a mentally tough person. I've handled a lot more than the *possibility* of a violent person coming over to my house. Some of the violent people lived at my house."

"I know these things. I would never want to put you through that again."

"You don't understand. Growing up with that much drama, I learned to adapt. It becomes a part of who I am. It's part of why I'm not in love with an accountant. I'm in love with a guy who used to star in a rock & roll band; a guy who now brings bad guys to justice. You need more than the usual amount of excitement in your life, and so do I."

"I never thought about it that way, but what you're saying makes sense."

"Does that mean I'm not homeless anymore?"

"On one condition."

"What?" she asked.

"That you get out of that horrible outfit immediately," I said with a grin.

"Do I still get the puppy?" she asked.

"I think that can be arranged."

Chapter 22

At 7:15 PM Leandra answered her phone. "What the hell is going on?" asked her anxious boyfriend.

"Calm down, honey. What's the matter?"

"Max hired a private investigator. He was at our apartment a few minutes ago."

"It was probably just a routine visit. I'll bet he's talking to everyone Max knows."

"He said he's down to three suspects, and the other two live with me," he said.

"How does he know that?"

"He said the guys that did the burglary went through the recent autograph file in Max's yard and tossed all of the autographs they didn't need."

"What idiots!" Leandra exclaimed.

"He also told us that he killed one of the guys involved in the theft. Is that true?"

"I'm afraid so, my darling. It was one of John's best friends. He's very upset. Stay as far away from that investigator as you can."

"I will."

"I'd just die if anything ever happened to you, my love," Leandra said. She had never before expressed her love with so much conviction. It had the desired effect.

"I love you, Leandra. Don't worry. Everything is going to be all right."

After they concluded their call, Leandra walked to the living room where John was watching television with their mother. She hadn't passed out yet; clutching the channel changer in one hand and a cigarette in the other.

"John, would you give me a hand with something?" she called from the kitchen.

"Can it wait till a commercial?"

"Right now, John," she said, and exited to the exterior landing at the top of the stairs.

"What's so important?" he asked.

Leandra recounted what she had just learned. "What are we going to do?"

"I spoke to Luis today. He said the cops are guarding Duffy around the clock. He needs to wait, for now. The cops don't have the manpower to stay with him for very long."

"In the meantime, I'll be going out of my mind."

"I'm not worried about you. What about that boyfriend of yours? Do you think he has the stones for this?"

"Sure," Leandra lied. "You should hear him talk about transporting all of that pseudoephedrine. The guy's got nerves of steel."

"He looked pretty scared on the pharmacy loading dock. I hope you're right."

Kelly prepared a crab omelet for breakfast on Thursday morning. The move-in was looking better and better.

"What are you up to today?" she asked.

"Shamansky wants me to come along while he braces Graham Weston, the memorabilia dealer who assessed the Varner's collection."

"The guy Ellen didn't want to be around?"

"She said he made her uncomfortable," I said.

"I trust Ellen's instincts. If she had a problem with him, I would expect there was something to it."

"I know what you mean. I'm sure her comment made me suspect that he could have tipped Donnie Daniels."

"Tell me about Weston."

"He's a wiry little guy who's a bit too hard-sell."

"How little?"

"He's about 5'2" and probably weights no more than 110 pounds," I said.

"How tall is Ellen?"

"She's at least seven inches taller."

Kelly started laughing. "I may be wrong about this, but I don't think so."

"What's so funny?"

"I think I know why Ellen felt uncomfortable."

"Why?"

"It's a short guy; tall, well-endowed woman thing," she said. "I'll bet that Ellen either consciously or unconsciously felt he was staring at her breasts."

"You never met the guy. How can you say that?"

"Remember meeting my friend Dalia at the Peterson cookout?"

"I think so," I said, uncertainly.

"Tall, good looking, nice figure; she works in finance at a car dealership."

"OK, I've got her now."

"We had lunch a few weeks ago and one of the topics was about how short guys have been getting away with ogling for years. Dalia runs into them all of the time. She said that the worst offenders are aggressive salesmen. When you described Graham Weston, he sounded exactly like the kind of guy Dalia was talking about."

We carried our breakfast dishes to the sink. "I think you just saved me about three hours that will come in very handy today."

"In that case, I'll take about 20 minutes back right now," Kelly said and crooked her finger, leading the way back to the master bedroom.

When I arrived at the office, Cory was waiting for me and seemed a bit flustered. Before I left Barnett's apartment complex last night, I stopped by Cory's van and asked him to keep an eye on the comings and goings of the roommates. There was a flurry of activity shortly after I departed, and Cory had a hard time because of the number of roommates.

"It sounds as if you could use some help," I said, and Cory nodded vigorously. "Let me work on it and I'll get back to you."

Cory went off to his darkroom to develop photos, and I called my father. I was still pissed about Dad instigating my current dilemma with Kelly, but I also had to agree with Mom that another Cold War would do no one any good.

"Any chance of getting invited over for lunch?" I asked.

"You're always welcome, son. What's on your mind?"

"I could use your help on a case. Do you think you'll have some time?"

"I'll check with my appointment secretary and get back to you at lunchtime," he said, feigning sarcasm.

I called Shamansky and said I wouldn't be joining him for the meeting with Graham Weston. The detective was quite amused by Kelly's theory.

"I'll bet you she's right. But he still could have tipped Donnie Daniels."

I brought him up to speed on my meeting with Barnett and the roommates. I also mentioned my intent to get Dad involved in the case.

"I think that brick wall might have knocked some sense into you."

"Any word on Luis Hernandez?"

"The Heartbreaker is still MIA. We've been running through lists of known associates, but he probably knows police procedure better than our rookies."

"He has a tie to one of the band members. Do you think you could help me make the connection?" I asked.

"Give me the names and I'll see what I can do. The dropped fork is pretty thin, but I can see how you got down to five suspects. My lieutenant shouldn't have any problem with a search of the databases," Shamansky said, and signed off.

I arrived at my parents' house just after noon and was greeted by Mom. "I'm so glad you're getting your dad involved. He knows he messed up with you and Kelly."

"Water under the bridge. Have you told him about Kelly moving in with me?"

"Not yet. I'm waiting for the right moment," she said.

Dad walked into the living room. "Do you want to talk before or after lunch?"

"How close are we, Mom?"

"About 25 minutes."

"Let's talk now," I said.

Dad led the way to the backyard. We sat in the lawn furniture, and I told him about how I narrowed the suspect list.

"I can see why Shamansky isn't ready to ask for a search warrant."

"Don't you think Barnett's reaction was a bit much for an innocent guy with nothing to hide?" I asked.

"He might have plenty to hide. I know the *bad boy* image is big with musicians who play the heavy crap that you enjoy. But from what you've told me, this band is into love songs and a softer sound. A gambling addiction might not play so well with their audience or their record company."

"Emo isn't exactly soft rock, but gamblers often have big financial problems."

"Just because he's a gambler doesn't automatically make him your guy. If it came down to needing a warrant to find the collection, there's no way you could get one on what you have now."

"That's why I'm here. There are three of them, and Cory won't be able to follow them all. Do you think you can help out?"

"I thought you had five suspects," Dad said.

"I knew that one of the three roommates was guilty when that fork hit the tile. Besides, Marni's family is rich, and Pedgy is like a brother to Max. He's godfather to their oldest son."

"Are you planning on tracking all three?" Dad asked.

"If possible."

"What happens if they all go their separate ways?"

"It sounds like you have an idea."

"I'm pretty sure Kerrigan would help me out. We could take two vehicles to Oceanside and hang together until they split up."

"Do you think Kerrigan would be willing?"

"He complains about being retired all the time. He'd love it."

"Do you think he'll get along with Cory?"

"We won't be sitting in Cory's van."

"Cory said he had a hard time finding a good vantage point last night. There are lots of assigned parking spots and not much for visitors. The place is at full occupancy, with half of the residents being Marines from Camp Pendleton. They're not the type to see a couple of guys sitting in a sedan for hours and not do anything about it."

"Between me and Kerrigan, we have over 60 years of police experience. I'm sure we'll figure something out."

"One more thing, Dad. The bunko detective handling the theft is David Darden. "

"Oh, geez," Dad said with a sour expression.

"I think you better tell me about your history."

"Do you remember when the daughter of State Representative Danford Gilliam got kidnapped?"

"Sure. You got a citation for that one."

"She was grabbed on the way to school when the kidnappers cut off her chauffeur on the street, dragged him out of the limo, and shot him. I caught the murder case while the FBI handled the kidnapping."

"I was at UCSD at the time. Everybody was following it."

"The commissioner knew the media would be all over every detail. He assigned me all of the officers that he had on the short list for making detective, to help with the legwork. Darden was one of those guys. He made it very clear to me that his father was best friends with a city councilman. Then he moaned and groaned every time I gave him a job that he thought was beneath him."

"A real team player," I commented.

"In spite of Darden, my team found out where the girl was being held, and in a joint effort with the FBI, she was returned to her family unharmed. When it was all over, the commissioner asked me who I'd recommend for Meritorious Conduct Citations. When Darden's name came up, I said he

135

was about as helpful as a hemorrhoid. After that, Darden got passed over for promotion until after the commissioner retired."

"I can see why you two aren't buds."

Jeannine was all smiles when I returned to the office. "I finished my research on The Tactile Tattoo."

"Great! Bring it into my office and we can go over it. Any calls while I was out?"

"Two. Ellen Varner wanted to let you know that Chris Barnett called last night and apologized to Max for fighting with him a couple of weeks ago. You don't need to call her back. She just thought the timing was a little strange and you should know."

"Who else called?"

"Kelly," she replied. "She wants to know if you would consider a poodle. Personally, I think poodles are very cute."

"Cute is not a characteristic I intend to look for in a guard dog," I replied. "Tell me about the band."

"I can definitely see why those three guys are roommates. They have very similar backgrounds. All three attended Catholic high schools, all are considered gifted musicians, all three have social networking pages that list very similar interests, none of them has ever married, and all three have girlfriends," she said.

"How do you know they all have girlfriends?"

"I found a Society Page item on them in the North County Times. They participated in a fundraiser for one of the local hospitals. Here's a copy of the picture that ran along with the caption."

"It doesn't list the girlfriends' names in the caption. Are they mentioned in the article?"

"No. It was mainly about the event," she said.

"What else did you find out?"

"Garvey Thompson is a practical joker. He's thought to be good for morale. It sounds as though he's popular with the other band members."

"Did the article give any details?"

"It said that he picks on Jake Fuller for being very tight with a buck."

"What did Thompson say about him?"

"He said that Jake still has his postgame snacks from T-ball," she said, and we both laughed.

"The reporters are gonna love him," I commented. "What else do you have on Thompson?"

"Just that he is considered a maximum effort drummer. He always gives 110%. That's about it."

"Who's next?" I asked.

"Let's do the tightwad next, since we were just talking about him."

"Go for it."

"Jake Fuller appears to be the polar opposite of Garvey Thompson, personality-wise. He's described as quiet, serious, and focused on achieving his goals."

"Any bio stories on Fuller in the local papers?"

"No. I looked through the stories from when the first album was released to see if I could get some quotes. There were plenty from the others, but nothing from Fuller."

"How about Chris Barnett?"

"He's very verbal during live shows. It's kind of an interesting dynamic at their concerts. While Marni sings lead on every song, she rarely talks to the audience in between songs. Barnett does most of the talking, and Thompson throws in some playful comments that seem to go over well," she said.

"Did any of the articles call Barnett the leader of the band?"

"Whenever they mentioned leadership they talked about their manager, Dr. Dumajian."

"What about Marni?" I asked.

"A local magazine had one of those *Up and Comers* articles that did a four-paragraph profile on her. I got the impression it was written before the first album got slammed by the critics."

"What did it say?"

"That she has an adoring male fan base, but is too committed to her singing career to settle down. She even turned down a full scholarship to USD. The Entertainment Section of the local paper did a small piece that called her the next Ashlee Simpson."

"Entertainment Section articles are usually pretty light. Did you find any business news?"

"Just a rehash about how their first album bombed financially. Nothing you hadn't already told me."

"Keep digging. I know Dr. DD by reputation. I want to know a lot more. I'm going to introduce myself on the way to Oceanside. Do you have his office address?"

"Right here," she replied.

I explained to Dr. DD's receptionist that I was working to recover Max's collection and was granted an audience with the man affectionately known in my circle as *The Albino Werewolf*. Although he isn't an actual albino, his status as an actual werewolf remains questionable.

Rising from his desk, Dr. DD extended his hand and said, "Delighted to make your acquaintance, Mr. Duffy."

"Thanks for seeing me without an appointment."

"I presume it's a matter of some urgency. Considering the horrible misfortune that Max incurred, I'm quite willing to clear a spot in my schedule. Have a seat."

Dr. DD aimed a perfectly manicured finger at a club chair opposite his desk.

I said, "I was in the music business before I became a PI, and know a little bit about how it works."

"Don't be modest, Jason. I attended a couple of Tsunami Rush concerts. I've done business with your favorite club owner, Bernie Liebowitz, for many years. In fact, I was at his club the night you performed with Doberman's Stub. What's your point?"

"I'm aware of the problems that have been hammering the industry since the words *file download* came into existence. It was one of several reasons why I opted out of the business. Second chances are practically non-existent anymore. I was hoping you could shed some light on why an exception was made for The Tactile Tattoo."

Dr. DD stood up and pressed the finger pads of each hand together. "There is a cornucopia of talent in that band. Even the infamous national magazine critique that exsanguinated the debut album gave kudos to the instrumentation. The reason they got their second chance is twofold. First, the fatal flaw was readily identifiable and fixable. Second, the demo for the new album tested higher than a Dead concert attendee on 4/20. Simply put, it was deemed to have unlimited upside potential."

I stood to be at eye level with Dr. DD, leaned forward, and rested my knuckles on the desk. "I spoke with all of the band members and got the distinct impression that there was something they weren't telling me."

I then walked around the room as I described the driveway scene, and how I narrowed the suspects to the five musicians working on the album.

"Your accusations are outrageous!" thundered Dr. DD. "I hope your lawyer is as talented as your old lead guitarist because you're going to need a virtuoso when I get you into civil court!"

"Calm down. I don't think it was a conspiracy. It was probably just one of them in a bind for money. Does anybody spring to mind immediately?"

"Get out!" screamed Dr. DD. "And don't come back!" The Albino Werewolf's murderous expression made me glad we were two weeks away from a full moon.

I met with Dad, Kerrigan, and Cory at a convenience store parking lot at the end of the block from the East Bank Apartments. The complex was built into the side of a hill on the eastern end of Oceanside. It consisted of four two-story buildings; two on each side of the street, which ended in a cul-de-sac. The buildings on the right side of the street were about 20 feet above street level and the buildings on the left were 10 feet below street level. The boys lived on the first floor in the second-to-last apartment on the left, just below the cul-de-sac.

"Too bad we can't park in that cul-de-sac," said Dad. "We could be looking right into their living room without turning our heads."

"Actually, there are only a couple of spots on their side where you can park and keep an eye out without turning your head like an owl," Kerrigan stated.

Cory whispered in my ear. "Cory said you're welcome to join him in the van. There's plenty of room and no rubbernecking necessary." In spite of the whispering, a few epithets escape.

"No thanks. We'll manage just fine," said Dad, who raised his eyebrows and gave a knowing look to Kerrigan.

Cory again whispered in my ear. "In that case, Cory put orange cones in the parking space next to the Dumpster on the east side building. You can back into the space and see the top of the stairs leading down to the boys' apartment from there."

"Next to a Dumpster in August? Thanks Cory. We owe you one," said Dad.

"Since Cory's the only one who'll be able to see the front door, he'll call if someone is leaving. He's been tailing Barnett, so I think it's best to switch it up."

"Let me take him," Kerrigan said excitedly. "I always wanted to check out one of those Indian casinos."

"All right, you can have him. I'll take Thompson," Dad said.

"Cory, that means you have Fuller. If he leaves, one of you two needs to move into Cory's parking space and watch the door," I said.

"We were doing stakeouts when you were in diapers, son. I think we can take it from here."

"Cory, why don't you go back to the van, I have a couple more questions for these guys," I said, and Cory left. "Actually, it's a technical question."

"Shoot," Dad said.

"I'm trying to figure out where the collection is stashed. Shamansky is checking a database of storage facilities. I want to get a look inside the band's practice room. Is a warrant needed for that?"

"Not if you have the owner's permission," Dad replied.

Kerrigan added, "The practice room is the owner's property.

If he thinks something illegal is in there, he or his appointee can have a look."

"Thanks for your help. Call me if there are any developments," I said.

Chapter 23

I arrived at my office at 9:15 the following morning, after picking up Jeannine at her apartment. We found Detective Dave Darden standing at the entrance to the building. It was immediately apparent that he was not happy. We went directly to my office, where he declined an offer to sit down.

"I thought we had an agreement!" he shouted in his high-pitched voice.

"I can understand why you're pissed, detective. But I didn't put the plan together with Graham Weston. I found out about it the day it went down. At the time, I wasn't sure it was legit, or if Weston was just scamming me to get in good with Varner."

"At what point was I going to be informed?" Darden asked.

"My plan was to see if the perp showed, then tail him to wherever the rest of the collection was stashed."

"Your little plan didn't work out so well, did it?"

I was starting to get angry. "Hey Darden, did it occur to you that if we'd been together, one of the twenty-some shots Daniels got off might have ended up in you?"

"Not for a minute! I would have busted him as soon as he walked out of Weston's shop!" he shouted.

"Did you figure he left his gun in the car and didn't suspect the possibility that Weston might have ratted me out?"

"You think you have all the answers, Duffy, but you don't. I know why you didn't call me. You were afraid I'd bust him before you could get the collection back. I'm on to you, hotshot."

"Is that what you came over here to tell me? You're on to me?"

"No. I'm here to tell you that you're interfering with an ongoing police investigation. I don't want you near any of the collectible shops or even talking with anyone in the business until I close this case. Do you understand me?"

"Does this mean I can't call you Dave?"

Darden walked into the reception area, turned back and said, "Asshole." Then, he immediately looked at Jeannine, tipped his hat and said, "Sorry ma'am," on his way out the door.

"What's wrong with his voice?" Jeannine asked.

"I'm guessing his testicles never dropped."

That was no way to start the day. I decided I needed to work on my relationship with SDPD. So I called Shamansky and arranged an early lunch at his favorite bistro.

I was chatting with Larabee's hostess when Shamansky walked in. He appeared agitated, and didn't schmooze with the June Cleaver look-alike.

When we were seated Shamansky asked, "What the hell's the matter with you?"

"What do you mean?"

"The chief just pulled the surveillance team that's been keeping an eye on you. From what I gather, you told Darden you were no longer cooperating with him."

One of Shamansky's favorite waitresses got halfway to our table, then reversed course after seeing his expression.

"Darden ambushed me this morning. Before I could sit down, he was screaming at me for not asking his permission to do my job."

"I told you he was pissed. That was your cue to make nice," Shamansky said.

"Why should I have to suck up to him?"

"Because we're obviously dealing with some very dangerous ex-cons. We have no idea how big this is, or how many people are involved," he said.

Our waitress noted a calm moment and jumped in to quell Shamansky's agitation. By the time we placed our orders he was a new man.

"Were you able to run a check on area storage facilities?" I asked.

"It's in progress."

"How far along are you?"

"We've cleared about half so far. But that's just under the names of Daniels and Hernandez. I doubt they would actually use their real names."

"Then why bother?"

"Police procedure," he replied. "Plus, I emailed or faxed a photo of them to the ones that gave contact info. Who knows? Maybe it will ring a bell with some underpaid clerk hoping to collect a reward."

"What about the visitors list at George Bailey?"

"Nada. But I did get a list of every prisoner released this year who did time on "B" Block."

"Did any names stand out?"

"No, but it could come in handy if more of those guys are involved. It also gives me some places to look for Hernandez."

"How did your conversation go with Graham Weston?"

Shamansky snorted. "I shouldn't laugh, because I'm still not sure if Weston tipped Donnie Daniels about you. But Kelly was on the money about the booby ogling."

"How could you tell?"

"I took a tall, well-endowed officer along with me and told her what to look for."

"What happened?"

"She damn near cold-cocked him," Shamansky said. "The guy strikes me as a little sleazy, not just horny."

"I know what you mean. I'll try to find out what Max sees in him," I said. "Did Weston relay his conversation with Daniels?"

"He did, and it all sounded plausible. But I kept getting the feeling the guy was jerking me around."

"Did you accuse him of tipping Daniels?"

"I did, and I expected him to get very defensive, but he didn't."

"What did he do?"

"At first he took another gander at Officer Renfro's rack. Then he asked if you suggested that he blew your cover. I got the impression he was more concerned about earning a commission than about whether or not he was in trouble."

"It sounds like he was distracted by Officer Renfro."

"Speaking of racks, Weston had an 8"x10" glossy of The Tactile Tattoo on his counter. That Marni Hawley is a knock-out."

"The press compares her to Ashlee Simpson," I said.

"I'll bet she's the topic of conversation with the other band members' girlfriends."

"They seem to be friends. In fact, Kelly saw one of them give her a page from a fashion magazine. Besides, she was with a good-looking guy at the last show that I saw."

"If you say so. But I remember how my second ex responded the first time I was assigned a female partner. I think jealousy is a part of human nature," said Shamansky.

"What do we do now?"

"*We* don't do anything when it comes to memorabilia dealers."

"Ah yes, my persona non gratis status."

"You have plenty of other angles to cover, not the least of which is your own ass. Let me deal with Darden and Weston. How is your dad doing?"

I told him about the volunteer surveillance work until the check arrived. We agreed to keep in close contact now that the protection had been lifted.

Leandra stared absently at a shelf full of aspirin bottles she had just restocked. She felt a hand on her shoulder, turned, and saw Poppy looking into her eyes with a sympathetic expression.

"It hurts me to see you suffer. What's going on, Leandra?"

"I'm just worried about the future."

"I thought you were going to be a millionaire rock star's wife, and live happily ever after," Poppy said.

"Making it to the top isn't as easy as we thought."

"That's why it pays so well. Can you stand some advice from an old man?"

"Poppy, you've been like a father to me. Of course I want to hear your advice," she said, and meant it.

"I hired you after you told me you won an award for being at the top of the freshman science class. I could see from an early age that you could be a natural in pharmacology with a little hard work. And you did apply yourself right up until you decided your boyfriend was going to be a big-shot star. Then you stopped thinking about your career, and started figuring out how you were going to spend your millions. My sage advice is to apply yourself to your studies as if the big money isn't going to happen. If it does – great! You can buy a chain of pharmacies as a long-term investment. If it doesn't happen, you have a wonderful fallback position where you'll never have to worry about making a good living."

"That makes a lot of sense, Poppy."

"College registration is coming up soon. I'll be glad to build your work schedule around your classes if you promise to give it your all."

Leandra put an arm around Poppy's waist and pressed her cheek into his chest. "Thank you, Poppy."

The Painted Pony Casino Lounge was near maximum capacity on Friday night. I met Dad, Kerrigan, and Cory on the far outer ring of the parking lot and gave them tickets to The Tactile Tattoo show.

I said, "Cory, be sure to get in a position where you can photograph anybody near the backstage entrance who passes a message to any of our suspects. Dad, you and Kerrigan will be seated next to the wives and girlfriends section. Here's a picture of the girlfriends. If any of them are at the show, see if you can get close enough to eavesdrop."

"What are you going to be doing?" asked Dad.

"Justin managed to get me a seat at the table of Colonel Bradford Sterling. He's the owner of the band's practice facility."

"I heard of him. He owns Leatherneck Motors. Will you be making your pitch for accessing their room?" Dad asked.

"That's the plan. Let's meet back here after the show. I want to hear what the girlfriends had to say."

Ten minutes later I introduced myself to the colonel at his VIP table, just below the stage. Sterling wore black from feet to fedora, and accented it with an emerald green scarf.

"Thanks for agreeing to meet with me, Colonel."

"It's a shame what happened to Max. He saved up to take care of his family. But instead of being rewarded, he's the victim of a crime. It's a sad commentary on our society, Mr. Duffy," said the colonel, who appeared to be in his late sixties.

"Did Max tell you I'm a private investigator, hired to help recover the collection?"

The band started to play. "He did. I'm a law and order guy. I've been backing politicians for years that have the balls to stand up to those spineless judges who let pond scum back on the streets because the jails are too crowded. They disgust me."

"I'm glad to hear that, sir. We could use your help in bringing to justice the people responsible for the burglary."

"Whatever I can do," he replied.

"I need to get a look inside The Tactile Tattoo's practice room."

"Whatever for?"

"One of the band members was in on the burglary."

"I find that very hard to believe, Mr. Duffy. I hope you're not planning on running to the press with that ridiculous accusation."

"That's why I'm here today. The suspect has two roommates who are also in the band," I said before the colonel cut me off.

"I should bring my attorney in on this issue," he said, shifting in his seat.

I was about to plead my case when I heard my father, who was standing on the other side of a velvet rope divider. "Jason!"

"Who's that?" asked the colonel.

"It's my dad and his ex-partner from SDPD. They're helping me out."

"I think we can make room for a couple of guys my age," he

147

said.

The colonel tapped the shoulder of the man directly in front of him, said a few words, and the two men occupying the seats in front of them immediately exited.

"Come on over and have a seat," the colonel called to Dad and Kerrigan.

"We didn't mean to break up your meeting," Dad said.

"Not a problem," said the colonel.

I did the introductions and the colonel was downright effusive in his extension of hospitality. It appeared he was buying time to decide how he was going to act on the bombshell that was just dropped in his lap.

"Let me ask you a question, Jim. We're a couple of law and order, old school guys. How would you handle this if you were in my shoes?"

"What's that, Colonel?" asked Dad.

"This band has been a regular customer of mine for the past three years. I rent practice space to a total of 12 area bands. If any of them gets wind of the fact that I let your son snoop around, I could be looking at a slew of instant vacancies. Do I demonstrate my belief in the Constitution by saying, *innocent until proven guilty?* Or, do I try to weed out the bad apple before my place gets raided by the cops?"

Dad replied, "I'm a big believer in the Constitution. But the law says it's your responsibility to take action if it's brought to your attention that an illegal activity is taking place on your property."

The band launched into one of its loudest songs. The colonel said, "Gentlemen, can we continue this conversation in the coffee shop?"

We agreed, and walked past a few rows of video poker machines. The crowd had the kind of boisterous intensity you would expect at 10:00 on a Friday night. We made our way to a rear table in the coffee shop, which was nearly vacant.

The colonel said, "As you can imagine, I'm concerned about the negative publicity that could come from my helping to put a musician behind bars."

"We can appreciate that, Colonel. Let me assure you that our primary focus is on the recovery of Max's collection. Unfortunately, the band member has involved some ex-convicts who play with guns. The longer this thing goes on, the more likely it is that it will end badly," I said. "I want to take a look through the practice room and see if there are any signs of where the collection might be stored."

"You don't think it's in their room, do you?" he asked.

"No. Since your facility is open 24 hours a day, there are too many potential witnesses around. Besides, I think it's just one band member who's involved. The collection is too big to stash in that room without immediately raising a lot of questions. Plus, Max is in there every day." I said. "I would be looking for a storage locker key, an address book, an appointment calendar, or maybe just a note."

"I'm not sure if I can legally give you access."

Kerrigan saw a chance to join the conversation and interpreted the law in a clear and professional manner.

Dad added, "The best case scenario is if we can locate the collection, get the thief to fess up, and have him cut a deal with the DA's office before one of his accomplices gives the DA all he needs."

"Wouldn't he be better off coming forward on his own?" asked the colonel.

"That's probably not going to happen," I said.

"Why not?" he asked.

Dad answered, "Because the ex-cons he's working with have tried to kill Jason twice. One of them got killed in the process. The band member is probably worried that he'll go up for murder if he comes forward."

"Or, if he has any sense, he's probably afraid of the scumbags he's gotten himself mixed up with," added Kerrigan.

"The sooner we get him away from those ex-cons, the better the chance that he won't get tied into a homicide," I said.

Colonel Sterling stood up and said, "This is a real mess. I'm going to need the advice of my attorney before handing over any keys."

"I thought you said you were a law and order guy," I said.

He replied, "I am. The law gives me the right to get the advice of counsel. It also gives the police the right to get a search warrant. Good evening, gentlemen."

"That son of a bitch!" Dad exclaimed.

Kerrigan added, "I have half a mind to drive up to his car lot tomorrow and tell all of his hot prospects what kind of guy they're dealing with."

I asked, "What if I use the Harry Houdini skills I learned at UCSD to get in?"

Dad replied, "If you get Sterling's consent, whatever you find in that room will be admissible at trial. If not, a good lawyer could call anything you find afterwards *fruit of the poisonous tree*. Tainted evidence does more harm than good."

I pulled out my phone and said, "I'm texting a message to Jeannine, asking her to come into the office with me tomorrow morning and fire up her computer. Something tells me Colonel Sterling isn't quite squeaky clean."

"What time are you picking her up?" Dad asked.

"Between 8:30 and 9:00."

"Since Darden got your protection pulled, I'll tag along. Cory should be able to keep an eye on the boys in the morning. After a Friday night show they'll probably snooze into the early afternoon if they're anything like you were after an engagement," Dad said.

Chapter 24

I knocked on Jeannine's door at 8:45 on Saturday morning and felt a wave of anxiety sweep over me when she failed to respond. In her well-ordered, obsessive-compulsive world, Jeannine is extremely predictable when it comes to her job. She sent a return text last night saying she was fine with coming into the office this morning. She has never once been late, and on the rare occasions when she was sick, she always called at exactly 7:30 to give a detailed account of her condition. I dialed her house number and got no answer.

I dialed her cell phone, got voice mail, and briefly considered trying to kick the door down. A last minute flash of common sense prevented that mistake when I remembered the four deadbolts that secure the door. Reluctantly, I exited her apartment building and went to my office on the next block.

As I approached from a parking space just east of my building, Dad and Kerrigan walked around the corner.

"Have you heard from Jeannine?" I asked.

"No," Dad replied. "Is something wrong?"

"She didn't answer her door. She always answers her door."

"Maybe she's sick," Dad offered.

"She always calls."

We speed-walked to the hallway entrance, and I shoved the key in the door. When I stepped inside, I saw Jeannine face down on the reception desk.

Dad shouted, "Jeannine!" But she didn't move.

I rushed around the desk and placed my index and middle fingers on her carotid artery. When I did this, she jolted to an upright position.

"What are you doing!" she yelled.

"What am I doing? What are you doing? You nearly gave me heart failure. I thought you were dead. You weren't at home. You didn't move when Dad shouted at you. What's going on?"

Jeanine smiled and said, "I really scared you."

I responded by staring at her incredulously.

"I'm sorry, but I woke up in the middle of the night with a great idea and I knew if I went back to sleep I would forget about it in the morning. So I came over here to check it out," she said.

"What if Luis Hernandez had been watching your building or this building?" I asked.

"I'm sorry, Jason," Jeannine said and yawned. "I just got to sleep about an hour ago and I'm not thinking straight."

"I'll walk you home. You can tell us all about your idea when you're rested."

"I've got to tell you now. When we were working the Terry Tucker murder, your Army friend Glenda MacPhearson gave me access to a database that's now available to the public. I looked in it to see what I could find out about Colonel Sterling's service time in the Marines. Since he made it all the way to the rank of colonel, I was expecting quite a bit of information. But there was no record of a Colonel Bradford Sterling. Around 2:30 this morning I found out that he was actually a colonel in the Merchant Marines. Then I went home to bed."

"Good work. How did you end up over here again?"

"Before I could get to sleep, I realized that our new information wouldn't really give us any leverage with him unless we could prove that he intentionally misled the public into believing he was a member of the USMC. So I came over here at 3:30 and started searching the files of the local papers."

"I imagine he generated quite a few hits on your search engine," I said.

"You're not kidding. That man's a huge publicity hound. But he's very careful about how he phrases his affiliation with the Corps. I went through the San Diego Union-Tribune, the North County Times, Orange County Register, LA Times, and even the old Oceanside Blade, but there was nothing we could point to and say he blatantly lied."

"So we're still at square one with the guy?" Dad asked.

"Around 6:00 AM I got into the Military Press and did a search for the year he opened his car dealership." Handing a couple of pages to me, she added, "I printed it out and highlighted the good part."

Handing it back, I said, "Why don't you read it, Jeannine. It's your discovery."

For the first time in the six years that I had known her, after sleeping on the desk, she looked disheveled. This is unheard of for Jeannine, who always appears to be ready for a modeling assignment.

She read, "Colonel Bradford Sterling is honoring the Corps by naming his new dealership Leatherneck Motors. When asked what motivated him to do so he said, 'I wanted to do something special for my fellow Marines, and hope they will help make the business a success by supporting one of their own.' So, Camp Pendleton, let's get behind this distinguished vet."

"Great work, Jeannine. I'd say we've got the distinguished colonel by the short hairs," I said.

"I'd love to be the one to break the news to him," Dad said.

I replied, "I'd say a conference call is in order."

After twenty minutes of kicking around how to approach him, my father made the call. Unfortunately, the colonel had his secretary tell Dad he would be in meetings all day and to take a message.

"That sonofabitch!" Dad yelled.

I said, "I'm giving Jeannine a well-deserved morning off. Dad, how about if you and Kerrigan take a ride up to the dealership and deliver the news in person? Then you can relieve Cory."

"With pleasure!" Dad exclaimed.

"I have to make a few calls. Dad, would you drop Jeannine off at her apartment on your way out of town?"

"Are you ready, Jeannine?"

"Let me get my sweater out of the restroom," she said,

making her way gingerly across the room.

"Brace yourselves," I said.

A scream ripped through the office that could probably be heard on the first floor. In response to Kerrigan's quizzical look, I said, "She just looked in the mirror."

After their tune-up last night, the band was scheduled to do a final practice session on Saturday afternoon, take Sunday off, and start recording their album on Monday. Max said that for the dress rehearsal they would play the 12 album cuts in the order they would be recorded. He was told that he could invite Ellen, which probably meant the band members would be inviting their significant others as well. Cory reported that the guys stayed home last night after returning from the concert at 2:30, and that no suspicious characters were seen at the stage door.

It was date night, but I felt my presence was needed in Oceanside. If all went well with Colonel Sterling, I would be swinging by Sterling Studios in the wee hours. Considering our recent problems, I called Kelly to see what we could work out.

"I have Dad and Kerrigan helping with my case, and they need me to work with them tonight. How about if we move some of those boxes of yours this afternoon?"

"You sound worried. Is it going to be dangerous?"

"I am worried, but not about the case. I'm worried that you'll be pissed that I'm not spending date night making amends for last week."

"Don't be silly. Every night is going to be date night by the end of the month; which, by the way, is the day after tomorrow."

I realized that I forgot to arrange a truck and a helper for tomorrow.

"How many trips do you think the move will take?" I asked

"That depends on what size truck you reserved."

"I was just planning on using my friend's pickup," I said, feeling reasonably sure one of my friends would come through. When she started to protest I said, "I just had an idea. Let me

154

call you back."

It took four calls until I was able to reach Randy Dyer, former roadie for Tsunami Rush. "Are you still in the business, Randy?"

"Still livin' the dream," he replied. "I do freelance for four local bands, and even did a tour with a power band warm-up act in April."

"Do you have a lot on your plate for tomorrow?" I asked.

"I was just gonna chill at the beach."

I decided to let that one go. "Any chance you could help out an old buddy and earn some extra cash instead?"

"Did you put the band back together again?"

"It's something even more unlikely. My girlfriend is moving in with me and I really need a big truck and some big muscle. What do you say?"

"Do you have any idea how many times I get asked to help people move?"

"Yeah, but how many will pay you $100 for your time and $100 for the truck?"

"Are you kidding? They all want a free ride." Randy mulled the offer for a moment. "We had some really good times, Jason. I'm glad you finally decided to try a serious relationship. OK, I'll help," he said, and we worked out the logistics.

I called Kelly back and gave her the good news. The plan called for us to pack both of our vehicles with breakables and electronics for transport to my place this afternoon. Once we unloaded, I would head to Oceanside, and Kelly would stay at my place.

I arrived at Sterling Studios at 5:00 PM and learned from Cory, who was in Dad's Riviera, that Ellen Varner was the only one of the better halves on hand for the dress rehearsal.

I roused Dad and Kerrigan from a snorefest that could be heard 50 feet from the van. The moment Dad opened his eyes he broke into a smile and pulled a key from his shirt pocket. "Guess who's back on the law and order bandwagon?"

Kerrigan chimed in, "I'll give you a hint. He does a wicked

impression of Jackie Gleason when he says, 'Hum-in-a, hum-in-a, hum-in-a.'" We all laughed as I pocketed the key.

"I'll be going in later tonight, once we account for everybody."

I gave them a status report and Kerrigan said, "None of the girlfriends showed up. This might be boy's night out. We could be in for a long one."

We talked about coverage and contingency plans. Then we watched Ellen depart and return a half hour later with a Kentucky fried feast and a case of beer. An hour later she walked out the front door and jogged to the van.

"They're right behind me, so I'll make it quick. Marni and Pedgy are coming over to our house to watch a couple of movies. One of them is *The Last Waltz*, so they should be tied up all night. If anybody leaves early I'll give you a call."

She took two strides toward her car when the band rolled out the door. Jake Fuller staggered toward Marni's Camero.

"Looks like Fuller's got a snootful," commented Kerrigan.

"What did you expect? He's a cheapskate with a shot at a freebie," Dad said.

Max and Pedgy appeared to be having a disagreement as they trailed the pack.

The top was down on the Camero, and Thompson jumped in the back with Fuller while Barnett took the passenger seat. Holding onto Marni's headrest, Thompson stood and started singing *We Are the Champions* at the top of his lungs, and his roommates joined in. Fuller struggled to his feet, clutched Barnett's shoulders for stability, and fell back to a sitting position when Marni gunned the engine.

Dad said, "We may not have to watch these guys at all. They'll be spending the night in the drunk tank if a cop gets a look at them."

But they managed to navigate home without incident, arriving around 6:00. Marni dropped them off in front of their apartment and left immediately.

Cory parked on the cul-de-sac in front of their place while Dad and Kerrigan pulled in across the street and halfway down the block. I parked a few spaces behind Dad and joined Cory. Just after 7:00 we heard shouting coming from the apartment.

"You're not going back there until you pay me what you owe me!" screamed Fuller.

"Fuck you! That's how I celebrate! You'll get your money!" Barnett responded, and made his way toward the door.

"Oh no you don't!" yelled Fuller.

Barnett was about to close the screen door when Fuller burst through and tackled him into the upward-sloping front lawn.

I had the passenger window down to hear what was happening, and was so close to them that I risked being spotted. Cory jumped into the back of the van the instant the action started. I slunk down in my seat and peeked out the corner of the window.

"Get the hell off of me!" Barnett yelled. "Go scrub a fry pan or something!"

Thompson appeared at the door and watched them roll around on the ground.

"Guys, guys, you're bumming me out here! This is supposed to be a night to celebrate, not to fight. This ain't Wrestlemania, dudes."

Barnett laughed at that last comment, and Fuller stopped fighting.

"He's right, you know," said Barnett.

Fuller started arguing again and Thompson said, "Jake, settle down. I have an idea. We deserve a night out. Why don't we go with him? Chris can play a few games while we hit the lounge, and we can check him out every so often to make sure he doesn't lose his shirt."

"You're encouraging him," protested Fuller.

"No I'm not," replied Thompson. "I just think we should hang together tonight. What do you say?"

Fuller stood up and brushed freshly mown grass off of his pants and shirt. "Just this one time, but I don't want to stay out till all hours."

Barnett said, "I don't want him standing behind me all night complaining about how much I bet."

Thompson replied, "We're going as band mates and we'll all pull together to have a good time. That means no complaining about bets and no fights about leaving when Jake and I are ready to call it a night, OK?" The combatants agreed.

Fuller said, "I'm driving. If Chris drives we'll never get out of there."

"If you drive we'll be off the road before we get to the end of the block. Besides, I don't want to hear you whining to go home ten minutes after we get there," Barnett said.

"I'll drive," said Thompson. "We'll stay no less than an hour and a half, and no more than two and a half hours."

"That seems reasonable," Barnett said.

"I'm going to be bored out of my mind if we have to stay that long," Fuller said.

Barnett replied, "There's karaoke in the lounge starting at 8:00. You're just drunk enough to sing your Neil Diamond songs. You'll be fine."

Fuller let loose with an off-key slur of *Song Sung Blue,* and they all went inside to change clothes.

Ten minutes later we tailed the band mates in Cory's van.

I said, "Surveillance inside the casino could be a little dicey since the boys know me."

Dad replied, "Me and Kerrigan will take the lounge. Most of these casinos have slot machines everywhere. You can sit at a slot somewhere behind Barnett. He'll be focused on winning. You should be fine."

"What about when Fuller and Thompson come to check on him?"

Dad said, "We'll sit between them and the door. When they get up, I'll walk straight toward you and give a hand signal."

We pulled into the lot of the Oceanside Native American Dreamcatcher Casino and were directed to a parking space somewhere in the next county. We had two cars between Thompson and us as we approached the casino, but both cars continued going straight when Thompson turned, so we were forced by the parking attendants to close ranks and park alongside of them. The boys were all drunk enough not to notice.

I brought along a Padres cap, and pulled it down low on my forehead. I walked behind Kerrigan, whose 240 pounds on a 6'2" frame provided excellent cover, should one of the boys do a sudden about-face.

Barnett led the way through a couple of huge rooms filled with slot machines, video poker, and blackjack tables to a somewhat smaller room with craps tables in the middle and slot machines on the perimeter. He assumed an open spot in the middle of one of the craps tables, where he could place the more complex bets.

"I'll be here for the duration. If I decide to switch rooms, I'll let you know."

"Where's the lounge?" Thompson asked.

"Which one?" Barnett asked.

"The one with the karaoke show," Thompson replied.

"That would be the Turquoise Lounge. It's off of the next room, halfway down, on the left."

Dad and Kerrigan walked down opposite sides of the room, appearing to check out the various slots while maintaining a safe distance from Thompson and Fuller. I sat at a machine about 12 feet behind Barnett. Cory sat at the machine next to me, fed $20 into the slot, and began pushing buttons. I did the same, but at a much more relaxed pace. Unfortunately, we were at the machines closest to the men's restroom and had to put up with the sound of flushing and the occasional smell of ammonia pads.

The first half hour was uneventful. I went through $20, so I decided to check in with Dad. The Turquoise Lounge was only about a quarter full. Thompson and Fuller were seated at a mahogany and silver bar with lots of turquoise inlay. They were focused on a television set flashing the words to *Ebony and Ivory* as a deeply tanned, Caucasian, blond woman sang a duet with a red-haired, light-skinned man.

I sat at my father's table with my back to the boys. "What's going on?"

"I told your dad we should try *When Irish Eyes Are Smiling*, but he's being a big chicken," Kerrigan replied.

Dad said, "They're talking about a song they'll be recording on Monday."

"Anything else?"

Kerrigan replied, "Yeah, Fuller's trying to get Thompson to pick up the bar bill since he didn't want to come here in the first place."

"There's nothing exciting to report with my guy. Just thought I'd check in," I said, and exited.

I was back at my slot machine no more than five minutes when two very large, very muscular men stood behind Barnett. "I hope you're winning," said the shorthaired blond man in a deep voice.

Glancing over his shoulder, Barnett looked none too pleased to see them. "I'm about even, gentlemen."

"I think you need a bathroom break," said the dark-haired guy with a Harley-Davidson tattoo on his thick neck.

"Stay here," I said to Cory, and ducked into the restroom.

On the left were six urinals, with only one in use. On the right were three stalls and three sinks. I walked quickly to the last stall, left the door slightly ajar, sat on the toilet and pulled my feet up onto the seat. A few seconds later the restroom door opened.

I heard the blonde ask, "Are you almost fuckin' finished, or what?"

There was an immediate flush, and no running water in the sink. I heard footsteps walk down the row of stalls.

"Block the door," I heard the dark-haired guy say from directly in front of my stall. I wondered if these could be more ex-cons from George Bailey. As the thug walked back he said, "I thought after our last talk, you were gonna stay out of places like this until we got our money."

"We finished the prep work for the album today. I'm just doing a little celebrating with my band mates," Barnett said.

"That's one of the reasons I'm here tonight. Why don't you tell me how this payback plan of yours is supposed to work again," he said.

"After we record the album we go on tour. I get paid $2,000 a week. I give you guys a grand a week for ten weeks and we're even."

The blonde chimed in, "The boss sees two big problems with your plan. First, you're gonna get about 40% taken out in taxes. So, after you pay us the grand, that will leave you with about $200 a week while you're on the road. He thinks you lack the self-discipline to make all of your payments on time."

"Yeah, but I'll also be getting royalty checks from the CD and download sales."

"That brings me to the boss's other problem. He said that after an album is recorded it takes time to mix it, press the CDs, and get them in the stores. He said it could be six months to a year before it gets released," said the blonde in his ominous bass tone.

"He's right. These things don't happen overnight," Barnett said. "But this album is getting fast-tracked. The recording company thinks it has tremendous potential and wants to get it out there immediately."

"I think you're full of shit," said the dark-haired thug.

Barnett made a noise that revealed his surprise that these goons were aware of the fatal flaw in his plan. After stammering he said, "Our songs are based on famous mystery novels that are in the public domain. That means anybody with a library card can come in and steal our idea. The record company doesn't want its ass hanging out any longer than it has to."

"How soon till we get our money?" the blonde asked.

"Our record company does sample testing while we're still recording. They told us to record our top two songs first. If the test group has a problem with them, there's still time to make changes. If they like them, we're good to go. If they absolutely love them, then our manager asks for an advance and I pay you off immediately."

"Let's say your little fairy tale dream comes true. When will you get the word on the advance?" asked dark-hair.

"I should know something in two weeks," Barnett said.

161

I heard the restroom door rattle. Then someone yelled, "Hey Jack, get security. Somebody's gettin' a blowjob in the restroom!"

"We'll finish this later," the dark-haired thug stated, and the three of them filed out. A few seconds later I ducked out before the Pervert Patrol arrived.

I kept a close eye on Barnett, who was obviously shaken by the encounter. I expected him to cash out at any moment, when I saw Dad headed my way, giving the sign that the roommates were right behind him. I nodded at Dad, pulled my cap down, and lowered my head. Thompson and Fuller stood right behind Barnett, about seven feet in front of me.

"Are you winning?" asked Thompson.

"I'm up about twenty bucks. Did Neil get hit with any tomatoes?" Barnett asked.

"Asshole," Fuller said.

"We decided to keep a low profile," Thompson said.

Suddenly, my world exploded. A bell sounded in my slot machine that scared the bejesus out of me. Bright lights flashed in my face. Before I realized what was happening, the three band mates were staring at me.

A few patrons yelled, "How much did you win?" So much for discreet surveillance. I was sorry my father had to be there to see it.

Barnett walked over to me and asked, "Come here often?"

I replied, "Are you kidding? This is my favorite place."

A hostess appeared and said in a loud, game show announcer voice, "Congratulations! You just won five thousand dollars!"

"Let's get outta here," Barnett said to his band mates, and they exited quickly.

I looked to see if Dad was going to continue the tail, but he shook his head. Once the roommates were out of sight, Dad walked over and said, "Let them go. I'm sure they'll head straight home."

I cashed out and walked alongside Cory while Dad and Kerrigan walked behind us. As we neared the exit Dad said to

Kerrigan, "This doesn't surprise me. He always had to be the star."

"A fly on the wall, he ain't," replied Kerrigan.

We made our way slowly to the van in case the boys were in the parking lot discussing what they had just seen. But the space next to Cory's van was vacant.

Once inside the van I said, "We lose as a team and we win as a team." I then handed ten hundred dollar bills to each of them. "Here's one thousand apiece and one for the IRS."

It was agreed that Dad and Kerrigan would return home for a decent night's sleep and be back at 9:00 the next morning.

"Sorry you're getting stuck staying up all night again," Dad said to Cory.

Instinctively, Cory let out a response laced with four-letter words that caused the two ex-cops to squint. I jumped in to interpret.

"He's telling you that he has a new device that he'll train on their apartment door. It's a focused motion detector. If the door opens, an alarm goes off in the van, waking him up. If the door remains shut, Cory gets a good night's sleep."

"Amazing," Dad replied.

I wasn't sure if he was referring to the device or my ability to understand Cory. Either way, everyone was happy about the windfall and departed in a good mood.

Chapter 25

Just before midnight on a Saturday night, most of the bands with practice rooms at Sterling Studios would either be at their gigs or networking the club scene. I saw no one as I headed into the main reception area. The glass display cases, filled with guitar strings, picks, bass drum pedals, and numerous electronic devices, provided the main source of light at that hour. I started down the hall toward The Tactile Tattoo's practice room when I heard a toilet flush in the men's room just ahead on the left. Realizing that I had only a couple of seconds if the guy failed to *lave sus manos*, I ducked into the women's room directly to my left.

My senses were immediately assaulted by the unmistakable thump of bathroom stall sex. A female voice quivered, "We'll only be a couple more minutes." When I didn't respond she added, "But if ya really gotta go – don't mind us."

I peeked out the door in time to see a guy with a florescent green Mohawk turn left and head in the opposite direction of The Tactile Tattoo room. In my best falsetto, I let out an indignant "Hmmp!" and walked out. Nothing says *I love you* like getting poked in the back by the blunt knob of a bathroom stall clothes hook.

My ten years of experience as a musician brought me into several of these practice rooms. Tsunami Rush used to rent one near the Sports Arena in a facility that housed 24 bands. While all of the rooms reflected a look that was unique to the band and its genre, most of them had one thing in common: a footlocker for each of the band members.

I had seen everything from drug stashes to hair extensions in those lockers. A few years ago, I jammed with an 80's band that had a bald lead singer who slammed down a six-pack in less than an hour. Once he had his buzz on, he went to his footlocker, pulled out a 12-inch rubber dick, dropped it down the front of his spandex pants and said, "When ya got one of these, ya don't need the big hair."

True to form, The Tactile Tattoo had four footlockers arranged in a roundtable configuration at the far end of the room, serving as chairs when closed. Using the lock picking skills I acquired at UCSD, I had no trouble gaining access. I could tell that the first one I opened belonged to Chris Barnett by the set of Ernie Ball Super Slinky strings sitting on top. Taped to the back of the lid was an 8"x10" glossy picture of his girlfriend wrapped in a towel. Barnett was not lacking for inspiration with this hottie. The rest of the footlocker was filled with sheet music, clothes, and a distortion device that was being cannibalized for parts. I tossed the electronic gizmo back in and heard a strange echo in the bottom of the box. After probing the base with my fingers for a few seconds, a false bottom came out and I found a flat metal box, about the size of a laptop computer. Inside was a combination of newspaper articles, printouts from the Internet, and handwritten notes. I spent the next ten minutes reading.

Barnett had discovered that Dr. DD was known as The Vinyl Slasher in the mid-60s. I once read a story about Howard Stern where the author said he thought Howard might have gotten some of his shock jock persona ideas from The Vinyl Slasher. Apparently, he was absolutely vicious in all of his record reviews. More than a few careers bit the dust as a result of a Slasher attack.

From Barnett's research it seems Dr. DD's career failed to launch like Howard Stern's because lawyers were lining up to sue him, the radio station, and the corporation that owned the station. An out of court settlement was reached that included the disappearance of The Vinyl Slasher.

Dr. DD reinvented himself as a band manager after Woodstock. He saw a major opportunity by working the other side of the street, helping bands with name recognition that had fallen out of favor with their fan base. His first big resurrection project was one of the bands he put out of commission as The

Vinyl Slasher. In fact, three of his biggest clients were bands he ruined in his past life. Two are still active clients today. There was no indication of what Barnett was doing with this information.

Marni's footlocker looked to contain the expected combination of sheet music and makeup. Unlike Barnett's locker, the flip-top held no picture. I was about to close the lid when I noticed an envelope peeking out of a music tablature notebook. Inside were folded pictures of supermodels cut out of magazines. I decided to ponder their significance later.

In Garvey's footlocker, under a half dozen sets of drumsticks, was a large brown paper bag full of novelty store prank items. Most bands have someone who can lighten the mood and keep everyone loose. I thought that guy was Garvey Thompson until I picked up a rubber rat and noticed that it felt heavier than it looked. Upon closer inspection, I noticed an incision in the rat's belly, reached in, and came out with a small box of bullets.

Jake's locker was packed with bass strings, effects pedals, a direct-box, a graphic equalizer, XLR cables, picks, and polishing cloths. I also found a savings book with $8532, made in small deposits over a five-year period, and an empty prescription drug bottle. It was in the name of Jonathan Fuller and was for a very high dosage of Lasix, used in treating heart problems.

When I worked as a counselor at the outpatient mental health center, I had a client who died of a heart condition. I used to monitor his meds closely and remembered his dosage as being substantially less than what was indicated on Jake's bottle. Could this be the same guy who was rolling around in the grass a few hours ago?

A search of the remainder of the room proved fruitless. I carefully returned everything to its original place and shut off the lights. After quietly making my way down the hall and past the restrooms without being seen, I was practically bowled over by a statuesque brunette in a scoop-backed pink top when I entered the reception area. My mind scrambled for a quick cover story.

She asked, "Do you have any aspirin, or anything? My back is killing me."

"Sorry," I replied.

When she turned to walk down the hall, I noticed a bruise that was about the size of a nickel on her shoulder blade.

Chapter 26

My phone woke me from a sound sleep at 8:00 AM. Cory was in a panic because all three roommates just walked out the front door and got into their own vehicles. Dad and Kerrigan were not due back in Oceanside until 9:00.

"Tail Barnett and call me as soon as he gets where he's going. I'll call Dad."

Two minutes later I finished relaying the information to my father.

Dad asked, "Did Cory say if they were dressed up?"

"No. Why do you ask?"

"You told me all three of these guys went to Catholic school. I'm sure they're on their way to mass. If you put in an appearance once in a while maybe you'd be able to figure this out on your own." For the second time in a few hours Dad had seen my detective skills as decidedly less than impressive.

"Why would they take three vehicles if they're all going to the same place?"

"I'd guess that they have different things to do after mass," Dad said.

"How soon will you get to Oceanside?"

"Kerrigan's already here. We can get there in about 45 minutes."

"I'll call you when I hear from Cory," I said.

"I have one request."

"What's that?"

"If Cory tails them inside the church, ask him to hold off on participating in the responsorial prayers," he said, and hung up.

Sure enough, ten minutes later Cory called to say they all entered St. Sebastian's Church on Elm Street.

"Here's what I want you to do," I said. "Wait for Dad and Kerrigan. They'll be going into the church. I need you to find a spot where you can get pictures outside the front of the church. I don't really expect a rendezvous at mass. But it's possible that the last to leave could meet up with somebody after the others are gone. I'll tell Dad you have whoever leaves last."

At 10:30 I received a call from Dad, reporting that he had just tailed Barnett to the Oceanside train station where he picked up the three girlfriends and transported them to the apartment.

Randy Dyer is a native San Diegan who could double as a cast member from the movie, *Deliverance*. He's 6'3" tall, about 285 pounds, has scraggily brown hair, and muttonchops that feed into a wild mustache. He usually presents himself as a gruff, no-nonsense guy, which is understandable for someone who spends a lot of time behind nightclubs at 2:00 AM. But Randy can also be generous, kind, and very protective. Considering the events of the past couple of weeks, Randy was a very welcomed sight. He gave me a hand prepping my house for the Kennedy merger. By noon we arrived at Kelly's condo, and a mere 90 minutes later we were ready to make the first of two runs. Kelly packed bag lunches for each of us, which we ate in the truck.

We were in the process of loading the last of Kelly's stuff on the second run when Dad called. "Kerrigan just came up with something that might be important."

"What?"

"We tailed the boys and their girlfriends to a diner on Mission Avenue where they met up with Marni and Pedgy. Kerrigan and I followed them in, but they were seated halfway across the dining room, so it was hard to hear what they were saying. Cory stayed outside with his camera."

"What did Kerrigan find?" I asked.

Randy secured the back door of the truck.

"After the meal was over, I was about to start the tail when Kerrigan suggested we look through their trash. I thought it would be a waste of time, but when you have a partner you've got to run with his ideas some of the time."

"I think I'm about to get schooled in that area with Kelly."

"You have no idea, my son."

"What was in the trash?"

"By that point, the waitress had already started to clean up. Kerrigan flashed his *Retired Detective* shield and the waitress let him go at it. What a mess. They sure do enjoy their condiments," he said. "Anyway, he opened a napkin that was covered in catsup, and a note fell out."

"What did it say?"

"It said, 'Duffy's friend is outside with a camera. You might want to catch the next train after we eat.' It sounds to me like the girlfriend is in on it," Dad said.

Randy interrupted, "Can you finish your conversation on the road?"

"Sure." I covered the phone with my palm, handed Kelly the RXS keys, and asked, "Can you drive?" She nodded and we were off.

"Are you still there?" Dad asked.

"I'm here. Did you see who passed the note?"

"No, we were across the room and didn't have a good angle."

"I'll check with Cory to find out if he saw anything."

"What was in the practice room?"

"I hit the mother lode in the deep dark secrets department."

"Such as?" asked Dad.

"Garvey Thompson had a white rubber rat with a slit in its belly. Inside were six bullets. What do you make of that?"

"If I thought there was a chance he was one of the burglars, I'd say it was pretty significant."

"But?" I prompted.

"But we know that all of the band members were together in Oceanside on the day it happened."

"Don't you think it's an unusual item for an innocent man to have in his locker?"

"Where were you the day your Civics teacher talked about the Second Amendment? Do you have any idea how many gun owners there are in the US?"

"I get your point, but still think we should follow up on it."

"Go ahead and tell Shamansky, but don't get your hopes up too high. By the way, what did you tell me was your reason for getting a revolver and a carry permit when you were in the band?" Dad asked.

"Some club owners paid in cash, and I was in a lot of alleyways at 2:00 AM holding the money while our truck got loaded."

"I gotta run," said Dad.

"What's going on?"

"Fuller is about to drive off with his girlfriend. Kerrigan has them. I flashed a sign to Cory, and I think he knows he has Thompson. I've got Barnett. I'll call back when I find out where they're going. Call me if Cory saw the note being passed."

"Will do," I replied, and hung up.

I called Cory and filled him in on the plan. He didn't see the note get passed. We discussed contingencies on how to proceed if the suspects opted to stay in or go out.

"Is there a chance we'll be able to use any of that high-tech surveillance equipment to hear what they're saying inside the apartment?" I asked.

Cory said that he already tried, but they constantly run a noisy air conditioner when they're home, so there's no chance of electronic eavesdropping.

After we unloaded the truck, Kelly and I took Randy to The Sizzler, his favorite restaurant in the world. He ordered two entrees: their largest steak and a chicken fettuccini alfredo.

Randy regaled Kelly with tales of the glory days of Tsunami Rush. I did my best to participate in the conversation, but my mind was being bombarded with thoughts of how to identify the band member who wrote the note. Maybe we could analyze the writing. Maybe the police could get DNA off of the napkin. Both of these ideas had merit, and both had serious flaws.

While Randy was on his third trip to the salad bar for another round of chicken wings, I said to Kelly, "Thanks for

171

carrying the ball in this conversation."

"I know you have a lot of things going on today. I appreciate that you're here, and didn't leave me with Randy when your dad called," she said.

"I nearly screwed this up once, I don't intend to do it again."

Randy followed his plate of wings with two deserts and a beer. I recounted a couple of Randy tales, which pleased him to no end. We agreed to keep in touch, and parted company in my driveway.

On their ride back to the apartment from brunch, Leandra listened to her boyfriend tell of his encounter with Jason Duffy at the casino. He was definitely nervous, but maintained a bit of false bravado. They acted as natural as possible for an hour of socializing. After Marni and Pedgy left, the couples adjourned to their bedrooms.

The Rock Star's bedroom was just off of the kitchen at the front of the apartment, while the other two were in the rear. With the air conditioner rattling, it was clear they could talk freely without being overheard.

"I can't believe how stupid we were," he said. "We didn't have to rip Max off."

"I thought you agreed it was the only way to be sure our secret never comes out."

"That autograph might have never made it out of Max's file cabinet. Now Max is financially ruined, his kids might not be able to go to college, John's friend is dead, and my band mates are getting suspicious of each other. And, all of this is happening at a time when we're supposed to be at our best, going into the studio tomorrow."

Leandra said, "Max can't afford to pay Duffy indefinitely. This is going to go away soon. You'll see."

"I hope you're right. But for now, I'm feeling so stressed I can hardly concentrate. Studio time is really expensive and we're only getting one week to lay down the tracks. If I make a lot of mistakes the record company might back out of our deal."

"You're going to do fine. You go into another world when you play."

"I never had to perform under this much pressure before."

"Maybe I can give you an attitude adjustment," she said.

"How are you gonna do that? You'll be at work."

Leandra handed him a pocket-sized photo of herself, kneeling on her bed, wearing a lacey blue bra and panties. The bra was unhooked and dangled just above her nipples. The panties were slung so low that she might have been wearing a tool belt just prior to taking the picture.

"Maybe if you put this where you can see it while you're recording, it will take your mind off of your troubles." His grin said it all. "But if your band mates see it, don't expect any more presents for a very long time."

"We can't have that," he replied, and they fell into each other's arms.

I was expecting our first night of cohabitation to be filled with unbridled passion and attentive lovemaking. In reality, we were both exhausted from the move and spuriously stuffed after watching Randy put on the feedbag. Kelly opened a bottle of wine and toasted the start of our new living arrangement. While we sipped, I told her what was going on in the case, and the contents of the footlockers.

"I need your women's intuition on something."

"OK."

"All of the guys have pictures of their girlfriends prominently displayed on the inside lid of their footlockers. Marni was with a guy at one of the shows that we saw, but his photo was buried under a pile of sheet music. I found an envelope filled with pictures of pretty girls cut out of magazines. What do you make of that?"

"It sounds like you think she might be a lesbian," Kelly commented.

"What do you think?"

"It's possible. Or, she might be bisexual. But it's also possible that she's thinking about changing her hairstyle or considering the clothes the models are wearing. Did you ever see her kiss her boyfriend?"

"To be honest, I never paid much attention to her when she wasn't singing."

"Oh c'mon, she's a knockout. I find it hard to believe you weren't giving her a second look."

"Are you kidding? I was with you both of those nights that we saw the band. If I wanted to see a real knockout all I had to do was have you catch me giving her the twice-over and you would have gone Jimmy Marcello on my ass."

Kelly responded with a two-handed tickle maneuver. "What happened with Jimmy Marcello? You never did give me any details."

"It's a long story and he's no longer a suspect. One thing Dad learned today is that the girlfriend knows about my involvement in the case."

"I wonder if she had to pour half a bottle of wine into him before he told her about what was happening?"

"I wouldn't be surprised."

"Too bad you can't just take them all out for drinks before you ask your questions," she commented.

Chapter 27

Shamansky called on Monday morning to say the Lasix prescription found in the footlocker was actually for Jake's father. We speculated on the prospects of bartering memorabilia for a heart on the black market. It seemed pretty remote for a guy who had no apparent connections to the underworld. We also discussed the more likely possibility that it could finance a costly operation. I said I'd look into it.

I called the office of the physician listed on the prescription bottle found in Jake's locker. After dialing *67 to block caller ID, I reached a receptionist and said, "This is Curt Refice from County Medical Transport. I'm scheduled to pick up a Jonathan Fuller and take him over to University Hospital for an angiogram, but somebody put the wrong address on my pickup sheet. I see Dr. Aziz is his primary. Can you give me the right address?"

"I can't give out patient information over the phone," she replied.

"Can I ask your name?"

"Amelia Robeson."

"Usually, I'd say fine and ask you to call the U. to reschedule him. But he was in my van last week, and frankly, he looked so bad I'm surprised he's still with us. I don't want to get drawn into a lawsuit over this. So if the family calls up after he dies and says they think it could have been prevented if only he had that angiogram, I'm going to give them your name. OK?" I asked.

After 10 seconds of silence she said, "Hold on." A minute later I was given an address followed by a quick dial tone.

As I was getting ready to visit the Fullers, the bass player from Tsunami Rush, Kyle Kramer, called to say he was having lunch with our drummer, Derek, and would I care to join them.

I hadn't seen them in over a month, and accepted the invitation.

The Fullers lived six blocks north of Balboa Park in an older section of town. The entire house could have fit into Marni's living room. I felt badly about disturbing the family under the circumstances. But I reminded myself that there was a decent chance that Jake could have been in on my rendezvous with the hitman, and rang the doorbell. A stout woman in her early fifties opened the door.

"Are you Mrs. Fuller?"

"Yes, what's this about?"

"I'm a field agent with CLAM Concert Promotions. My company is considering the sponsorship of a tour by The Tactile Tattoo. I'm doing a background check on the band members. Could you spare a few moments?"

"This is for Jake?" she asked.

"Yes, ma'am. May I come in?"

"Of course. Have a seat on the couch."

As I entered I made eye contact with Jonathan, seated in a wing chair next to the front window. A blue oxygen tube dissected his face. We exchanged nods.

Over the next twenty minutes I asked a series of questions ranging from Jake's interest in music memorabilia to his favorite place to go when he wants to be alone to write music. It became apparent early in the conversation that no matter the question, the answer was always the same: Jake should expect to be canonized as a saint. No pertinent answers were disclosed.

The trip wasn't a total loss. Jake's mom seemed to have a good handle on the names of his friends. The only *Donnie* she knew of was a miserable junior high boy that put a depilatory cream in Jake's hair gel in 8th grade.

I thought I had a lead when I asked, "Does Jake know a Luis?"

"Oh my, yes," she replied.

"Can you tell me the nature of their relationship?"

"Jake asked Louise to go to Father Mike's freshman pool party. She was quite the little missy. But do you know who that little stinker ended up going with?"

"Depilatory Donnie?"

"Jake was crushed."

"I'd say Donnie and Louise got what they deserved. Thanks for your time. I'll let my boss know that your son won't give us any trouble."

On my way back to the RXS, I wondered if Louise saw a doctor about puberty reversal after Donnie creamed her bathing suit. It was definitely the kind of topic Kyle would enjoy at lunch.

Just after noon I walked into A Taste of Athens and was given the ball-buster greeting I had come to expect. Kyle couldn't wait for the obligatory small talk to end, and waived our waitress over immediately. He ordered a falafel, and Derek asked for a spanikopita. I ordered a roast pork sandwich with gravy on a toasted roll.

"You're not doing much to dispel the *meat and potatoes* Irish diet stereotype," said Derek.

"Didn't you hear me pass on the fries?" I replied.

Tsunami Rush played together as a band for seven years. My earnings financed my college education and also supplemented my income as a mental health counselor in the years prior to becoming a private investigator. We used to get together once every month or so after the break-up to jam, relive the glory days, and drink beer. But since a famous band hired our lead guitarist, the get-togethers have been drastically curtailed.

Derek said, "I want to hear about your case. Is there anything interesting happening?"

"As a matter of fact, I could use your opinion on something." I told them about Dr. DD's secret identity as the Vinyl Slasher. "My dilemma is that if I tell Shamansky, I'm pretty sure it will have to go into a report that will eventually be accessed by the press. I wouldn't feel good about outing this guy. He's done a lot of good since his shock-jock days."

"I'll bet you'd feel differently if it was our band that he ruined," said Kyle.

"I went online and read some of his old critiques. I think he was right about the albums he slammed. Back then, if a band was hot, the record companies forced them to crank out albums as fast as possible. There was a lot of crap that came down the pike," I said.

Derek added, "Not to mention all of the bands that slacked off once the money and drugs started rolling in."

"Exactly. I read about 20 of his reviews and, while I'm not a fan of the shock-jock approach, I didn't read any that I felt were unjustified," I said.

"Some people need a pat on the back and some need the old sneaker in the padunkadunk," Kyle said.

I was in the process of agreeing when my phone rang. Glancing at Caller ID I said, "Yes, Jeannine."

"Michael, I'm calling to cancel our date for tonight," she said.

"You've got Jason, not Michael," I replied, and nearly hung up.

"I know. But, my mother was really sick this morning. I could barely get her out of bed," she said.

Something was very wrong. Jeannine's mother died five years ago.

"Are you all right?" I asked.

"No, don't worry about it," she replied. "I got the flowers you sent. They were pretty as a picture."

"Is there somebody at the office that you can't talk in front of?"

"Yes. I'd say as pretty as the picture you took of me in front of the oleander bushes out front."

I took that picture with the camera on her office cell phone. I activated my phone, opened her message, and a chill went through my body. I was looking at a shot of Luis Hernandez in my reception room.

"Don't panic, you're doing great. I'll figure a way to get you out of there and call the cops. Just keep playing it cool."

"Love you too, honey. I'll see you soon," she said, and hung up.

"What's going on?" Derek asked.

"Call 911 and tell them Luis Hernandez, the subject of a manhunt, is at my office right now!"

Derek called while I scrolled through the numbers stored in my phone. I found Heather Gains, a CPA who occupies the office next to mine.

I said, "Heather, it's Jason Duffy from next door."

"Well hello, Jason. Are you ready to do some tax planning?"

"I have an emergency, and I need your help."

She replied in her New York accent, "After the boost you gave my business last year, I'll be glad to do whatever I can."

"I need you to go next door and ask for me. When Jeannine says I'm not there, tell her you're working on my quarterly tax returns and you can't read my writing on several receipts. Tell her you need to get it in the mail today, and you want her to come downstairs to your office and interpret my hieroglyphics."

"But my office is right next door, not downstairs," she protested.

"I don't want the guy who's in there with her to know that," I said.

"This sounds dangerous," she said warily.

"Not if you're a convincing actress."

"Are you kidding? I starred in *The Jewish American Princess and the Pea*, at Public School #129. I killed 'em."

"Then break a leg, Heather," I replied, trying not to sound stressed.

Five minutes later I was weaving in and out of traffic on the freeway as fast as humanly possible. My only solace was that I reached Shamansky who said he would drop what he was doing and rush to the office. Twenty minutes later I bounded up two flights of stairs and into my office, where two uniformed policemen stopped me at gunpoint. After producing ID, they allowed me to look around. On Jeannine's desk I found her cell phone with Luis's picture prominently displayed. Next to it was an 8"x10" picture of Jeannine and Michael lying flat on the desk. Luis had put a bullet through Jeannine's forehead.

Nothing else seemed to be out of place.

I went to Heather's office and found it locked. After identifying myself, Heather opened the door. Jeannine was quite visibly shaken. Heather told me they were fine until they heard the gunshot.

"She thought you had returned and gotten killed," Heather said.

"Both of you were absolutely incredible. I'm very proud," I said.

I wanted to walk Jeannine back to her apartment, but knew the police would need a statement from her. Heather said it would be all right for her to stay until Detective Shamansky arrived.

Five minutes later Shamansky walked in and took command. I asked, "Do you think we could get rid of the picture of Jeannine before she comes back in here?"

Shamansky began giving orders. The criminalists were now on the scene. After taking numerous digital images of the desk, they bagged the photo and put it away.

"Do you want me to get her now?" I asked.

"Not just yet," he replied. "Let's go in there," he said, pointing to my interior office. After securing the door he said, "Before we bring her in here I suggest you get a plan together for keeping her safe."

"I was thinking about that while I was waiting for you. The band will be putting in a lot of 12-hour days. I'll have Dad and Kerrigan work out of my office until I have some other security measures in place."

"Any chance Hernandez got her address?" Shamansky asked.

"Nothing else seems out of place, and she took her purse to Heather's office."

"How secure are her locks?" he asked.

"The whole building is tight. I'll go through the drill about not opening her door to anyone. I'm sure she'll be very receptive."

We walked Jeannine back over to the office and Shamansky

was quite sensitive to her fragile state as he conducted his interrogation. When he finished, I walked her home and gave my security speech. She was greatly relieved when I told her Dad and Kerrigan would be around for a while.

When I returned to the office I called Drayton Claymore, a former mental health client that I helped find a position as a security consultant. Unfortunately, I was told that Drayton was no longer affiliated with the firm. My next call was to Andy Stelzner, my former supervisor at the mental health center.

"Andy, I need a favor."

"I knew that rock & roll lifestyle would eventually lead you back to our doorstep," he replied.

"Very funny. I need a phone number for Drayton Claymore. I tried calling him at Kitzer and Kitzer, but he's no longer there."

"You act surprised," Andy observed.

"I thought it was the perfect gig for him. What happened?"

"You know that stuff is confidential."

"I was his therapist."

"*Was* being the operative word," he said.

"I'm offering to help him out once again with another job. That would make me a volunteer. What happened?"

"He started having a problem at last year's company Christmas party. Old man Kitzer married a younger woman who showed up at the party wearing an outfit with a white fur collar. Drayton followed her around and told her she was wearing his lost kitten, Fluffy. Apparently, he kept petting the collar saying, 'I miss you Fluffy.' The guests thought it was hilarious, but the new Mrs. Kitzer was miffed."

"Don't tell me they fired him for that."

"It happened two months later. This time Mrs. Kitzer stopped by the office with her new poodle. Drayton planted a miniature camera on the dog's collar, believing Fi-Fi would lead him back to Fluffy. Mrs. Kitzer left the office and went straight to the women's dressing room of the Apollo Health Club while several of Drayton's coworkers monitored the incident," he said.

181

"How did Kitzer find out about it?" I asked.

"One of the young techs, who hated old man Kitzer and planned on leaving soon, put it out on the Internet the next day."

"What's Drayton doing now?"

"I think he's collecting SSI. What do you have for him?" Andy asked.

"I need him to design and install a security system." Andy gave me Drayton's phone number, and we agreed to have lunch soon.

Prior to making the call, I briefly stopped to consider how Drayton might get along with Jeannine, Cory, and Dad. Drayton was one of those mental health clients that didn't exactly fit the mold of one particular malady. Initially, he was diagnosed as a Paranoid Schizophrenic. He was referred through the court system after it was learned that he broke into three of his neighbor's homes and installed audio and video monitoring devices. He told the courts that he was sure they were conspiring against him, so he was just keeping an eye on them out of self-preservation.

Reading the court records convinced me that the initial diagnosis was correct. But Drayton's behavior defied expectations. He was the life of the party and found almost everything he encountered to have a humorous side. Invariably, he went overboard in communicating that to others. He told jokes, played pranks, and teased. His most annoying behavior involved puns and twists on what other people said. He spent several of our sessions doing nothing but a lame stand-up routine, where I played the straight man and Drayton did his best to turn everything I said into a joke.

I didn't miss working with him. However, I'd never seen anyone so well versed in electronic surveillance. Drayton not only knew every piece of equipment on the market, he also knew what each manufacturer had in development and when it should be available for purchase.

The notion of putting Drayton in the same room with Cory, Jeannine, and especially my father, was very scary. But it was the only way I could get a top-notch security system within a reasonable time and budget.

The phone rang three times. "Drayton, its Jason Duffy, your old therapist."

"I blew it Jason. I lost the job you got me. I should have been thinking Duffy and I was thinking Fluffy. My bad," he said.

"I hope you've been keeping up with the technology because I've got a little consulting job for you."

"Don't tell me old man Kitzer got over seeing his pooch video his kooch."

"No. I want to hire you to design and install a security system for my office as soon as possible. We had a bad guy pay us a visit today, and I realized how much I need your expertise. Can you come over to my office first thing in the morning?"

"I can come over right now," he replied.

"The cops are still here, so tomorrow will be fine." I gave him the address.

Toward the end of the day, Jeannine found a phone number for Chris Barnett's parents. I tried using the same ruse I had run on the Fullers and got my tympanic membrane stretched to the limit by an irate Mr. Barnett. Apparently, Mrs. Fuller gave Jake an accurate description of her grand inquisitor and the word was out. I wasn't terribly disappointed since the Fuller interview seemed like a waste of time.

Shamansky called as I was about to head home. "I just wanted to give you a bit of information that I thought you might find interesting."

"What's up?"

"I stopped by Darden's desk to fill him in on the events of the day and he told me Graham Weston has a sheet with the feds."

"What did he do?" I asked.

"He was busted for income tax evasion following an audit six years ago. I'm sure a lot of small businesses scam on their taxes, but it also shows a willingness to break the law,"

Shamansky said.

"I'm still not sure what to think of that guy."

"Did you ever find out what Max Varner sees in him?"

"No, but it just got bumped up on my priority list. I'll check it out. How are you doing with the parolees of "B" Block?" I inquired.

"We have twelve of them in San Diego and Orange Counties. I decided to do pop-ins at home instead of calling them on the phone."

"How come?"

"Because I wouldn't be surprised if one of them has the collection at his residence."

"Do you think you'll see it sitting on the dining room table?"

"I have a pretty good sense of what a convict looks like when he's holding. I've seen it a hundred times."

I wasn't a big proponent of the *watch their lying eyes* school of detecting. But I recognized the value of reading body language, so I didn't bust Shamansky's chops for trying to be intuitive. "Any luck so far?"

"Convicts with nothing to hide have no problem telling cops to take a hike. I tried to find out who Donnie was tight with on the inside, but no luck so far."

"Any plans for Weston?"

"I asked around and found a patrolman out of Western Division who's a rock memorabilia nut. I'm going to review the list of stolen items with him, and send him in for a buy. I'll let you know if anything interesting happens. Now, what can you do for me?"

"I'll call Ellen Varner and find out why Max does business with Weston."

"Let me know ASAP," he said, and hung up.

Ellen answered on the first ring. "I was just thinking about you. Are there any new developments?"

I spared her the details of our visit from Luis Hernandez. "We're getting close, but we have a few pieces of the puzzle that just don't fit. I was hoping you could help."

"What do you need to know?"

"I'm still not sure if Graham Weston was involved, but I've seen him in action and I can't figure out why Max does business with him."

"I know what you mean. I told you about leaving Big Bear because he made me very uncomfortable," she said.

"Yes, I remember. Do you know what Max sees in him?"

"I think so," she responded. "Max was best friends with the boy next door when he was a kid. They did everything together until they got to junior high. Max grew up to be a big, strong, popular musician, but his buddy stopped growing at 5'1" and was the butt of a lot of jokes.

"Max said he stuck up for his friend for a long time, but when he discovered girls he stopped hanging around with his old buddy, and eventually started a fight that ended the friendship. He felt badly about what he had done after he matured a bit. But by that time the boy had moved out of the area and Max was stuck with an unresolved sense of guilt."

"So you think Max overlooks Weston's shortcomings to make up for his past sins?" I asked.

"That's my best guess. I just wish the little creep would stop staring at my boobs all the time. That can get very annoying."

"I can imagine. Has Max said anything more about his relationship with Chris Barnett?"

"Not a word. Do you think he did it?" she asked.

"He's one of the suspects. But if Max says anything it could mean the collection gets destroyed. If you tell him, be sure to stress the importance of keeping it quiet."

"Max misses the collection terribly. He talks about it all of the time. He's like an artist who lost his life's work. I don't want to pressure you Jason, but I want you to know, our family is really counting on you," she said.

"I understand, Ellen. I wish I could guarantee that you'll get it back, but we're dealing with some very bad people who have little respect for your treasures or even life itself. There are some ex-cons involved, but that's not necessarily a bad thing. They should understand that the collection can be used as a bargaining chip for a reduced sentence if they get caught."

"I hope you're right. I'll say a prayer for you. I know you've been through a lot for us," she said.

"Thanks, Ellen. I'll be in touch."

I called Shamansky and gave him the details on Graham Weston. He was quite amused that Ellen picked up on the breast fixation. I offered to help interview ex-cons, but Shamansky felt his boss would have a problem with subcontracting the legwork to a PI.

Chapter 28

Having Kelly around was a real pleasure. However, on Tuesday morning I found myself not wanting to share the near catastrophe that happened at the office the previous day. Yet, I felt obligated to offer some explanation when she asked why I tossed and turned all night.

"I went to sleep with something on my mind," I replied, hoping she would take the hint that I didn't want to talk about it.

"What?"

I felt compelled to show her I was learning the importance of strong lines of communication in our relationship, but saw a big downside to telling her about the many risks involved in my job. I was sure she didn't feel the need to share every little problem that went along with being a second grade teacher. So, I opted to bullshit my way past this potentially disturbing topic. There was no need to worry her to death.

"I went to bed with a half-baked idea on how to identify the musician involved in the theft."

"Ooh, this sounds interesting. Let's hear it," she said, putting three slices of French toast in front of me at the breakfast table.

I slowly unscrewed the top of the maple syrup bottle, buying time to formulate a response. When I finished pouring I said, "Actually, you gave me an idea a couple of nights ago after we split a bottle of wine."

"What did I say?"

"You said it was too bad we couldn't pour a half a bottle of wine into the suspects before my questioning."

"How do you propose to do it?" she asked.

"That's the part that had me tossing and turning all night."

"What did you come up with?"

"I thought maybe we would host an open-bar PR event. I'll get Calvin Dawson to come and represent the tour promoters. Justin and Bernie could use their contacts to get the media out. Cory could take professional photos. Somebody could circulate with a video camera. And, we would have one table where we'd do interviews. We could invite the significant others to attend, since we're sure the girlfriend of the thief knows about what happened. We could let the suspect couples at the interview table know that the police are about to make an arrest, and that the PR firm was hired for damage control. We'd cover a few basics on how to deal with the press after the arrest. Then, our interviewer would find an excuse to leave them alone for a few minutes. A hidden camera and mic could record what they say."

"How do you know they'd talk to each other about it in a room full of people?"

"We'd set up the room to give the illusion of privacy. The table would be far enough away from everyone that they'd feel certain they wouldn't be overheard."

"Would it be admissible in court?" Kelly asked.

"I don't see why not. They'd be in a public place. We'll video the master of ceremonies telling them they'll be videotaped throughout the event. I don't think we have to expressly state where every camera and microphone is located. At the very least we'll know who did it, and can apply pressure from there."

"That's very good. I just wish you didn't have to work so hard all night."

It was a good idea. In fact, it was my best idea since I started working the case, and I got it trying to bullshit my way through breakfast. My muse works in mysterious ways.

Dad, and Kerrigan were standing in front of Jeannine's desk when I entered the office. I started to explain about the security system when Drayton Claymore arrived with an oversized attaché case.

"Drayton, this is my assistant, Jeannine Joshlin."

She offered her hand and Drayton kissed it. "Little Annie Fanny. I've read all of your comics. This is a real pleasure."

Jeannine has been exposed to enough outpatients at the mental health center that I was sure she'd recognize him as a fellow client.

"This is my father, James Duffy, SDPD retired, and his former partner Bob Kerrigan."

Drayton looked at Dad and asked, "Didn't you play the father on the sitcom *Frasier*?" Dad glanced at me and shook his head.

Kerrigan was out of handshake range and didn't move in to complete the formality. Drayton flashed him a serious expression and said, "Ten four."

"And, this is Cory Pafford, our resident photographer and stakeout specialist." Cory nodded.

"Cat got your tongue?" Drayton asked.

Cory dropped a couple of quick F-bombs and exited into his darkroom.

"Nice meeting you, Mr. Congeniality!" Drayton called. Then, turning to me he asked, "Want to look at some surveillance equipment catalogs?"

"Sure. Why don't you go into my office and unpack your briefcase. I'll be along in a minute."

After he exited, I said to Dad and Kerrigan, "I was thinking that one of you might patrol outside part of the time. But before you do that, I'd like both of you to check out the hallway and front of the building, then join me in my office. I want your opinions on what kind of surveillance equipment I'll need to keep Jeannine safe."

"Sure," Dad said, shooting a glance at Kerrigan. "Mind if I ask a question?"

"Go ahead," I said slowly, then looked at Jeannine, knowing that Dad was about to comment on Drayton's mental health status.

He got the message and took a second to phrase his question carefully. "Are you sure this guy is qualified to do the job?"

"Are you familiar with Kitzer & Kitzer? They did the

security systems for all of the courthouses in San Diego and Orange Counties."

"They're the best in town," Dad replied.

"Drayton was one of their top designers. He's an expert on every piece of security equipment on the market."

"If you say so," he said, rolling his eyes at Kerrigan.

I spent the next hour explaining what I needed and how much I could afford to spend. I also asked about mounting the equipment so that it could be transported to another location. Drayton was intrigued by my plan and insisted that his employment include participating in the party as the site engineer.

At that point Dad joined us in the office. "Where's Kerrigan?" I asked.

"He gave me some input on what we need. He's going to walk through the neighborhood to make sure Hernandez isn't sitting in a car waiting for you."

"What do you think?"

Dad replied, "At the least, you need a camera on the hall door and on the front entrance. You're not going to get much more than the entranceway if you mount one on the balcony, with all of those bushes out front."

I said, "I know what you mean. They're a big problem, and I'm not sure I can get the landlord to go along with mounting cameras in the hallway."

We looked at Drayton, who was staring at the ceiling with a strange smile on his face. "Maybe you could pile soda cans in front of the hall door, and put a big mirror on the balcony," he said sarcastically.

Dad asked, "Is he on something?"

"I think Drayton is trying to tell us we're thinking in the past, and there are some new innovations that can solve our problems."

Drayton clapped his hands, pointed at me, and exclaimed, "Exactamundo!"

"I told you how much I can afford. What can you do?"

Drayton replied, "Let's start with the hallway. I recommend

a two-directional door-sign camera set. It's a frame that holds a normal size door sign. The top and bottom are cylindrical brass scrolls, about the width of a double A battery. The top holds the battery pack and transmitter. The bottom scroll has a miniature camera at each end that will give you a clear view of the hallway from both directions."

"That sounds great. No landlord permission required, and the bad guys don't know we're watching," I said. "Do we need two monitors or can we get by using one with a split screen?"

"No monitors," Drayton replied.

Dad squinted. "Why have cameras if you can't monitor what they're shooting?"

Drayton replied, "The signal is transmitted to your computer screen. You can size the pictures however you want. I recommend three-inch vertical tiling on your desktop monitors and two-inch if you use a laptop. That way you can keep an eye on everything and still work on the computer."

"Amazing. Now if you can recommend something that can see through oleander bushes we'll be all set," I said.

"I checked it out on the way in. Where you see a big problem, I see an almost ideal situation," Drayton said, and waited for someone to play along.

After about 10 seconds Dad asked, "OK smart guy, what do you have in mind?"

"What you need outside is a view of the sidewalk and the parking spaces where somebody could stake you out. Your building is just one property off of the intersection; I'd estimate about 100 feet. You have the good fortune of having a telephone pole at the intersection on your side of the street. I can put a band track up on the pole with a mini-camera mounted on it that will give you a 360 degree view of your street and the intersecting street as well."

Dad asked, "Do you mean the camera will rotate around the track all day?"

"This isn't a choo-choo train, Jimbo. You control where you want the camera to look from your computer. If you had the big bucks to spend, I could put the monitor in your wristwatch and you could control it from anywhere in the world," Drayton said.

"Do you think the phone company is going to let you do this?" I asked.

"I wasn't planning on asking," he replied. "That pole just holds wire. I'll bet it hasn't had a tech on it in years."

Dad said, "Shamansky can get an SDPD tag that you can put on it to keep the cable people and phone techs away."

Drayton said, "I can set the system up with an audio alert in case no one is looking at the monitor. A tone will be heard on all computers set for monitoring as soon as someone appears in the hallway. You can turn it off when your emergency is over."

I asked, "Can we remove the cameras and bring them to the party?"

"What party?" asked Dad.

"I'll tell you in a couple of minutes."

Drayton said, "I have a lot of my own equipment. We can use my stuff for the party. What do you think of my recommendations?"

"They're brilliant," I said. "What do we do next?"

"Give me a blank check for Ballard Electronics and I'll be back this afternoon."

On his way out the door Dad said, "Nice job, kid. I have to admit, at first I had my doubts about you. But you really know your stuff."

Drayton replied, "Thanks, Marty. Say hi to Eddie for me." Then he was gone.

"Who's Eddie?" Dad asked.

"Marty Crane's dog. You remind him of Frasier's father. He's an ex-cop, too."

"Your mother watches that show once in a while. Isn't he the old guy that walks with a cane?" he asked.

"Frankly, I don't see the resemblance either. Let me tell you about the party."

"Please do," he said, with a hint of annoyance in his voice.

I spent the next ten minutes reviewing what I told Kelly in the morning. I left out the part about how I came up with the idea.

Dad asked, "How do you get Dr. DD to go along with this plan?"

"When the story breaks that one of his musicians was involved in the burglary of another musician's home, the press is going to have a feeding frenzy. At the party, we can give the band some sound advice on how to handle the media when they want to be evasive. We can also provide Dr. DD with professional quality photos from Cory, and the video from the party will be shot with a professional camera that can be used by a music video producer to determine shooting angles, wardrobe choices, color matches to skin tone, and things like that," I said.

"I doubt that Dr. DD will take a position where it appears he helped bust one of his musicians," Dad said.

"Maybe if I use the *one bad apple* analogy he'll see himself as a leader who needs to get the bad guy out of the band before he kills any chance of the new album taking off. If that doesn't work, I recently came across some information about the good doctor's past life that I'm sure he'd prefer remain in the past."

"It's always good to have a backup plan, son. How soon do you want to do this?"

"I'm shooting for Sunday afternoon. The recording is scheduled to wrap on Saturday. There will be a couple of down days while Engineering reviews everything and starts the mixing process. Retakes and overdubs shouldn't start until Tuesday at the earliest. No one will have to worry about hangovers affecting quality."

"Are you going to need an OK from Dr. DD today?" Dad asked.

"Definitely. Jeannine is going to have a hard enough time finding a banquet room on this short of a notice. We can't start spending the Varner's money until we know the band is going to show up."

"Why not set the party up for Saturday night?"

"Final day sessions are notorious for running late. Max told me about a wrap session that didn't end until 3:00 PM the following afternoon. Besides, I'm sure a lot of the guests we'll be inviting already have plans for Saturday night. Sundays are usually more laid-back and flexible."

"The band will be having an off day either way on Monday, so you might be able to convince Dr. DD that they'll see the party as a reward for their hard work."

Kerrigan walked into the office. "What's up guys?"

Dad replied, "We're hosting a party for the band." Then, looking at me he asked, "What's my role?"

"You'll be the Master of Ceremonies." Turning to Kerrigan, I said, "We're going to pose as a PR team. At the beginning of the event, Dad will address everyone, congratulating them on a great session. He'll introduce Cory as a professional photographer and tell them that Derek will be collecting bio information from the musicians and significant others."

Dad commented, "I like it. This way we can check out the girlfriend, now that Kerrigan discovered she was in on it."

"Jeannine will look for a large, rectangular room. We'll put you and Cory in the front of the room, the bar along a side wall, and an interview table in the back, as far out of earshot as possible. We can use a room divider or velvet ropes to make sure no one inadvertently wanders too close to the couple at the interview table."

"What do I do?" asked Kerrigan.

"I could really use you as the bartender. Do you think you could pull it off?"

"Does a bear defecate in the forest?" Kerrigan asked.

Dad interjected, "That's a definite yes."

"Great. It would help if we had some type of mixed drink theme where you could stiffen the drinks of our suspects and their girlfriends," I said.

"I'm told I make a mean martini," Kerrigan said.

"Terrific. If we have martini night, you'll probably get asked for all of those specialty drinks, such as appletinis, chocolate martinis, French martinis and lemon drops. Can you handle it?"

"Does a chicken have lips?" Kerrigan asked.

"I'm not sure," I replied.

Dad said to me, "He can do it." Then, to Kerrigan he said, "Let's take a walk. I'll fill you in."

I said, "Before you leave, there's something else." I told them of my uncertainty about Marni's sexual orientation and asked them to keep an eye out for how she behaves around her boyfriend and her band mates' girlfriends. I also conveyed this information to Cory later in the morning.

I called Ellen Varner and gave a five-minute summary of the party proposal, which she thought was a good idea.

I said, "I need to know two things. First, I want to get approval, because it will add quite a bit to your expenses."

"We can handle it. What's the second thing?" she asked.

"We're going to need a banquet room on short notice. Since you two are footing the bill, I thought you might want to participate in the planning phase."

After about 15 seconds she said, "I have a friend who works for a property management company that specializes in office spaces. She told me about a hotel they bought over the summer that they're converting into a commercial office building. I'm pretty sure she said it's a six-story building, and they're working from the top, down. If that's the case, the banquet rooms and kitchen might still be there."

"We're hoping to get approval from Dr. DD today. Can you call her now?"

"I'll call as soon as we get off of the phone."

"I'm putting Jeannine in charge of the party. If you can work with her on the catering and the bar it would be a tremendous help," I said.

"I'll do all that I can. I'm glad I can be more involved."

"Ellen, there's one more thing I've been meaning to ask you. The day you brought the beer and chicken to Sterling Studios I saw Max and Pedgy having a pretty heated discussion. Do you mind telling me what that was about?"

"I think I told you that Pedgy is Carl's godfather."

"I remember."

"Carl wants to go to Ensenata for Thanksgiving weekend

with his college friends. He asked Pedgy to put in a good word before he made the request. Max hated the idea."

I asked, "Because Max has been there and knows what goes on?"

"Max trusts Carl. He was mad because he wants to keep the family together for the holidays. Carl's going for spring break instead."

I thanked her, and she agreed to fill Max in on the party plan.

Over the next half hour I briefed Jeannine and Cory. They were both excited about their assigned roles. After the party discussion concluded, I described the new security system and alerted them to the fact that Drayton was also a client of County Mental Health. Cory recognized him from a socialization group that he attended briefly a couple of years ago.

I wrapped up the meeting by asking, "Any questions?"

"Who is Little Annie Fanny?" Jeannine asked.

"She's an attractive, blond comic strip character. I guess that means Drayton thinks you're pretty."

"Does he know I have a boyfriend?" she asked.

"I'll be sure to tell him."

By 4:30 Drayton had installed the hardware and was finishing up the software hookups to our three computers. He did a training session with Dad while everyone watched over their shoulders. Thankfully, Drayton kept his unique sense of humor to a tolerable level.

We were about to call it a day when Dr. DD returned the call. I told him that I just got the word from SDPD that an arrest was imminent. I transitioned into gaining consent for the party.

"Forget it! There's no way I'll expose my band to any such thing! Nobody's getting arrested. If the cops had anything, somebody would already be in jail!"

I tried the *one bad apple* scenario with no luck. As Dr. DD was about to hang up, I said, "I guess I'll have to turn it into a

Vinyl Slasher Fan Club party."

Nearly a full minute of silence followed. Then DD said, "That's ancient history. Nobody cares about that anymore."

I named the bands he had panned unmercifully that he continues to represent when Dr. DD said, "A little wrap party might be good for morale."

When I got off of the phone Dad asked, "So are we all systems go on the party?"

"He'll announce it to the band this afternoon, and make sure the girlfriends and Marni's boyfriend will be there, too. I told him to let them know that it was OK to drink with the media and show them a good time."

Chapter 29

Sleeping in on a Wednesday morning was a rare treat for Leandra. Poppy had been very supportive when she asked for a few hours off to attend registration at the community college.

He said, "I know how hard it is to get the courses you need at registration. I don't want you to miss any because you were in a rush to get back to work. I'll give you the day off with pay. Make me proud, Leandra."

She tried explaining that the school registered 100 level courses in the morning and 200 level courses in the afternoon, and all she needed were 200 level courses.

But Poppy had made up his mind. "Then you'll be the first one in line."

Leandra thought about how Poppy was the only one in her life who didn't want something from her. Even though the Rock Star appeared earnest in his love, she couldn't be sure if it was all motivated by his sex drive. Taking Poppy's advice made her feel like a kid bringing home an honor roll report card. She stayed in bed and imagined Poppy watching her graduate from college.

Around 10:00 AM there was a knock at the outside door. She was pulling on her robe when she heard John ask, "Now what does the San Diego Police want with me?"

Leandra had started to open her bedroom door, but froze when she heard John utter those dreaded words. With the door ajar and her back against the wall, she could hear every word, but could not be seen by the visitors.

The apartment was long and narrow, sitting above a six-car garage. The stairway from the ground floor led into the kitchen, which took up the width of the south end, just as the living room occupied the same amount of space on the north end. A hallway connected the rooms, with two doors on each side.

Nearest the kitchen was Leandra's room, with John's former bedroom between Leandra's and the living room. Directly across the hall was their mother's room. The bathroom was between the master bedroom and the living room.

"We were afraid the welcome wagon might have passed you by, way back here above the garage," retorted a middle-aged man.

"Then where the hell is my fruit basket?" John asked, playfully.

"We're saving the fruit basket for Luis Hernandez," the middle-aged man said.

Leandra let out a faint gasp that, in her paranoid state, she was sure was audible in the kitchen.

"That guy gets all the breaks. By the way, I didn't catch your names," said John.

"I'm Detective Shamansky and this is Jason Duffy. He's consulting with SDPD on my case."

"Pleased to meet you," John said in a voice that did not reveal surprise.

Leandra had never experienced a panic attack in her life, but she had certainly cashiered enough prescriptions for Xanax to know it was a common occurrence. Her thoughts began to race. She tried to remember how many photographs of her were displayed throughout the apartment, and if any could be spotted from the kitchen. The only one she could remember was in the living room, completely out of Duffy's view.

"We were hoping Luis might be spending a few days with you," Shamansky said.

"We're not exactly old friends," John replied.

"That's not what we heard," Duffy said.

"Hernandez was the meanest, toughest son-of-a-bitch on the cell block. I forged my alliances to survive. That's the way it is on the inside. Now that I'm out I don't have anything to do with him," he said in a way Leandra found quite convincing.

"Aren't parolees supposed to have jobs?" asked Shamansky.

"I work part-time at a garage a few blocks from here. I'm their body and paint man," John said. "When there aren't any

199

body or paint jobs, I stay here."

Duffy said, "John, I drank a huge coffee on the way over here. Can I use your bathroom?"

"Sure," John replied without enthusiasm, "this way."

While the two men moved toward the hall, Leandra quietly moved further behind the door.

"There you go," John said, and Leandra heard the bathroom door shut. There was a pause of a few seconds before she heard her brother walk by. When he returned to the kitchen, he asked the detective, "Who told you I was friends with Hernandez?"

"That would be the bartender who served drinks to the two of you last week," Shamansky said, and Leandra felt her knees weaken.

"You're a long way from Fisherman's Landing, detective. Nice try," John said.

She heard a toilet flush. A minute later Leandra heard Duffy walk past her door. Upon entering the kitchen he said, "I saw lots of women's products in the bathroom."

"I live with my mother and my sister. It helps having the support of the family. I consider myself one of the lucky ones. I don't intend to do anything that will get me put back in prison with people like Luis Hernandez. I've had my fill of that lifestyle."

"You'll let us know if you hear from him, right?" Shamansky asked.

"He's not going to call here. But if he does, I'm hanging up and changing my number."

Leandra heard the screen door shut, but could not get her body to move. She wanted to peek out the window and watch them drive away, but feared one of them would see her. She heard an engine turn over, and was about to move when the door stubbed her toe. She opened her mouth to yell, but nothing came out.

"Sorry, Leandra. I didn't know you were there," said John.

She held her hands up to her face and started to cry. "Oh my God!" she exclaimed in hushed tones.

"Please don't tell me you're falling apart on me."

Leandra regarded her brother closely. "You might have broken my toe," she said, angrily.

"Is that all? I was afraid you were losing it," he said, and gave her a strange look. For the first time in her life, Leandra feared her brother. She wondered if he would view her as another obstacle that needed to be eliminated, like Jason Duffy.

Her survival instinct told her to act tough. "If I lose my toenail I'm kickin' your ass with my other foot!" she exclaimed, and swatted him on the shoulder.

"I'd say we're even. I got up in the middle of the night last week and stubbed my toe on that stupid Kirby vacuum cleaner. Why don't we just use the new Dirt Devil?"

"Because half of Mom's walnut shells end up on the carpet. They can be as jagged as glass, and sometimes cut the bags. Let the crone pay for the bags. The Dirt Devil's great for the car and the tight spots."

Leandra walked down the hallway and into the living room. She was jolted when she glanced at the top of the TV set where her senior high picture was always kept. "Where's my picture?" she cried, in a voice that revealed her jangled nerves.

"I turned it down when Duffy went into the bathroom," John replied. "I figured he might have seen you at one of the shows, and I didn't want him making the connection."

Leandra took a deep breath and sighed, "Thank God. I thought he took it."

"It's right here," he said, propping it back up to its usual position. "There's nothing to worry about. Big brother's got your back."

The day trip with Shamansky revealed no obvious clues. All of the cons sounded like they were lying, which meant that no one got eliminated as a suspect. Edward Zipendale looked promising for a few minutes when we spotted a rock star shrine in his living room. But on closer inspection we discovered the collection consisted of cheap posters and unsigned, bottom-of-the-line guitars.

Jeannine made significant headway in coordinating the party

by the time I returned to the office. We had a caterer, a menu, a stocked bar, and permission from the hotel to drill a couple of holes between the party room and our control room next door. The wall is about to be removed as part of the remodel.

Just as the plans were coming together, Max called to say he had a conversation with the recording engineer and learned that there would be minimal changes and overdubs. Dr. DD told them the band could be free to do a pre-release buzz tour as soon as the end of next week. The three roommates talked about possibly taking a Mexican vacation once the overdubs were completed. If the party didn't produce some hard evidence, all of the prime suspects would be out of the area in just over a week. There's no way the cons would sit on their hands for the duration of any tour.

Duffy Investigations looked like the green room at a Lollapalooza Thursday through Saturday as we all hustled to prepare for the party. I outlined everyone's role, wrote an intro for Dad, and instructions for Kerrigan and Cory. I went into greater detail in writing the directions for Jeannine, to prepare her for the range of responses she might get when she dropped the bombshell about an impending arrest of one of the band members.

I also called Calvin, Justin, and Bernie, and told them that the party was a definite go. They agreed to follow up with the industry and media guests they had invited.

Ellen was right about the contractors working from the top down on the conversion, but she failed to prepare us for the mess the construction crew had made in the lobby. The office team took care of the clean-up operation. On Saturday, Kelly helped with the finishing touches by adding plants and other needed furnishings. I wished she could do the interviews with the couples, but the girlfriends had seen her when we sat with Ellen at two of the band's recent shows.

Shamansky called early in the evening with some interesting information about Marni's boyfriend. He learned that the guy is currently playing rhythm guitar for a new East County emo band. "You worked the local club circuit, Jason. Are bands in the same genre usually colleagues or rivals?"

"Occasionally you'll get a rivalry, especially with the tribute bands. But most rock band members understand that there's a lot of turnover in their field and it's best to keep doors open."

Shamansky said, "One more thing. I sent our memorabilia-loving patrolman into Weston's yesterday to try and score an item from the heist. He said Weston was worse than a used car salesman trying to save his job, but he didn't appear to have a line on any of the stolen merchandise."

Three hours later, as I was turning off my house lights and heading for the bedroom, Cory called to say Marni's boyfriend just dropped her off at her parents' house.

"Is there a reason you're calling me after midnight?"

Cory explained that, even though they were smiling at each other and obviously in a good mood, the boyfriend didn't even attempt a goodnight kiss. They both smiled, he said something, then he walked away with the smile still on his face.

Chapter 30

I walked into the banquet room at 10:00 AM Sunday feeling as if everything had fallen into place. My moment of satisfaction was shattered when Drayton entered the room and babbled nervously in techno-speak. From what I could discern, Drayton ran into one problem after another when he tested the equipment. The mics were picking up nothing but static, so no conversations could be recorded. I tried to settle him down and get him focused on troubleshooting. But Drayton had clearly hit a wall he had never encountered before and was not handling the stress of the looming deadline. The party was scheduled to start at 4:00 PM. Over the next five hours I was torn between dealing with caterers and everything else I had loaded onto my plate, and dispensing therapeutic mini-sessions to Drayton every 30 minutes.

By 3:00 PM I was exhausted from the constant stress. I took a restroom break and was in the middle of relieving myself when Cory walked in and reported that the boys should be at the party in about 45 minutes.

I explained the static problem. Cory approached the urinal next to me and responded to the complication with a string of expletives as one of the chefs walked in.

The chef shouted, "What the hell's the matter with you? Everybody around here is a nervous wreck. Is this some kind of drug party for that rock band?"

Cory zipped up immediately and left the restroom. I briefly explained the equipment problem and Cory's condition. A few minutes later I stood in front of the interview table when Cory tapped me on the shoulder. Without saying a word he gestured for me to follow him.

As we walked out of the building, Cory told me he went around back to take a leak and found the source of the problem.

A construction boom extended from the roof of the building, and a huge electromagnet was suspended at the middle of the second floor, about halfway between the interview area and our control room on the other side of the banquet room wall.

After telling my staff what was going on, Kerrigan informed us that his uncle was a heavy equipment operator and he knew enough to retract the magnet to the top of the boom. Within minutes, Drayton's mind returned to planet Earth and we were back in business. But the incident left me with the uneasy feeling of just how quickly things can fall apart.

Shortly after 4:00 the press began to arrive and headed straight for the bar. Justin helped Kerrigan keep the drinks flowing at a rapid pace. The new arrivals immediately saw Cory's two very distinct signs: *Martini Night*, and *Congratulations to The Tactile Tattoo*.

Wearing his best suit and tie, Dad greeted each guest in a professional manner. Jeannine stood by his side holding a bright blue clipboard listing all of the invited guests. As she checked off each one, she handed out promotional brochures.

Vibrations in his larynx triggered Cory's symptoms. While he can't will himself to remain silent, he only blurts out obscenities at times when he would normally speak in social situations. Drayton made a special mouthpiece that fit onto Cory's camera. Whenever Cory felt compelled to speak he was able to do so into the mouthpiece without being heard. My old band mate Derek Schmidt played the role of Cory's boss. Derek accompanied him everywhere, set up all posed shots, directed him to take candid shots, and answered all questions from guests.

The martini special was a huge hit. By 6:00 the decibel level had risen dramatically. Dad stepped to the microphone at the front of the room and shouted, "Let's hear it for The Tactile Tattoo!" Drayton and I had to pull the headsets away from our ears. "Is everybody having a good time?"

"When do we eat?" shouted one of the reporters.

"The food will be out soon. But before any of you band members spill cocktail sauce on your shirt, you need to see our photographer up here at the front of the room for promotional pictures. This isn't just a wrap party. We're here to have fun and celebrate, but we're also here for some other public relations reasons. Cory is an exceptional photographer whose work has appeared in National Geographic. Derek will be getting some bio information while Cory does his thing. We asked the band's loved ones to come along tonight for pictures and bios, since we know that some of them have participated in charitable events. All of this will be made available to the press in attendance today, as well as for future promotional purposes.

"Cory and Derek will also be making a video of tonight's festivities, which will be edited and passed along to Dr. Dumajian. So, try to keep the language at the PG level, since we'll be recording video and sound throughout the evening," Dad said.

"Does that mean we can't say shit?" yelled Darren Belliveau, a journalist from a local online music site. His colleagues roared.

Dad said, "We want everybody to loosen up and have fun. But keep in mind, Cory's the one who will be editing the video. I'm guessing the easier you make his job, the better he'll make you look in the video."

Dr. DD chimed in, "And for those of you already too drunk to understand what he's saying: The harder you make his job, the more he'll make you look like what Belliveau's not suppose to say."

When the laughter died down, Dad said, "Jeannine Joshlin will be conducting band member interviews at the back of the room, one couple at a time. We're going to do these alphabetically, including Max and Pedgy; A to Z up front for pictures and bios, Z to A at the back of the room for interviews. Please be sure to stay behind the velvet ropes in both areas until it's your turn."

"Here comes the food now. Journalists, keep an eye out for a review copy of the album. I'm told it will be mixed and mastered by the end of the month. We'll include a CD with pictures from today's event," Dad said. "Have a great time and let our staff know if you need anything."

Drayton bugged the bar with four miniature microphones spaced equally under the armrest. Behind the martini mixes he placed a button that Kerrigan and Justin could press to signal a conversation I might want to listen to in the control room. Each mic was numbered one through four and the number of beeps would tell me which one to monitor. The bartenders also had a signal for each other so that when one pressed the button he'd signal the other to stay away from that area to create the illusion of privacy.

Max and Ellen Varner were the first couple to be interviewed by Jeannine. I was listening for clarity when the bar signal buzzed three times. Glancing at the monitor I saw that I was listening to Doug and Marty, two friends of the band who served as volunteer roadies whenever The Tactile Tattoo played in the San Diego area. Barnett had asked Dr. DD to put them on the guest list.

"I heard Jake complaining about the PI Max hired to try to find his collection," Doug said.

"What does he care if Max is trying to get it back?" Marty asked.

"He said the PI thinks one of the guys in the band did it, and he's been following them around," Doug said.

"Why would he think that? Max's house is three hours away, and they've all been together almost every waking hour of every day since they started working on this album," Marty protested.

On the interview monitor I saw Max and Ellen leave the table and noted that Garvey Thompson and his girlfriend were next. Tapping Drayton on the shoulder I asked, "Can you record the conversation on bar mic three and the interview table at the same time?"

"Not a problem," he said, and flipped switches.

We had three monitors in the control room. Two were fixed cameras showing the interview table and the bar. The third could be rotated to focus on any spot in the room. I watched Jeannine lead Garvey Thompson and his girlfriend to a three-foot wide circular table. On it sat Jeannine's clipboard and a single rose in a cut glass vase. The microphone was built into the vase.

"Have a seat," Jeannine said.

The couple's careful movements told me they were probably on at least their third stiff drink.

"This was a great idea," said Garvey, enthusiastically.

"I'm glad you're enjoying yourselves," Jeannine said. "Unfortunately, this part won't be quite as fun. My job is damage control. I'm here to teach everybody how to deal with the press in a professional manner when you don't want to talk with them."

"I get along great with the press. Why wouldn't I want to talk to them?"

"We got the word a few days ago that one of the band members is going to be arrested in connection with the theft of Max Varner's collection," Jeannine said.

"What?" Garvey asked.

Jeannine said, "We understand that you have a close relationship with everybody in the band and your natural inclination will be to defend your buddy when the arrest goes down. I'm here to tell you that could be a major setback to keeping the band together and making a success of the recording you just laid down. We want to head off guilt by association right away."

"It's hard to believe a band member could be involved," stated the girlfriend.

"Our contact with the police said the arrest will happen before this time next week. From what I understand, the evidence is very compelling," Jeannine said.

"Then why haven't they made an arrest yet?" Garvey asked.

"Apparently, there are two or three accomplices that they want to tie in at the same time," Jeannine said.

After taking a gulp of his martini Garvey replied, "Aren't you worried that you're going to be telling the guy the cops are after that he's about to be arrested?"

"We don't work for the police. Our main concern is that the

image of the band and the record label don't get pulled down into a public relations disaster," Jeannine said. She flipped through some papers on her clipboard, and looked down at the floor next to her chair.

"I have a handout that will give you some very acceptable lines to use with the press. It's quite possible the major networks will cover the story, so please refer all questions to me. I'll be serving as the press liaison until the media frenzy is over. I must have left the handouts at the podium up front. Will you excuse me for a few minutes?"

"Sure," Garvey said, and Jeannine departed. Turning to his girlfriend he said, "I can't believe we let your brother ruin our lives."

Leandra replied, "It wasn't all John's fault. You decided to go along."

Garvey asked, "How stupid was it to throw away the autographs of practically everybody else at the scene of the crime and not think anybody would notice which ones he kept?"

"Yeah, well you're the one responsible for Max getting the autograph on the back of the pharmacy invoice in the first place," Leandra retorted.

"Whose idea was it to get mixed up with a meth lab chemist?"

"Excuse me for putting my neck on the line to try and help make your dreams come true," she said with a strong measure of irritation.

"I guess it doesn't matter who's at fault, I'm screwed no matter what. Maybe I should just turn myself in and get it over with," he said, dejectedly.

"Don't be ridiculous," Leandra said. "What have they got? I don't see where they could possibly have any physical evidence linking you to the crime. You never touched or even saw the collection. The invoice was burned. John might need to move south of the border, but I think everything will be OK."

"Then why would they hire this PR agency?"

"I'd guess some music fan cop called the record company to

give them a heads up on something he heard in the squad room, and they overreacted."

When Jeannine returned with the handout, Garvey smiled and asked, "Can we get back to the party now?" Jeannine nodded.

I called her cell phone and told her we had our man, so she could give an abridged edition of her meeting when she met with the other band members. She spent the next half hour giving them tips on dealing with the press without mentioning an impending arrest.

Just after 8:00 a loud siren screamed through the banquet room from the front of the hotel, and everyone ran out to the parking lot. My first impulse was to run outside, but I realized that Thompson and his girlfriend would probably see me.

When the siren wailed, Garvey grabbed Leandra's hand and shouted, "C'mon!"

They ran into the hotel lobby, but stopped when they reached a bottleneck at the front door. Leading with his front shoulder, Garvey knifed through the crowd, pulling Leandra behind him. When they reached the curb, Jake's girlfriend, Diane, ran up to them and cried, "It's Chris!"

Two Oceanside police cars pulled into the lot with their lights flashing and sirens blaring. As Garvey was about to break through the front of the crowd to where Chris was being treated by the paramedics, one of the cops called through a bullhorn, "I want everybody back on the sidewalk. The paramedics need room to work."

Jake returned to the sidewalk. "What's going on, Jake?" Garvey asked.

"He's unconscious. He looks really bad."

"What happened?" Leandra asked.

"He and Debbie were having a drink with me and Diane when he said he was going out to his truck to get some baseball scores on the radio. He probably had a bet on one of the games. I guess he was out there about 15 or 20 minutes when I heard the siren. By the time I got to him, Charley, the recording engineer, was talking to the paramedics. He said he was leaving the party when he saw two big guys beating the shit out of Chris. Charley yelled and pulled out his cell phone, and the two guys jumped into a red corvette and took off."

"Where's Debbie," Diane asked.

"The cops are letting her stay with him, and they said she could ride to the hospital in the ambulance," Jake said. "She's really a mess."

Al Tunney, a reporter for the North County Times, was standing next to them and heard what Jake had said. "Who did this? You guys are his roommates. Do you know what this is about?"

Jake replied, "One of the paramedics said that it might have been car thieves."

"In a red Corvette?" Tunney asked. "That doesn't sound right."

"Maybe it was a stolen Vet that the thieves use to outrun the cops if they get spotted," Jake offered.

"Yeah, maybe," Tunney replied. Everyone looked at the ambulance as the paramedics hoisted Chris into the vehicle.

Turning to Garvey, Jake said, "We're heading over to the hospital. Do you want to come with us?"

"We'll meet you there," Garvey replied. As he and Leandra crossed the lot he said, "Just when we thought the night couldn't get any worse."

I called Dad. "What's going on?"

"Barnett got a major tune-up in the parking lot. Probably the muscle you heard him talking to at the casino."

"Sounds to me like Barnett missed a payment deadline. How bad is he?"

"He was unconscious when the EMTs transported him. I didn't hear anything else," Dad said.

"Did Thompson and his girlfriend leave?"

"They followed the ambulance."

"Then let's shut the party down. No need to run Max's bill up any higher."

"I'll clear the room now, since most of the crowd is still

outside," Dad said.

"Do you see Jeannine?"

"She's standing right next to me. Do you want to talk to her?"

"Yeah, thanks Dad."

Jason, what just happened?" she asked.

"We'll talk later. Did you get the bio information from Derek?"

"Yes. What do you need?"

"What's Garvey Thompson's girlfriend's name?"

After a few seconds she replied, "Leandra Lundquist."

"Lundquist, John Lundquist, the welcome wagon guy," I said.

"Who?"

"I met her brother last week when I was visiting ex-cons with Shamansky. Come over to the control room once Dad sends the guests home and I'll tell you about it."

Chapter 31

On Monday morning I called Thompson, identified myself and said, "I heard what happened last night and we need to talk."

"I don't have anything to say to you" he replied, and hung up.

I called right back. When Thompson picked up the receiver, I played a recording of the conversation with Leandra, admitting their involvement. I restated my offer to meet when it concluded.

"The band is going over to the hospital to see Chris right after lunch."

"That means we won't have to worry about Jake walking in on the middle of our talk. I'll be there at 1:30," I said, and hung up.

I decided a staff meeting was in order and started by congratulating everyone for a job well done.

"Drayton gave me a DVD and the master of Thompson and his girlfriend admitting to their role in stealing the collection. I'll be playing it for him this afternoon. Dad, I'll need you or Kerrigan as backup while the other stays here with Jeannine."

"I'll go," offered Kerrigan.

"Great. I'm about to play the video and I want everyone's thoughts on why they did it, and who's in charge in their relationship."

After it ended I said, "Let's start with the crime. Why did Leandra's brother and Donnie Daniels steal Max's collection?"

Kerrigan replied, "It had something to do with the pharmacy receipt."

"I'll bet he's on drugs," Jeannine said.

Leandra didn't say receipt, she said 'pharmacy invoice.' I'm sure it's drug related, but I haven't figured out the link yet," I said.

"Did you tell Shamansky?" Dad asked.

"I want to find out which of the recent parolees on his list did time on drug charges. My problem is, once I tell him, I know he'll be obliged to tell Darden, who'll bust Lundquist before we recover the collection."

"Shamansky's going to be pissed if you keep him in the dark," Dad commented.

"I've been thinking about that and I'm not sure I agree. If Darden grabs Lundquist, Luis Hernandez is sure to make a permanent move to Mexico and Shamansky's case goes unsolved."

Dad replied, "He's a bright guy. I think if you lay it out for him, he'll choose the path that gets the more dangerous guy off the street."

"Would you feel comfortable presenting a hypothetical situation to him without tipping our hand?" I asked.

"Why me?"

"If he's been ordered to pass along anything I tell him relating to the case, he won't have to worry about disobeying a direct order."

"For a civilian, you've got a pretty good grasp of stationhouse politics," stated Kerrigan.

I assigned Cory to tail Leandra Lundquist. Then I spent a half hour with Dad discussing how to work things out with Shamansky.

Kerrigan and I arrived at Thompson's apartment on time and managed to find a parking spot directly in front of the building. We decided that Kerrigan would remain within earshot and make his presence known if Thompson freaked out while watching the DVD. Otherwise, he would keep an eye out for John Lundquist and Hernandez.

Thompson stood inside the screen door when I walked up. He opened the door and said, "Let's get this over with. I need to get to the hospital."

"I want you to watch this DVD. It's only a few minutes long. Then I'll have some questions."

Thompson watched with an expressionless stare. When his conversation with Leandra was over, I hit pause.

"Where is Max's collection?" I asked.

"I don't know."

"It's very clear from what you said that you were in on the theft."

Thompson said, "You don't have anything on me. They'll never allow that DVD in court unless you had a court order to make it, and I seriously doubt that you did."

Thompson displayed the look of someone saying *checkmate*. Apparently, he made a few calls after hearing the recording.

"You're right, Garvey. If I made that DVD without your knowledge it wouldn't be admissible. That's why I added a little reminder from earlier in the evening."

I restarted the video. It showed a view from across the banquet room of Dad telling everyone that they would be recorded throughout the evening. While Dad was delivering his lines, I walked over to the TV and put my finger on Garvey, who was obviously paying attention to what Dad was saying.

"It looks clear to me that you heard him say that everything would be recorded."

"Damn!" shouted Thompson, hammering his fist on the arm of his couch.

"Garvey, I've been checking on your background and I have a hard time believing this was all your idea."

"From what I understand, it doesn't make much difference whose idea it was."

"That's not true," I said. "Judges give breaks to people with clean records."

"And people like you lie to people like me all the time to get what you want."

"What I want is for Max to be able to afford to send his kids to college. What's it like, knowing that you'll be denying your band mate's kids an education. He's got one in college right now and another one is a senior in high school. I have a hard time believing that a good Catholic boy like you is getting much sleep."

"Life has gotten a lot more complicated since Catholic school," he said.

"I know it must seem as if everything you worked for is about to be destroyed, but it doesn't have to be that way."

"Are you saying there's a way out of this?"

"You won't get a free pass, but you live in a very forgiving country," I said.

"Maybe I won't get a sentence as long as a guy with a record, but my music career will be over for sure," he said, lowering his head.

"Are you kidding? Musicians get busted all the time."

"This album is our second chance. There won't be any third chances for us. If I can't tour in support of that album it's all over for me," he replied.

"So, maybe they hire a contract drummer to fill in for a while. Your name will be the one on the back of the CD. You could pick up your career as soon as you have this behind you."

"What about the cops?" he asked.

"You'd go through the arrest, trial, and maybe do a little time. It's not going to be easy. But your best shot involves taking responsibility right now."

"I think I'm just gonna wait till after the CD comes out and deal with it then."

"And do what? Deny everything in the meantime?" I asked.

"Why not?"

"Do you know why Pete Rose, the all time hits leader in baseball history, was kept out of the Hall of Fame all those years? It was because he kept denying that he bet on baseball. He kept lying to the investigators, lying to the commissioner's office, and lying to the public. He strung his fans along for years, asking them to believe in his innocence. Then, he finally gave a modified version of the truth when he was out of money and tried cashing in with a book." I walked over to the TV and ejected the DVD. "Are you planning on telling your parents the truth?"

"This is gonna break their hearts," he said, squeezing his eyes closed tightly.

"What would be worse: If you came clean and asked forgiveness, or if you lied to them and everybody else for a while, then changed your story after the facts were revealed at trial?"

"You were right about me losing sleep over Max. What you're saying makes a lot of sense. But I'm gonna talk to Leandra before I do anything. I'm sure the cops will want to talk to her and I'm not gonna let her get blindsided. I'll tell her tonight and see if she'll help me get Max's stuff back this week. Then I'll turn myself in," he said.

"It'll feel good getting it off of your chest. Guilt can be a tremendous burden."

"Tell me about it," he replied. "Can I hang on to that DVD to show her?"

"You know it's a copy, right?"

"I know. It's just that if I show her the way you showed me, it will take a lot less time making her understand why I need to tell the truth and get the collection back."

I handed the DVD to him and he placed it on the coffee table.

Jake Fuller burst through the door and let out the kind of yell that might be expected from a lottery winner. The scream faded when he recognized me.

"What the hell's he doing here?" he asked.

"Don't worry about it. Everything's cool," Thompson said. "What are you so excited about?"

Focusing on Thompson he replied, "Dr. DD stopped by the hospital to say we're gonna be the warm-up band for the Aorta Event Invitation tour! It starts in 6 weeks. He got the studio to put a rush on mixing and mastering. We'll have it available for digital release around the time the tour starts."

"Things are happening really fast," Thompson said to Fuller. Turning to me he said, "Give me one of your business cards. What time will you get into your office tomorrow morning?"

"Nine o'clock," I replied, handing him the card.

"I agree with what you said. I'll call you first thing tomorrow," Thompson said, and shook hands.

I walked outside and saw Kerrigan leaning against the side of the RSX.

"How did it go?" he asked when I reached the top of the stairs.

"It sounds like he'll be giving a confession tomorrow."

"Good work kid. You're a chip off the old block." I never thought I'd hear those words. "Can I buy you a beer?"

"I'll celebrate when Max gets his collection back."

As we rode back to the office Kerrigan asked, "How does the Catholic boy with the whoopee cushion turn into a crook?"

"To make it big in the music business, bands need talent and a ton of drive. I heard Thompson described as a 110% effort drummer. I also heard he was the main composer on most of their songs. He must have felt like it was his baby and he'd do whatever it took to make it thrive and grow. The pranks are just part of his personality and a way to not come across as a taskmaster when he's pushing the others to build on his ideas."

Kerrigan asked, "Even to the point of hiring a hitman and dealing in hard drugs?"

"I'm starting to think the girlfriend with the ex-con brother played a big part in reversing his parochial training."

"What?" asked Kerrigan.

"Do you think his girlfriend got him to break the rules?"

Kerrigan replied, "Does a fat dog fart?"

Leandra was in the process of restocking contact lens products when Poppy told her she had a phone call. Her friends and family usually called her cell phone and left a message that she would return when she took a break. She was expecting bad news when she answered the phone. "Hello."

"It's Garvey. I need to see you tonight. Can you come up to my place after work?"

"Is it Chris?" she asked, fearing he may have died from his injuries.

"He's gonna be in the hospital for a few days, but he'll be OK."

"Good," she said, perplexed as to why he called the

pharmacy.

"We spent the day together yesterday. I've got some things to do tonight. Can't this wait?"

"I'm turning myself in tomorrow. I thought we should talk first. I'm gonna keep you out of it. But I'm sure the cops will want to talk to you, so I thought you should hear what I'm gonna say."

Leandra was stunned. She tried to speak but nothing came out. She swallowed hard and said, "I need to do a couple things for my mother. Does this mean it could be our last night together for a long time?"

"Probably," Garvey said flatly.

"Then let's do something special. Do you remember last year when you were on tour and we didn't see each other for almost two months? You flew out here on your day off so we could spend one night together."

"I'll never forget. It was probably our most romantic night ever," he said.

"Let's go back to that same little motel over by Balboa Park and spend the night together."

"Perfect," he said. "What time?"

"Why don't you check in around 7:30 and I'll come by as soon as I can. If I don't answer my phone, just leave a message with the room number."

"I love you, Leandra," he said, and hung up.

When I got back to the office, Dad was seated behind my desk and Shamansky was in the client seat.

"Was there a mutiny while I was gone?" I asked.

"Just keeping it warm for you, son," Dad said, standing up quickly.

"How did your meeting with Thompson go?" Shamansky asked.

Over the next 10 minutes I gave them the details.

Shamansky said, "The way I see it, Thompson is going to be giving Darden what he'll need to close the case. My concern is Luis Hernandez and John Lundquist, since it's clear Lundquist is the one who contracted with Hernandez."

"I get the impression Thompson's girlfriend has been leading him around by the nose," I said. "I don't see him conspiring to do a murder."

Shamansky replied, "I'm not looking to hang him on the conspiracy charge if he doesn't confess that he was in on it. The sticky part will be with the girlfriend. We've seen a lot of similar cases and they all go down the same way." Turning to Dad, Shamansky asked, "Should I tell him or do you want to?"

"Go ahead, Walt. You're on a roll."

"Thompson will be operating on the assumption that, if he can keep his girlfriend out of it, she'll remain faithful to him while he does his time. Then, when he gets out, they'll get married and live happily ever after," Shamansky said.

"He told me he's waiting till tomorrow so Leandra doesn't get blindsided."

I'm sure they'll be cooking up a story tonight," Dad said.

"Is that going to be a problem for you?" I asked Shamansky.

"It shouldn't be. Guys like Thompson are usually victims themselves. They don't have criminal minds and are usually pretty easy to deal with during interrogation if they don't lawyer up," Shamansky said.

Kerrigan asked, "Do you think there's a chance he'll run?"

"No," Shamansky replied. "Jason did a good job of building his hopes that he could still have a career down the road if he plays it straight."

Jeannine tapped lightly on the half-open door. "Come in, Jeannine," I said.

"I've been digging for information on Leandra Lundquist and just found out that she works at Popakalitis Pharmacy on El Cajon Boulevard."

Shamansky stood and said, "That should explain the meth cook reference. I'll find out if they reported any problems recently. Call me in the morning when you hear from Thompson."

An hour later Shamansky called. "When I got back to

Metro, I ran everything past the captain. Then, two minutes ago, Darden showed up at my desk and informed me that his team will be taking over surveillance of Thompson and the Lundquists. He added that if he sees you or Cory anywhere near them you'll be spending the evening as a guest of the city."

Chapter 32

Leandra arrived at The Conquistador Motel at 8:30 PM. She wore her sexiest mini-dress and combed her hair in a new style.

Garvey asked, "What kept you? I thought you'd be here an hour ago."

"You don't think this look just happens, do you?"

"I left five messages. Why didn't you call back?"

"I was rushing to get here as fast as I could. Answering the phone would have slowed me down, so I turned it off," she said.

"I'm sorry. I didn't mean to snap at you. It's just that this will probably be our last night together for a long time and I wanted everything to be just right."

"How can you expect everything to be just right when you're talking about ruining both of our lives?" she asked.

"We can't go on living a lie. Too many people know what's going on."

"What are you talking about?"

"I'll show you," Garvey said.

He walked to the television and turned on the DVD. Just like his afternoon viewing, he stopped it after their conversation ended. Leandra brought up the same question he had asked about its admissibility in court, and Garvey played the final segment. He even pointed to the two of them paying attention when they were told about being recorded throughout the evening.

Leandra's mind whirled as she tried to process what she saw. "Play it again," she said, and Garvey did so.

This time she focused all of her attention on her own responses to see if anything she said could be construed as an admission of guilt or complicity. It was clear from the DVD that she knew what was going on.

"Duffy said the judge will go a lot easier if Max gets his collection back," he said.

"Of course he's going to say that. He works for Max. Jason Duffy is doing what's best for his client. He doesn't care about you."

"Maybe it *is* good for him. But getting the collection back to Max will be good for me too, and not just with the judge. I haven't had a decent night's sleep since the break-in. For now, he's my band mate. It was like ripping off a family member."

"So, what's your plan?"

"My plan is for us to talk about how I can turn myself in without getting you in trouble. Then I'll admit I made some mistakes, take my lumps, and start over," he said.

"Just because you *want* to keep me out of trouble doesn't mean you *can* keep me out of trouble. You mentioned the pharmacy invoice on the video and I work at a pharmacy. Does Duffy know about the meth operation?"

"I'm gonna tell the cops I saw the pharmacy order one night when I picked you up from work, and knew when it would be delivered" he said.

"Then admit to stealing the order off of the loading dock?" she asked.

"I'll say I knew you'd be handling the order, and I made sure you were distracted in another part of the store while I took the drugs."

Leandra was about to tell him how clever the police are in their interrogations, and about how they'd keep pressing him for details until his story fell apart. She tried picturing him in an interrogation room and realized his plan had no chance of keeping her out of it.

"Do you think you can pull it off?" she asked.

"You know I'd do anything in the world for you, Leandra."

She didn't say anything for a couple of minutes. Her mind drifted back to her high school gym class locker room. Coming back from the shower, before turning the corner to the row of lockers where she would get dressed, she overheard a group of four classmates talking about her. They said she'd probably end up in jail like her big brother.

"Leandra, are you listening?" Garvey asked.

"Sorry, Rock Star. This is just a bit overwhelming for me."

"I know what you mean," he said, sitting down on the bed next to her. "I can't believe the stuff that I've done. I even bought bullets for my dad's Army pistol the day I drove the drugs up to the cook's house."

"You brought a gun? Do you have it now?" Her jaw slackened.

"I never even took it out of my parents' house. I realized I was never going to use it after I bought the bullets."

She put her hands on his shoulders and said, "Your muscles are tighter than your snare drum. Why don't you take your shirt off and I'll give you a nice massage."

"I want to wait until after we make love," he said, and she nodded. In silence they got undressed and made tender but passionless love.

When they finished Leandra said, "Roll over on your stomach. I want to give you a massage after I pee."

Garvey complied in silence. Leandra grabbed her purse and walked to the bathroom. In a couple of minutes she returned with her right arm shielded from his view.

Garvey sprawled in the middle of the bed, his face turned toward the bathroom door. Leandra walked around the bed and knelt down alongside him, away from the direction he was facing. She started at his shoulders and slowly massaged her way down his back. Looking closely at the back of his thighs she spotted a vein close to the surface.

"I love you, Rock Star," she said.

Holding a hypodermic needle in her fist, with her thumb on the plunger, she injected an air bubble into his vein. She expected him to react violently. But Garvey simply turned back to her, glanced at the hypodermic needle she was holding, and made eye contact with a pained expression on his face. They gazed at each other until the air bubble hit his heart and jolted him into the hereafter.

Without shedding a tear, Leandra spread the sheet on the

floor and eased Garvey's body off of the bed and onto the sheet. She dragged him to the bathroom, pulled him into the tub, and washed him from head to toe. She then pulled him onto a towel, dried him and dressed him in his usual sleepwear – a T-shirt and boxers.

After checking to make sure no one was in the parking lot, Leandra left the motel, returned to her apartment, and made sure her mother was still passed out in front of the television. She glanced at the clock and saw that it was 9:55. So far, so good. She tossed the laundry in the washer, turned it on, returned to the living room, and noted that the red light on the DVR was illuminated, indicating it was still recording.

Consistent with their routine, Leandra woke her mother up at 10:00, walked her to her bedroom, helped her into her nightgown, and tucked her in.

"John has a birthday coming up in a couple of weeks. Do you think we can afford to take him to Mr. A's for dinner?" she asked, knowing her mother would not approve.

"Don't be ridiculous, Leandra. That's one of the most expensive restaurants in town," she protested.

"But it's his first birthday with us in a long time," Leandra said, hoping to ensure that her mother would remember the conversation.

"No," her mother said flatly, and pulled her covers up to her chin.

"Hold on a second, Mom," Leandra said, then opened her mother's bedroom door and shouted, "John, turn the oven off for me."

"What are you making at this hour?" her mother asked.

"John's been asking me to make chocolate chip cookies for the last two hours. So, I finally gave in," she replied.

Mrs. Lundquist shifted in the bed, squinted at her clock/radio and said, "At 10:20? You'll be up all night if you eat chocolate at this hour."

"Don't worry Mom, I'll be fine. We can talk about where to take John on his birthday in the morning," she said.

Leandra kissed her on the forehead, turned off the light, and shut the door. She switched the laundry from the washer to the dryer, and baked cookies while she waited. She was certain her mother hadn't noticed that John wasn't home.

At 11:00 she left the apartment with a large duffel bag containing the laundry, cleaning supplies, and the Dirt Devil vacuum cleaner. She found street parking a block away from the motel and slipped back into the room unnoticed. She then put on a pair of rubber cleaning gloves, made the bed, pulled Garvey back onto it, and readjusted the bedding to look natural. She positioned him so that he would look as if he had given himself the injection.

Leandra went to work dusting, scrubbing, and vacuuming everything in the room. She rolled Garvey over in the bed and vacuumed him thoroughly with a nozzle attachment to get any stray carpet fibers off of him.

After stuffing the unclean towel in her bag, Leandra slipped out of the motel and walked to the next block where she had parked her Mustang. She battled the emotions of remorse and relief as she drove. Before she reached her neighborhood, Leandra stuffed the towel in a residential trash bin, set curbside for pickup in the morning.

John was in the living room watching television and drinking a beer when she arrived home at 12:15. She told him what had happened, starting with the party and ending with the alibi.

"I recorded the television shows we would have watched if we were here between 8:00 and 11:00. I think we should watch them now," she said.

"We'll be up till 3:30," he protested.

"I doubt if I'm going to sleep anytime soon," she said. "I think you should go on a camping trip in the morning. The cops are sure to come by. Once they see the DVD from the party they might arrest you. I'll give them your alibi and Mom will vouch for you, too. If they don't believe it was a suicide, I'm sure they'll think Luis did the hit. They shouldn't get too worked up about not having immediate access to you."

"How will I know what's going on?" he asked.

"You can take Mom's cell phone. She doesn't know where it is half of the time anyway."

They watched television for the next three hours with very little conversation. A couple of times Leandra felt tears well up, but she wouldn't let John see her cry.

Chapter 33

I picked Jeannine up at 8:15 and began the day by sketching out contingency plans on how to proceed, depending on Thompson's ability to get the collection in his possession. I hoped Leandra had helped her brother to stash it at the estate where they live, and that she'd be willing to trade it for help with charges against them.

Nine o'clock came and went without a call. At 9:30 Shamansky phoned to find out if I'd heard from Thompson.

"Did you ask Darden if he's still in the apartment?"

"He said the vice president made an unscheduled visit to the Naval Air Station on North Island last night, and all of his men got put on security detail."

"Shit!" I exclaimed.

I told Shamansky I'd call back soon. Garvey and Leandra left the party before filling out an information card with Derek, but I did have cards from Barnett and Fuller. After reaching their answering machine, I left a message to call immediately.

I called Tri-City Hospital, and was connected to Barnett's room. I asked for Garvey Thompson without identifying myself.

"Who's this?" asked Barnett.

"It's Tom Mulhern with Modern Drummer Magazine. Is Garvey Thompson there?" I asked.

"No, Mr. Mulhern, he isn't."

"I tried calling his home number but got the machine. Then I checked with the studio. I understand you're his roommate. Do you have any idea where he could be?"

"I've been wondering the same thing myself. He was supposed to come by here yesterday afternoon and never showed up, or even called."

"Is that unusual for him," I asked.

"He's a great guy and a terrific friend. I thought he might have gotten called into the recording studio for an overdub. Now I'm really worried."

"Is there anybody else who might know where he is?"

"Maybe he went somewhere with his girlfriend."

"Do you have a phone number for her?"

"Yeah, it's in my phone," he said. A minute later he gave me her cell phone number. "Are you writing an article about him?"

"I've got to talk to him before I say anything to anyone else."

"I understand," replied Barnett.

I tried calling Leandra and got voice mail. Disguising my voice with an authoritative tone, I used the Modern Drummer Magazine ruse. I left Jeannine's cell phone number, and instructed her to answer: "Modern Drummer."

Shamansky called back at 11:00. "I'm getting worried about our boy. With Luis Hernandez in the picture, I'm going to take a ride up to Oceanside."

"Do you want company?" I asked.

"Sure," he said. "Do you know if there's an onsite property manager?"

"Yes. Cory parked in front of the office one day and the manager came out and asked who he was waiting for."

"I'll pick you up in an hour," he replied, and hung up.

Shamansky was running late. Just after noon Leandra Lundquist called.

"Thanks for calling back. I need to talk to Garvey Thompson right away, and Chris Barnett said you might know how to find him," I said in a disguised voice.

"If you're with Modern Drummer why do you have a local area code?" she asked.

"We have a local line in every city where we have a distribution outlet," I replied, hoping my bullshit sounded plausible.

After a brief pause she said, "I went to a party with him on Sunday, and haven't talked with him since."

"I can't find him anywhere. Is it unusual for him not to call?"

"He calls most days when he isn't on the road, but not always. I'm starting to get worried. Will you ask him to call me when you find him?"

"I'll do that," I said, and hung up.

When Shamansky arrived I filled him in on my conversation with Leandra on our way to the car. He had picked up sandwiches at the local deli and we ate in silence while making our way through downtown La Jolla and up Torrey Pines Road. As we entered Interstate 5 North, I ran through my ideas on how to proceed, depending on Thompson's access to the collection, as well as possible ways of bringing Luis Hernandez to the surface.

"Guess which pharmacy had a huge order of pseudoephedrine stolen off of its loading dock recently?" Shamansky asked.

I mulled this information a minute and asked, "How do you see the drugs fitting into this?"

"All I can figure is that we don't know who all of the players are yet. Besides Hernandez, Lundquist, and Daniels, maybe there's a druggie ex-con in on it, too. Right now my main concern is Thompson. I don't like the way he just disappeared the day he was supposed to confess," he said.

"A lot of guys in that situation might go out and tie one on," I suggested. "He could be passed out in the back seat of his car in front of some dive bar."

"I hope you're right," Shamansky said.

When we reached Carlsbad, one town south of Oceanside, Shamansky received a call. He wasn't saying much on his end of the conversation, but it was obvious that the news was bad. He changed lanes and got off at the first possible exit. After entering 5 South he ended his call.

"Thompson's dead. They found him at a motel near Balboa Park."

"Damn it! What was the cause of death?"

"The coroner just got there so nothing's definite, but they

found a needle on the bed," he said.

Shamansky turned on his lights and siren. We streaked down the freeway at 85 mph, and arrived at the scene a half hour later.

We entered the motel room for a brief look before the forensics team took over. The body was still on the bed, but covered. Shamansky removed the cover and crouched to have a better look at the needle's point of entry. I looked, but didn't move in for the close-up.

There was no sign of a struggle. I noticed that the room was equipped with a DVD player.

"Can you look inside the DVD player to see if the disc I gave him is in there?"

Shamansky removed a pen from his pocket and pushed the flap out of the way. "Nothing."

"I'll bet if you ask at the front desk you'll find that he rented this machine."

"I'll check it out. I'm going back up to Oceanside before I call it a day. I'll let you know if it's still there," he said. Then he bent forward over a small dining table and looked intently. "Not even the slightest hint of a partial print." He walked into the bathroom and performed a similar inspection of the vanity and toilet flusher. "Somebody cleaned up in here, too."

"Gentlemen, you're standing on my carpet," boomed a voice from behind. We turned to see the forensics supervisor and a tech. "We've got a scene to process."

Shamansky replied, "We're done for now. I'll be outside. Let me know what you find." After we walked out of the room he said, "I'll have to stay here. Can you catch a ride back to your office?"

I called Dad while Shamansky walked to the motel office and confirmed that Thompson did rent the DVD player when he checked in at 7:15 PM.

I gave Dad the details on the ride back to La Jolla. When we arrived, I called a staff meeting and repeated what had happened for everyone. I finished by saying, "I felt like he was more of a victim than a perp."

"That can happen when you get in with the wrong crowd," said Kerrigan.

"If I let Darden take him down yesterday he'd be alive today."

"He would have been out on bail in a matter of hours, and this still might have gone down the same way," Dad said. "You can't blame yourself, son."

"I can't help it. I was actually starting to like the guy."

Dad said, "Jason, he was obviously in on stealing the collection, and involved in some drug deal. Who knows, maybe he even knew about Luis Hernandez's plans for you. Don't spend too much time feeling sorry for this guy. He doesn't deserve it."

Jeannine asked, "What happens next?"

"I'm sure Shamansky is gonna pull John Lundquist in for questioning later today," Kerrigan commented.

"That will probably force the collection underground," I said.

"Won't he tell where it is, since the party video makes it clear that he took it in the first place?" asked Jeannine.

"He could say Donnie Daniels had it from day-one and it disappeared when Daniels died," I said.

"That's exactly what a con would say," Kerrigan said.

"Cory, I want you to head over to the Lundquist's. Keep a low profile if Darden's men have it staked out. Kerrigan, I need you to go over to the pharmacy and follow Leandra when she leaves."

After Jeannine returned to her desk I said to Dad, "Thompson was definitely salvageable. I screwed up."

Considering our newfound camaraderie, I was expecting Dad to sympathize and maybe share a story from his career that would make me feel less guilty.

Instead, Dad said, "Boo hoo. If you want to save the world go back into social services." He then stood up and added, "I'm gonna take a walk."

In his own insensitive way, Dad was right. I wasn't doing anybody any good sitting around feeling sorry for myself. After spending a couple of years working at a mental health center, helping people get in touch with their feelings, it went against the grain for me to push my own out of the way. But I realized that the window of opportunity on getting Max's collection back was getting smaller by the hour. I spent the next 45 minutes working out a plan of action, and called Shamansky.

"I have an idea on how to get the collection and all of the suspects together. You said you'd be going back up to Oceanside to check out the apartment. How about meeting me at Tri-City Hospital while you're up there?" I asked.

"I have to stop for dinner at some point," he said, obviously fishing for an invitation to the Larabee's of the North County.

"And hospital cuisine immediately came to mind?" I asked.

"It's been a long day, Jason," he said flatly.

"I'll pick something up. You'll love it. We can eat it in the Crown Vic at 6:00 while I brief you on the plan."

"It better be good," he said, and hung up.

I wasn't sure if he was talking about the plan or the dinner. To be on the safe side I called The Fish Market, by the Del Mar Racetrack, and placed a *to go* order for 5:30. If this didn't get Shamansky in the right frame of mind to approve my plan, it just couldn't be done with food.

At 6:30 we walked into Barnett's hospital room. When he saw me he shouted, "I'm not talking to you! Get out of here!"

I replied, "This is Detective Shamansky. He's investigating Garvey's murder. I know you're pretty upset right now, but we need to talk."

"I told you, I'm not talking!" he yelled, on the verge of losing it.

Shamansky sat down on the edge of the bed next to Barnett and in a quiet voice said, "If you weren't so quick to throw Mr. Duffy out of your place a couple of weeks ago, your buddy would probably still be alive. So shut the fuck up and listen or you could be suffering a relapse in the next few minutes."

"Are you really a cop?" he asked, and Shamansky flashed his badge. "How would it look if I called the press and told

233

them I was being threatened by a cop, in my hospital room, the day I found out my best friend was murdered."

Shamansky replied, "Probably not nearly as bad as it will look to your record company when I tell the press the reason you're in the hospital is because you were beaten up by your bookie's goons for massive unpaid gambling debts. I don't think your bookie's going to be too thrilled with the publicity either."

Barnett's jaw dropped and all color drained from his face. "How . . ." was all he could manage to say.

I asked, "Do you remember the conversation you had with those guys in the restroom at the casino the night you saw me there?" Barnett nodded. "I was in the last stall and heard every word."

"I'm dead, too," he said with a vacant stare.

"Not necessarily," I said, and proceeded to tell him the plan.

Over the next hour we prepped Barnett for a call to his bookie. We taught him how to propose settling the debt with a part of the stolen collection.

Barnett sounded steady as he presented the plan to his bookie. Afterwards, he listened for a couple of minutes, then said, "OK, I'll call you tomorrow," and hung up.

"What did he say?" I asked.

"He said he'd rather drag me through the streets of Oceanside on a rope tied to his back bumper, but he has bills like everybody else. So, he's gonna call a fence he knows and I'm supposed to call him back in the morning," Barnett said.

Chapter 34

Leandra was drinking coffee at her kitchen table on Wednesday morning when the phone rang. "Hello."

"Leandra, its Chris. I'm so sorry about what happened to Garvey."

Leandra started to cry. "Oh, Chris, you must know what I'm going through. He was really close to you."

"Do the cops have any idea why it happened?"

"A couple of detectives came by yesterday and asked some questions. But they don't know much at this point."

"What was he doing at that motel?" he asked.

"We met there once last year. All I can figure is that he was planning on surprising me with a special night when something went terribly wrong."

"I'm afraid it might be my fault."

"What do you mean?"

"The guys that beat me up at the party work for a bookie. I owe him $10,000 and don't have the money."

"So they beat you up. What does that have to do with Garvey?"

"I told him when he visited me at the hospital that they gave me until Friday to come up with the ten grand or they were going to kill me. He told me about Max's collection and your brother. I called the guy I owe and asked him if he'd take memorabilia to pay off the debt. He said he'd give me twenty cents on the dollar. Garvey was going to get in touch with your brother and try to set it up."

"Do you think my brother killed him?" Leandra asked.

"No, not at all. It's my fault. I told Garvey the name of the guy I owe. He probably figured since I was in the hospital that he'd take care of everything himself. I'm sure the same bastards that beat me up, killed Garvey."

"Oh my God, you might be right."

"Do you think I should call the cops and tell them?" Chris asked.

Leandra was tempted to say yes to direct suspicion away from herself and her brother. On the other hand, once it came out about John stealing the collection, they would be watched constantly, making it almost impossible to move it. "Not just yet. Does this mean those guys are still planning to kill you?"

"Just because they killed Garvey doesn't let me off the hook."

"It's bad enough having to go to one funeral this week. I don't think I could handle two."

"What are you thinking?"

"I might be able to work this out with my brother if you could get the people you owe to buy the whole collection."

"How much are we talking about?" Chris asked.

"It was recently appraised at $2.3 million. At twenty cents on the dollar that would be $460,000," she said. "You can have the $10,000 for brokering the deal."

"I understand it's now up to $12,000, since I missed my payment deadline."

"Then $12,000 it is," she said. "I'll talk to my brother tonight. See if they'll take the whole collection and call me when you know."

"They'll probably want to know when and where you want to do this," he said.

"Let's find out if they'll go for it before we work out the details. I'm sure my brother will want to be in on that decision."

"OK, I'll call you tonight," he stated, and said goodbye.

Leandra got dressed and went to work. Poppy told her to take the week off, but after one day of being alone with her thoughts, she looked forward to occupying her mind in a familiar setting.

At lunchtime she called John. "Are you still in the county?"

"Why?" he asked warily.

She told him about her conversation with Chris. "I think we

should do it and put this thing behind us."

"Twenty cents on the dollar? I was thinking about traveling around the country and moving it piecemeal in small markets."

"How long do you think it will take before a wanted poster of you is in every memorabilia shop in the country?" she asked.

"That could be a problem. I was looking at the collection last week and there sure are a lot of very unique items. I guess going through a fence is a good idea," he said. "What about Luis?"

"Chris said that the guy we'll be dealing with has two leg breakers who will probably be at the exchange. I think we should pay off Luis to provide protection and get him out of our lives. Since he knows we have the collection, I don't see him going away."

"How much do you think we should pay him?" he asked.

"Let's tell him we're getting ten cents on the dollar and offer to do an equal three-way split. Do you think he'll go for it?"

"How much does it work out to?"

"We tell him the guy who set it up gets $20,000 and we get $70,000 each. Actually, $12,000 gets taken out of the pot to square Chris with the buyer. That leaves $189,000 for each of us. What do you think?" she asked.

"I think you make a better crook than I do."

Just before Leandra was about to put her mother to bed, Chris called to say the deal was on, provided the buyer found the exchange arrangements to be acceptable.

"He wants a full inventory of everything you have. He'll take it to his experts and, if they agree with the appraised value, we have a deal. Did you figure out where you want it to go down?" he asked.

"I have a pretty good idea, but I won't know if it's a go until tomorrow. I'll call you then."

"Thanks again for saving my life," Chris said. "Call me when you know."

"I will. Take care of yourself," she said, and disconnected.

After hearing from Leandra on Thursday morning, Barnett called and told me the exchange was set for Monday at 10:00 AM.

"I thought you were scheduled for a long nap in a clam bed if you don't pay up by tomorrow."

"I guess it's more important that they have an inventory of what they're getting, and check with their own experts to make sure they agree on the price."

"Have they set up a location yet?" I asked.

"Leandra wants to do it at the pharmacy where she works."

"How are you doing?"

"The ribs won't be healed until October."

"How's the rest of the band holding up?"

"Everybody's sick about Garvey. I'm glad we don't have to play right now. Dr. DD said he'd start looking for a drummer for the tour pretty soon."

"I'm surprised you didn't put the bite on Dr. DD for the money you owed Augustine," I said.

"I doubt that he'd give me an advance before seeing if the album takes off."

"Yeah, but I'll bet the Vinyl Slasher might pony up the bucks."

"You're full of surprises, Duffy." After a brief pause he said, "OK, I knew about Dr. DD's past. But the guy hung with us in the bad times. I also know that he's financially on thin ice."

"How do you know that?"

"Jake has a family member with a medical condition."

"His father's heart problem?"

"Yeah. Jake's been saving up for a transplant operation. He went to Dr. DD about a loan. That's when we found out about his money problems."

"Are you sure he wasn't just blowing Jake off?"

Barnett replied, "He got one of his big-name acts to schedule a fundraiser. It's going to be at the Apollo Theater in New York next month."

"I've got to run. Give me a call when you have more

details."

I called Shamansky and brought him up to speed on the new developments. "Why did he call you? I'm the one with the connections in the DA's office."

"I think you scared the shit out of him, Shamansky."

"I must admit, I'm pretty good at the *bad cop* role."

"What's happening with the coroner's office?"

"They're still working on him."

"What killed him?"

"An injected air bubble stopped his heart. Whoever did it tried making it look like a suicide," Shamansky said.

"Any sign of a struggle?"

"None whatsoever. His lack of resistance leads me to believe it was somebody he knew and trusted. Are you sure Barnett was in his hospital room Monday night?"

"Max told me that the whole band, minus Thompson, was there until they got kicked out at 8:30. What was the time of death?"

"Between 9:00 and 10:00."

"It's at least a 45 minute drive without traffic, and that's if you're dressed and sitting in your car with your needle and cleaning supplies," I said.

"OK. He's clear. Did your stakeouts turn up anybody else that was close to Thompson?"

"He spent his spare time with either his roommates or his girlfriend."

"I checked out the girlfriend and her record is perfect. Not even a speeding ticket. I have a hard time buying that she could commit murder," he said. "Any other ideas?"

"How does this sound? Thompson gets the room expecting Leandra to come by. He hears a knock on the door, opens it, and there's her brother and Hernandez. They tell him they're going to shoot him up with some drug, but instead give him the air bubble."

"Then why no struggle?" asked Shamansky.

"What if Hernandez holds a gun to Thompson's head while Lundquist tries to calm him down. He shows him the needle and tells him it's full of truth serum so they can be sure of what he told the police. Then, he pulls back on the plunger to take in some air, and shoots the bubble."

"I'll run it past the coroner. It sure sounds more plausible than the girlfriend."

I said, "I'm not sure I buy that theory myself. But since you asked for alternatives I thought I'd share it with you."

"It's definitely worth considering."

"Did you run a sheet on the bookie?"

"His name is Arnie Augustine. He's 46 years old and has been in trouble since he was 12; mainly for gambling operations and assault."

"Is he mobbed up?"

"He's more of a mob wannabe. He acts like a gangster, probably to get his losers to pay up, but there are no signs of any actual ties. The real tell is the lawyers he's used when he was popped. None of them appear to be in the fraternity."

"Is there any way of finding out if he has more leg-breakers besides the guys that I saw at the casino?" I asked.

"The Oceanside PD doesn't have the personnel to keep a close eye on him."

"Don't they have a vice squad?"

"Of course they do. But in a city that borders one of the largest Marine bases in the country, their priority is to keep the troops from getting AIDS from skanky hookers."

"So, what do we do till Monday?"

"Keep an eye on the Lundquist place if Darden's team isn't covering it. Let me know if John shows up or if Leandra meets him anywhere. I'll line up my team for Monday morning. I want to get somebody inside the pharmacy that doesn't look like a cop," Shamansky said.

"How about Chief Carson from Big Bear? He's old enough to be believable, waiting around for a prescription, and he's eaten his way out of the cop look. I'm sure he'd love to be in on the bust," I said.

"Give him a call. I'll be in town over the weekend. Let me know what he says."

Leandra received an inventory of the collection via email before work on Friday. She forwarded it to Chris, who was now out of the hospital and staying at the apartment. An hour later Chris called and left a voice mail that he forwarded the inventory to the bookie and got confirmation that it was received.

Chapter 35

Chris called Leandra at noon on Saturday. "We've got a problem. Arnie's people don't think the collection is as valuable as Max's people."

"I was afraid he'd try this. What do they think it's worth?" she asked.

"One point five mil."

"So he wants to give us $300,000 for the whole collection?"

"That's what it adds up to," Chris said.

"My brother has the collection, and I know this isn't going to work for him."

"Does that mean I'm getting thrown to the wolves?"

"No, it doesn't mean that. He is my brother and I have some influence. Let me talk to him and I'll get back to you when we figure things out."

"Thanks Leandra. I owe you my life."

I finally had a chance to deal with the redistribution of my stuff now that Kelly had settled in. My office/spare bedroom was packed with extra furniture and 18 boxes of assorted items Kelly collected over the years. Last weekend the room was officially designated as a storage facility and ceased being an office. The only overnight guest we could accommodate would be a cat – a small cat.

I started by loading my neighbor's pickup truck with junk I had relegated to the garage, and made a run to the dump. Before I attempted to move the office items into the garage, Kelly rewarded my efforts with a tasty lunch and promised an especially romantic evening. As I carried the first box out of the home office, my cell phone rang. Caller ID showed it was Jeannine's cell phone.

"Help!" she squealed in a high-pitch whisper.

"What's the matter?"

"I'm at the office. Luis Hernandez and another guy are trying to break in. I can see them on my computer screen," she gasped.

"Is the other guy John Lundquist?"

After a moment she said, "Yes."

"They're probably looking for the original of the video from the party. Let's make it easy for them to find."

"Where is it?"

"Top left hand drawer."

"Got it," she said. In a higher voice she added, "I just heard one of the deadbolts!"

"Before they pop the other one, put a sticky note on it saying 'Make copies ASAP.' Then hide in the darkroom."

"OK," she said, and I heard her put the phone down.

While she did this, I called 911 on the house line. When the operator came on, I gave my name and office address.

"My office is being broken into by Luis Hernandez, who's wanted for attempted murder. My assistant is in the office and will probably be killed if he finds her."

The operator started saying something when Jeannine came back on the line. "They got in before I could get to the darkroom. What should I do?" she asked, in a whispered panic.

"I just emptied out my credenza. Can you fit inside?"

A moment later she whispered, "I'm inside but the door won't shut all the way."

"Hold it as closed as you can get it, and try not to shake."

Instead of hearing Jeannine's voice I heard Hernandez say, "It's probably in here. This is Duffy's office."

Lundquist asked, "What's that on his desk?"

"This is it. Let's get outta here."

"Not so fast. There might be other copies."

"I don't think so," said Hernandez. "The note on it says, 'Make copies ASAP.' I think we're done."

"I want to check that darkroom you told me about before we go."

"All right," said Hernandez. "I'll keep looking in here.

Maybe I'll find some petty cash."

I heard a shaky, high-pitched hum that I recognized as Jeannine getting ready to freak out. I disconnected my home line from the 911 operator and was grateful that Kelly had put my office number on speed dial. While I waited for the answering machine to kick in, I heard a loud thud. Since I didn't hear Jeannine say anything, I hoped Hernandez dropped something on top of the credenza.

When the answering machine finally beeped I said, "Duffy, this is Detective Shamansky. Our surveillance camera just picked up Hernandez at your office building. Don't answer the door if you're there. We have a black & white less than a minute away. It looks like we finally got him."

"Let's go!" I heard Hernandez shout.

I breathed a sigh of relief. But my stomach came back up into my throat as I called Jeannine's name and got no response.

"I gotta go," I said to Kelly, who had been watching the entire time.

"I'll drive," she said. "You can call Shamansky on my phone."

"OK," I said, and we ran to the Acura. Kelly did her best impression of a NASCAR driver while I tried three numbers before reaching Shamansky.

"This better be good, hotshot. I'm in a hammock listening to the game and drinking a beer," Shamansky said.

I gave him a quick summary. "Can you find out if your guys got there yet?"

"I'll call in from the house phone. Hang on," he said.

While I waited for Shamansky on Kelly's phone, I called Jeannine's name over and over into my phone. There was no response. Kelly kept crossing the double yellow lines to pass cars on Ingraham Street in Pacific Beach.

"We're clear in here," said a male voice in the background of Jeannine's phone. I tried shouting into the phone, but no one responded.

I then started shouting into the Shamansky line and heard, "Easy does it, buddy. I'm not deaf."

"I can hear cops at the scene, but they don't know Jeannine's in the credenza."

"I'm trying to get patched through right now. If you can hear the cops, listen up and you'll probably hear my call any minute."

By now Kelly was on La Jolla Boulevard, about a mile from the office. I heard the call come in when we were within two blocks. As I listened, Kelly roared into the parking lot. I jumped out of the car and ran up the stairs. Dropping the two cell phones into my pants pockets, I ran into the office and saw one of the uniformed officers lay Jeannine on the carpet. I couldn't tell if she was unconscious or dead.

"Jeannine!" I shouted, running to her side and dropping to my knees. I touched her hand and it was cold, though her eyes were wide open.

"She's still alive," said the officer.

Emergency Medical Services arrived three minutes later.

"What's wrong with her?" I asked a paramedic.

"I think she's in shock."

"With her eyes wide open?"

"We'll know more once the doctor examines her," he said.

"Where are you taking her?" Kelly asked.

"Scripps Green," he said, and started wheeling her out of the room.

"Kelly, will you get her medical card out of her purse and bring it to Admissions? Shamansky's on his way. I need to fill him in."

"No problem. I'll see you there."

I found pictures of Hernandez and Lundquist, and showed them to the first officer on the scene. Unfortunately, he didn't see either of them on his way in.

Shamansky arrived wearing blue jeans and a Porky Pig T-shirt. I brought him up to speed on what had happened since our last conversation.

"Do you have any more copies of the video?" he asked.

"No," I replied. "Drayton made a quick DVD of the confession and Dad's disclosure that the party would be recorded. But then his computer crashed when Kerrigan moved the electro-magnet back into place. I tried copying it here at the office, but my software isn't compatible with whatever Drayton used."

Shamansky was obviously pissed that he hadn't received a copy of the confession the day after the party. But with Jeannine on her way to the ER, he just shook his head.

"If everything goes as planned on Monday I guess it won't matter."

I said, "That's the only hard evidence we had on Leandra Lundquist. If things don't go down just right she could skate on the conspiracy charge."

"She just lost her boyfriend and any chance at a life of leisure. I'd hardly consider it a skate," Shamansky said. He then got on the phone and five minutes later said, "We have squad cars on all of the roads out of La Jolla. We're checking all of the vehicles heading out of town, but no sign of them."

"I need to find out what's going on with Jeannine."

"Let's take a ride up there now," Shamansky said to me. Then, to the officer he said, "Call me when Forensics is done, and stay here till we get back." He gave the officer a business card.

While Shamansky drove, I looked closely at everyone who was shopping, strolling, and driving through La Jolla. All I saw were well-dressed pedestrians and one luxury car after another. Nothing merited a second glance.

As we approached the hospital, I dialed Kelly's number and heard her cell phone go off in my left front pocket. We caught up with her in the ER waiting room.

"What's going on with Jeannine?" I asked.

"They're doing some tests."

"I should tell her doctor the medications she's on."

I walked to the front counter. A clerk called the head nurse, and I told her Jeannine's meds and dosages.

"I'll get this to her doctor right away," she said, and I returned to where Kelly and Shamansky were seated.

We kept the conversation off of the case while we waited

for someone to come out and tell us what was happening. Finally, a white-haired physician arrived and said, "She hasn't regained consciousness yet. At first I was afraid of a head trauma, but that wasn't the case."

"What is it doc?" asked Shamansky.

"We're not exactly sure at this point. But the list of her medications was helpful in giving me a pretty good idea. She's in a catatonic state. Most of the current research suggests that these states are brought on by an imbalance of dopamine, serotonin or noradrenaline. Kelly told me what happened. Under that extreme stress, the medications she's taking probably accelerated the production of one of those chemicals and caused her to shut down."

"How long till she comes out of it?" I asked.

"It could be any minute or it could be years. Once we figure out which chemical is out of balance we can use drugs to try to correct it. But there's no guarantee that the catatonia will lift immediately, or at all."

"Oh my God," Kelly said quietly.

"She appears to be in very good health, so that's definitely in her favor. But you also need to know that once someone's had a catatonic episode, the chance of having another is much greater. She'll probably have to stop driving and working around dangerous machinery," the doctor said.

"Jeannine doesn't drive, and she works in an office."

"Good," he replied. "It will also help if she remains around people she trusts and who care about her well being."

"Can we see her?" I asked.

"The testing should be done in about two hours. She won't need to go to the ICU. We'll get her set up on a Med/Surg floor and let you know where she's at. You're welcome to stay till the end of visiting hours," he said, and walked down the hall.

Shamansky said, "I've got to go relieve the patrolman at your office. I can lock up if you give me a key."

"I brought Jeannine's purse," Kelly said. "Do you want her key?"

"No," I said. "Take mine. I have another one at home."

While I peeled it off of my key ring, Shamansky asked, "Is there a chance your intruders saw any notes on our Monday morning operation while they were nosing around your office?"

I suddenly felt as if our plans had gone down the Royal Quiet Flush. I had been drafting out contingencies on a legal pad late Friday afternoon and thought I left them sitting on my desk. How could they have missed them? Then it hit me.

"Not to worry. If Jeannine was there for more than five minutes before the break-in I'm sure everything was put away in a neat file folder in a desk drawer. I could hear them on the phone the whole time they were in the office. They were looking for videos and had very little time for any reading."

"Thank God for that. Make sure you get plenty of sleep no matter how long it takes Jeannine to come around. If you show up on Monday morning looking like you were in a sleep deprivation experiment, I'm not letting you anywhere near that pharmacy," Shamansky said, and walked out the door.

Kelly said, "You should call your dad and tell him what happened."

I took her advice, and my parents arrived about an hour later.

"What was she doing at the office by herself?" Dad asked. "The reason Kerrigan and I have been over there every day is to make sure she's safe. Why would she just drop over unprotected, like the night she got the dirt on Colonel Sterling?"

"That was pretty good work, you must admit," I said.

"It was so good we forgot to scold her for blowing off the safety precautions. Maybe if we came down on her a little harder she wouldn't be in the hospital right now."

A nurse told us Jeannine was in room 418. It was a semi-private room with no one in the other bed. She was lying on her back, staring at the ceiling.

Mom broke the silence. "I can't believe, after all the poor girl's been through today, that her makeup is still perfect."

Dad said, "Maybe if we muss it up a little she'll wake up to fix it."

I exchanged glances with Kelly. I had been telling her for over a year that Dad always says the wrong thing at the wrong time. She simply shook her head, conveying that she didn't want me to start anything.

We stayed until a nurse told us visiting hours were over. The four of us went to Trophy's restaurant for a late dinner.

"I'm glad they don't have a dress code," Mom said, noting our chore attire.

I was hoping we could watch the end of the Padres game at this sports bar/restaurant, to take our minds off of Jeannine's condition. But the hostess must have taken our sartorial slovenliness into account when she seated us next to the open kitchen. I considered it the perfect ending to a horrible day.

Around 3:00 PM Leandra got a call from her brother. "I just wanted to say hi. I can't stay on the line. I'm about to go into the Pirates of the Caribbean for the 4th time. See you soon." He hung up before she could say a word.

Leandra thought for a moment and concluded that her brother was afraid the phone was tapped, or being triangulated through area cell towers. He surely wasn't at Disneyland. Hearing him say *Pirates of the Caribbean* struck a very familiar note.

Then it hit her. The estate of Mrs. Winthrop Ballington was bordered in the rear by a canyon that was intersected by the I-15 freeway. There were two eight-foot by 20-foot terraces leading down the hill into the canyon. On the lower terrace was the entrance to a grotto that connects to the neighbors' properties that face the canyon. The grotto extended to the base of the canyon where only those who know of this closely guarded secret could access a hidden exit. Mrs. Ballington told her mother that the grotto network was built during World War II, right after Pearl Harbor. San Diego was considered a prime target for attack at the time.

John and his neighborhood buddies would say they were going to play Pirates of the Caribbean when they were teenagers and wanted exclusive access to the grotto. This signaled the younger kids to stay clear of the grotto or face the wrath of the pirates. When he said it was his 4th time, he must have meant four o'clock. She just wasn't sure if he meant AM or PM.

At 3:40 PM, with her hair bound in a scarf like a cleaning lady, she wheeled the Kirby vacuum cleaner into the main house, so that the cops assigned to watch the property could see her. She started the vacuum and worked directly in front of the living room window for about 10 minutes. Then she slipped out the back door and across the lawn, which was blocked from the street by the main house and a huge hedge. Leandra walked down eight steps to the first terrace that held a wrought iron table on a neatly mown lawn. Usually, there were four chairs at the table. Today there were only two.

She descended eight more stairs to the lower terrace and looked into the darkness of the grotto, which appeared to be a mere shadow from the freeway below. Her eyes did not adjust quickly after leaving the bright sunshine for the blackness of the grotto, but she felt John's presence.

"Where are you?" she asked.

"Three more steps, and don't fall over the chair," he replied.

She took three tentative half steps. John struck a match and lit a citronella candle to help her.

"Thanks," she said, and sat down on the cold wrought iron. "Are you eating OK?"

"I'm fine, and you will be too when you see what I've brought for you."

"I wasn't expecting a present," she said. "What is it?"

He handed her the video he had stolen earlier in the day. "It's the original and only remaining evidence of your admission at the team party. I took it from Duffy's office this afternoon."

Leandra beamed. "Oh my God, I don't believe it!"

"Come with me," he said, removing a flashlight from his pocket.

They walked to a section of the grotto Leandra had never seen. When she was 11, one of the older boys brought a dead rattlesnake out to the street where the younger kids were playing, and said he found it in the southernmost part of the grotto. He said it was where all of the snakes lived.

"Aren't there snakes over here?"

John responded, "We made that up to keep younger kids out of our clubhouse."

They entered a small, empty, rectangular room. At the far end, John disappeared behind a wall that looked to be one continuous slab of sandstone. It actually partitioned off a small maze that led into a much larger room with a few beams of sunlight filtering through the ceiling. Five old lawn chairs and a hibachi sat under the main shaft of light.

John found a rusty can of charcoal lighter fluid, and sat in a beach chair next to the hibachi. After breaking up the video he placed it in the hibachi, covered it in fluid, and tossed a lit match on it. A huge flame shot up about four feet. They watched in silence as it turned into black smoldering plastic. John stirred the ashes, put more fluid on the bits that hadn't burned, and struck another match.

"What's going on with the bookie?" he asked.

"He's trying to shake us down," Leandra replied, trying to sound tough.

"How?"

"He told Chris his experts evaluated the collection at only one and a half million."

"Then tell him the deals off and to go fuck himself," John said.

"I think we should tell him we'll give him $60,000 worth to pay off Chris's debt and keep the rest to sell off piecemeal in a few years at full price."

John replied, "Let me see if I've got this straight. You killed your boyfriend, but you want to give away $60,000 to get his buddy out of trouble?"

Leandra slugged him in the arm and exclaimed, "Jerk!" She then turned away and smothered a sob.

He walked over, put his hand on her shoulder, and said, "I'm sorry. But I still don't get it."

By this point Leandra had composed herself. "I think we can still put a deal together with this guy. We just need to show him we're willing to walk away from it if he tries squeezing us."

"I've been thinking about his offer, and 20% is top end for a fence. He must have a buyer lined up who's willing to pay at least 70 cents on the dollar, maybe even full price, for him to offer that much in the first place."

She said, "By offering to give him the $60,000 to bail Chris out, we're telling him that we're not desperate for the money. If we tell him to take a hike, he may kill Chris, and that would definitely be the end of us doing business."

"Maybe the guy spends a lot of time in Tijuana and enjoys haggling prices."

"I could have Chris make the bailout offer. Then, after Arnie responds, concede that the original estimate might have been a little high, but nowhere near as low as what they're offering," she said.

"That should open the door for a counter offer. On the other hand, we could tell him we've got a guy working with us who was a hitman for a Mexican drug cartel and see if that motivates him to stop screwing with us," John said.

"All that would accomplish is to tip our hand. We know this guy has full-time muscle working for him. He's either going to play it straight on Monday or he's going to try to rip us off. If he thinks we're small-time he won't get too clever or call in extra muscle. If he plays it straight after we settle on the collection's value, we just do the deal, take our money, and say goodbye to Luis Hernandez forever. To earn his share I think Luis should hide in the bushes in front of the pharmacy. If Arnie tries pulling a fast one, he can pop out and turn the tables on them. Just make sure he knows to only pull his gun as a last resort. I plan on continuing to work there after this is over."

"Why do you want to do the deal at the pharmacy in the first place?" he asked.

"It's my turf. I won't have my work jacket on, so I'll look like a regular customer. But if I need to, I can go out the back door. I also want Arnie to know he's being videotaped by the security cameras."

"That should keep him from pulling guns during the exchange. The only vulnerable area will be outside of the store."

"That's why I want Luis in the bushes near the front door," she said.

"What about your boss or other employees? Won't they think it's strange that somebody's giving you a briefcase?"

"Poppy is going to be at his home office, preparing for a meeting with his CPA. The only other employee in the store will be the pharmacist who helped us with the meth deal. I guarantee he won't say a word. Ginger doesn't come in until noon."

They spent a few more minutes hammering out details. It was decided that once Leandra was alone in the store with the cash, she would hide half in the storeroom. A few minutes later she'd meet with John and Luis in the parking lot of the restaurant down the street to split up the remainder of the cash and pay off Luis.

She said, "At least we won't have to pay off stupid Donnie."

Leandra returned to her apartment by way of the main house, where she collected the vacuum cleaner. She checked on her mother, called Chris and told him what to say to Arnie and how to say it. She let him know that they were looking for a minimum of $400,000 after paying off Chris's debt if the deal was going to happen. She also told him he had better do a good job of selling it because her brother wasn't too keen on giving away all that money to help someone he doesn't even know.

Chapter 36

Before leaving the restaurant last night, I promised my parents that Kelly and I would accompany them to church in the morning. I always hated going with them because they both do things that really annoy me. Dad always has to be a half-second ahead of everyone else on the responsorial prayers. Mom says it's because he's a natural leader, but I think it comes off as *holier than thou.* Mom is fine during the service, but always spends way too much time afterwards critiquing what her fellow parishioners wore and whether or not the women had their hair done. It's been about ten years since I attended with them, and nothing has changed. Dad continued in his role as *Leader of the Pack* and Mom did her impression of Academy Awards commentator on the red carpet at IHOP after mass. During the service I spent a lot of time pondering whether or not Jeannine should continue working at the agency, if and when she recovers. The office has proven to be a dangerous place in my first two years as a detective. Jeannine has been there for all of it, and I didn't think there was any way to completely ensure her safety.

I knew that Jeannine's world revolved around her job and she'd be devastated if she couldn't come back. Also, the doctor said she should be around people she trusts and loves. I didn't see that happening in another job, or in being cooped up in her apartment. Despite the setting, divine guidance never happened and I left church with one more stone around his neck.

When we got to IHOP, Dad took the pulpit and started sermonizing on how I might have more good fortune in my life if I accompanied them to church on a regular basis. I was pissed at him and needed to change the subject, so I dropped the bomb about cohabitating with Kelly. By the look in her eyes and the high heal grinding into my foot, I could tell Kelly

254

was not enamored with my timing.

"Do you know what the pope says about unmarried couples living together?" Dad asked.

"These are man-made laws that have been evolving for many years," I replied.

"Those laws are in place for a very good reason, and have served as an excellent guide to live by for hundreds of years."

"How many hundreds of those years did the church say it was OK to own slaves?" I asked.

Before Dad could explode, Mom asked, "Does anybody know why Jeannine went over to the office alone?"

"I stopped by the office before church and checked her computer," I said. "She found out that the guitarist Marni's been seeing, Mick Halpin, isn't her boyfriend. He's her half-brother."

Kelly said, "They must be very close to spend that much time together."

"Mick plays rhythm guitar for a new band in the East County. I think she's hoping he can take over for Pedgy when his contract is over, and become a permanent member of the band. That's probably why she's become such good buddies with Pedgy."

Dad's lips were so tight during this exchange that they appeared completely white. Ignoring the new topic he turned to me and said, "So, you think you know better than the Catholic Church." The conversation deteriorated quickly, and my parents decided to check up on Jeannine later, instead of accompanying us to the hospital.

We arrived with high hopes of seeing Jeannine awake, alert, and ready to pose for the cover of a magazine. But she was lying in the exact position with the same expression as last night. The only difference was that someone had scrubbed off her makeup.

"Jeannine," I said, and took her hand. No response.

Kelly gave it a try. "Jeannine, everything's all right. You can come out now." It was a clever approach, but Jeannine remained motionless.

About a half hour later an angry voice came from the doorway. In spite of his tone, I was happy to see my former band mate and Jeannine's boyfriend, Michael Marinangeli. Michael paced along the side of Jeannine's bed.

"She gets into a lot of dangerous situations working for you, doesn't she?" he asked. "You damned near got her killed last year on the Terry Tucker case."

"In all fairness, Michael, you were the one who brought her along to that audition." He crossed the room quickly, and I stood. When his arms came up, I thought he was going to take a swing. But instead, he slung one arm around me, put a hand on Kelly's shoulder, and in a quivering voice said, "Please tell me she's not going to die."

We stayed for the remainder of the day, talking with her and each other, hoping the sound of familiar voices would help pull her back. Michael had been on the road in Boston with Doberman's Stub when he got the news.

My parents arrived around 4:00. Dad was still in a surly mood. I explained to Mom the various things we had tried to rouse her.

I said to Dad, "The warm and nurturing approach clearly isn't working. Maybe if you yell at her for a while it will get her attention."

Mom was about to reprimand me for making such a suggestion when Dad yelled, "Jeannine, get out of bed! It's time to go to work! Jason needs you right now! Wake up!"

A nurse in the hall heard Dad, rushed in, and scolded him for shouting and waking other patients. She also told him that his visiting privileges were over for the day. Dad gave me a disgusted look on his way out the door.

I shrugged and said, "It was worth a shot."

Leandra received a call from Chris just after noon. "What did Arnie say?"

"I told him the options you laid out. At first he acted pissed. Then he said he'd just take the $60,000, provided he could pick out the merchandise. I explained that it wasn't my friend who has the collection, it's her brother, and that he's not too enthused about giving anything away without getting something in return."

"How did he respond to that?" she asked.

"He argued for a while, but eventually came to realize that I had no say on what happened to the collection. I also told him the guy who has it isn't hurting for money and would probably just sit on it for a few years while it grew in value."

"Did he believe you?"

"He told me he'd call back and hung up. Twenty minutes later he said he'd have $400,000 tomorrow at 10:00 AM and I'd be off the hook after I introduced you."

"I want you to come by the pharmacy at 9:30 to make sure Arnie doesn't sneak his thugs in early, posing as customers," Leandra said.

"Won't I look suspicious hanging around that long?"

She replied, "The boss will be out, and besides, people hang around all the time waiting for prescriptions to be filled. You'll be fine."

"OK, I'll see you then."

Chapter 37

Shamansky agreed to let Dad and I onsite for the bust since we had initiated the plan and may be needed if anything unexpected arises. I arrived at my parents' home at 6:45 and ate breakfast. Thankfully, Dad didn't feel the need to resume his sermon on cohabitation.

At 7:30 we met Shamansky in the parking lot of the neighborhood grocery store where he was drinking coffee with his four assigned officers. He had a detailed map of the area around El Cajon Boulevard where the pharmacy is located. He wrote initials where each man was to be located prior to Leandra's arrival at 8:30. Dad and I were to be in the command van with Shamansky, directly across the street from the pharmacy.

Chief Carson arrived at 8:00 and was briefed by Shamansky, who handed him a prescription that would take a while to fill. He would enter the pharmacy at 9:50.

Morale was high and everyone exuded confidence until Darden showed up and tried taking over.

"What the hell are they doing here?"

"Jason set the whole thing up," Shamansky replied in a louder than usual voice.

"I don't care what he set up, he's a civilian and this is a police action," Darden said to Shamansky. Turning to me he said, "Get out of here."

"Who the hell put you in charge, Bunko Boy?" Shamansky asked, and his four men laughed. "Homicide's running this show."

Darden was clearly miffed, but realized he was second in command at best. "I'm not arguing that it's your command. I'm here for two things: To collar the people who stole the collection and to make sure things are done by the book."

Looking down at the map with the initials he said, "I see you've placed the two civilians in the command vehicle across from the pharmacy. That's not by the book. If you're going to insist on that, you'll be talking to the captain in the next five minutes." He then crossed his arms, stuck his chin out, and a smug look formed on his face.

Shamansky knew he was going to have to compromise. "I need them in the area."

"Why?" asked Darden.

"Jason has a relationship with Chris Barnett, the guy who's the link between the buyer and seller. If he gets cold feet the whole deal could go south. Jason could talk him into holding up his end," Shamansky said.

"He can stay in the area, but not in the command vehicle or any of the adjacent properties," Darden said.

"I want him right here," Shamansky said, laying his index finger on the map. "There's a real estate agency across the street, two doors down from the pharmacy, with a side parking lot."

Darden took a few seconds longer than necessary before nodding his head.

Shamansky said to me, "If you go over now, you can back into the front parking space. You should have a great view from there."

I fought my natural inclination to take a verbal shot at Darden and simply said, "OK, we're on our way."

As usual, Leandra arrived at 8:30 to prepare for the opening at 9:00. The pharmacy is one of two businesses in their building. The other is a maternity shop, which has the same frontage space as the pharmacy, but Poppy leases the rear half of their store to accommodate the behind-the-counter side of the pharmacy operation. This left the maternity shop with no rear entrance for deliveries. When they moved in five years ago, the building owner installed a retractable metal garage door between the two businesses, and built a small storage area in the front to handle deliveries and unpacking of boxes. He also built a driveway leading up to the metal doorway. The maternity shop owner was thrilled that she got a lot of window space without the overhead of unneeded square footage. Last Friday, Leandra asked if a U-Haul truck could park in the driveway for about a half hour, around 10:00 AM on Monday. Since the maternity shop doesn't even open until 11:00, and wasn't expecting any deliveries, the owner was happy to help out. This would enable John to back the truck up, open the rear doors, and allow Arnie to see his merchandise from inside the pharmacy before turning over his briefcase full of cash.

Shortly after Leandra arrived, Parker Willis strode through the front door and started prepping the pharmacy. She walked over to him and said, "Parker, I need you to keep an eye on the register around 10:00. I'll be taking off my lab coat for a few minutes to handle a personal issue. It should only take 15 minutes or so."

"With Poppy working on his taxes today, I'm the only one back here and I have a pretty big backlog of prescriptions," Parker replied.

"Give me a break, Parker. You take longer bathroom breaks than that. This is something I have to do. Don't give me a hard time."

"Make it quick," he said, and walked away.

Only two customers had come into the store before Chris arrived at 9:30. He looked nervous and still had bruises from the beating he had taken.

"Do I have to stick around for the whole thing?" he asked.

"I'm sure Arnie won't want you to be a witness. Once you do the introductions, ask if you can leave. He should be glad to get you out of the way," Leandra replied. "I need to keep working until he shows up. Act like a shopper and keep an eye on the window. Let me know when you see him coming."

As planned, at 9:50 Chief Carson handed his prescription to Parker and asked, "How long is it going to take?"

"At least 45 minutes. I have a couple in front of you and this is a compound mix."

"I brought my paper along to do the crossword puzzle. No

hurry," Carson replied. He sat in one of the waiting area chairs facing the shopping area.

At 10:04 Arnie Augustine walked into the pharmacy. Instead of a briefcase, the only thing in his hand was a large cowboy hat. He was tall and lean, with slicked-back, salt and pepper hair that emanated from a well-defined widow's peak. He wore cowboy boots, jeans, a western shirt, and a sport coat that was probably added to conceal a handgun. Leandra tossed her lab coat behind the counter and walked over to Chris. She noticed that John had backed the U-Haul into the driveway.

Chris's face was shiny with sweat as he made the introductions. "Can I go now?"

Arnie replied, "Wait till I have a look inside that truck."

Leandra said, "Before we open up the truck, it looks like you forgot something."

Arnie's expression soured as he turned to Leandra. "I didn't forget anything. The first time I do business with someone I take precautions. Believe it or not there are a few dishonest people out there who'd rip me off if they got the chance."

After dealing with her brother over the past few weeks, Leandra had gotten pretty good at acting tough. "But you're a nice guy who'd never hurt a fly?"

"I'm the salt of the earth, little lady," he said with a grin.

"Then let's have a look under that sport coat," she said.

Arnie opened his coat enough to reveal his Berretta Model 92 pistol. "The Boy Scouts taught me to be prepared."

"I can understand how you feel uncomfortable doing business with someone for the first time. I feel the same way. I'm sure you can understand that this deal isn't going down with you holding all the cards, weapons, and money," she said.

"I'm just protecting my end."

Leandra picked up a newspaper from a nearby rack. "If you want your end to be doing any business today you need to drop that gun into this newspaper right now."

"That's not gonna happen," Arnie replied.

Leandra lifted the phone she had been holding in her left hand and hit a button. "The deal's off. Get the truck out of here

261

right now."

Arnie said, "Hold on. We got off on the wrong foot. Call him back and tell him to stick around for a minute. I think we can work this out."

Leandra speed-dialed again and said, "Stay here, but don't turn the truck off. If anybody comes anywhere near the truck, assume it's a rip-off."

Leandra held the newspaper out to Arnie again. This time he dropped the Berretta into the paper.

"We're good for now, John. Stay on the line." Then, to Arnie she asked, "What about the money?"

"It's nearby. Let's have a look in the truck first. I'll have my guy compare the contents to the inventory. If everything checks out we'll bring the money in."

"How about if John opens up the back and you look from here?"

"Do you really want him bringing each item up to the window so I can be sure that I'm getting what's on the inventory sheets?" he asked.

"Let's do it this way: John will open up the truck and go back to the driver's seat. With it running, your guy can do his thing. But if I see a gun, John takes off. When your bean counter is done, he walks across the street where we can see him while the money guy comes in. In the meantime, Chris leaves now and you're out of his life, permanently. Does that work for you?" she asked.

"I don't mind doing business with a smart gal. Let's do it."

Leandra turned to Chris and said, "Keep in touch and stay out of trouble."

"Thanks, Leandra," he said, and beat feet out the door.

As they watched Chris leave, they saw John swing open the two rear doors on the U-Haul, and return to the cab. Arnie made a call and a minute later a large blond man climbed into the rear of the U-Haul, pulled out some papers, and proceeded to poke around the mass of memorabilia. Leandra checked the wall clock. Seven minutes later the blond man gave Arnie the thumbs up from the back of the truck.

As Arnie called the bagman, Leandra spotted Poppy crossing the street, clutching his tax briefcase. Her mind raced to think of how she could explain the U-Haul and the fact that she wasn't wearing her lab coat. When he reached the shrubbery, Luis Hernandez jumped out, stuck his gun in Poppy's chest, and pulled the trigger. He grabbed the briefcase out of Poppy's hand and sprinted across the street.

Leandra screamed, dropped what she was holding, and ran to Poppy's side. She held him in her arms and cried, "Poppy!"

The view from the first parking space of the real estate agency was probably better than what Shamansky and Darden could see from the van, with one exception. An 8' by 6' patch of shrubbery sat in the east corner of the lot to help drivers spot the entrance to the parking area on that side of the building.

It was a little disconcerting to see Arnie Augustine walk into the pharmacy empty-handed. But the notion of *honor among thieves* went away a long time ago, if it ever existed in the first place.

"Where do you think the money is at?" I asked Dad, who sat behind the wheel of his green Riviera.

"I'm sure there's a bagman with a cell phone within two blocks, probably sitting in Arnie's car," Dad said.

They saw John Lundquist leave the cab of the U-Haul and open the back doors.

"Do you think Shamansky knows where he's at?"

"I'm sure he does. Walt said Arnie drives a black Caddy, just like the old Mafiosos. He may not actually be connected, but he sure works at creating the image."

"How does Shamansky find the Caddy?"

We watched the blond goon from the casino climb into the back of the U-Haul.

"When we were over at the grocery store parking lot, did you see the two guys in shorts and T-shirts?"

"Yeah. What's that about?"

"They're posing as joggers. They'll run the neighborhood until they find the bagman. Whoever finds him first will stay with him while the other looks for more accomplices and eventually moves into place for the bust," Dad said.

"Where do they keep their guns?"

"Fanny packs."

"A cop with a fanny pack? Who could imagine?"

"That's what undercover is all about."

We watched as a man of about Dad's age crossed the street carrying a briefcase.

"This can't be the bagman," Dad commented.

"It's the pharmacy owner. Cory took pictures of everybody who works there."

Just before the owner reached our blind spot we saw Luis Hernandez jump out of the shrubbery and commit murder in his signature style, causing me to put a hand to my chest. Hernandez snatched the briefcase and sprinted directly toward us. With our windows down we clearly heard the call, "Stop, police!"

Hernandez tossed his .25 caliber handgun, pulled an Uzi sub-machine gun from his belt, and squeezed off a short burst in the direction of the pharmacy. Dad started the car as Hernandez shot.

Return fire was now coming in our direction. The real estate office building was made of brick and extended to the corner of the parking lot and the sidewalk. Hernandez rounded the corner into the parking lot to use the building as a shield. When he did this, Dad threw the Riviera into drive, stomped on the gas, and hit Hernandez in the side of the right knee, causing him to go airborne and drop the Uzi.

Dad slammed on the brakes and I jumped out of the car with my gun drawn. Hernandez was sprawled on his back and began pushing himself toward the Uzi, which came to rest against the real estate building a few feet away.

"Stop!" I screamed.

Hernandez looked at me and said, "I thought I killed you." He pushed himself a little closer.

"If you move again," I said, as Darden rounded the corner, "I'll put a bullet in your heart just like you tried to do to me."

"Drop it, Duffy!" Darden screamed.

I glanced to my right and saw Darden aiming a 9-mm Glock at my face.

"He's trying to get the Uzi," I yelled at Darden.

"Put the gun down or I'll blow your fuckin' head off right now!" Darden screamed. He was fully focused on me and seemed intent on punishing me for being involved in his case.

As I lowered my gun Dad yelled, "Look out!"

A shot rang out and Darden clutched his stomach. I brought up my .38 and shot Hernandez in the neck just as he was bringing a handgun to bear on me. Hernandez was dead before his head hit the pavement. His right pant leg was hiked up over a calf holster.

Dad was out of the car and helping Darden when Shamansky ran into the parking lot. His view of what just happened was completely obscured by the real estate building.

Shamansky managed to say the word, "What," when the U-Haul drove past the lot. "Jim, stay with Darden."

I jumped behind the wheel of the Riviera, which was still running, and Shamansky dove into the passenger seat. I had to break hard when we reached the street because an unmarked Crown Vic zoomed by with one of the jogger cops behind the wheel.

"Shouldn't he have a partner?" I asked, pulling out behind him.

"We're spread pretty thin. The bagman took off in the Caddy right after the shooting. Arnie went out the back door of the pharmacy, and we've got a guy covering Leandra, who's still crying over her dead boss."

We could see the U-Haul doors swinging open and closed as the blond goon squatted on both knees for stability while aiming his gun in the general direction of the Crown Vic. With a wave, the jogger cop acknowledged that he saw Shamansky behind him. Now that he had back up, he tried to stop the truck by shooting out the tires. When he squeezed off his first round, the blond goon opened fire, and the jogger cop swerved hard after his windshield was hit. The Crown Vic sideswiped a parked car and took out a fire hydrant before coming to rest against the *Bargain of the Week* at a Toyota dealership.

"Is he OK?" I asked.

"I saw the airbag deploy. Keep going."

When we got to within 50 feet, Shamansky leaned out the window and began firing at the goon, who grabbed one of the U-Haul doors to use as a shield. When his gun was almost in a firing position, the truck hit the brakes and he lost his balance. We had reached an intersection and heavy traffic forced Lundquist to come to a full stop. The goon jumped from the back of the truck and made a run for it on the passenger side of the street.

Shamansky jumped out and yelled, "Stay with the truck!"

A few seconds later I heard shots ring out as the truck started moving. I slid down in the seat, trying to create the illusion that the car had been abandoned to chase the goon. The U-Haul made a right at the light, and I advanced to the corner in time to see it make a left into an alley. It was headed in the general direction of the Lundquist's apartment, so I drove past the alley, made a left at the next light, raced to the end of the block and turned into a convenience store parking lot.

The truck turned right coming out of the alley, and left at the convenience store intersection. We were now in the Talmadge section, which is mainly residential and has very light traffic at that time of day. I was able to pursue from almost a block away, and John gave no indication that he spotted the tail.

John appeared to be headed straight for his apartment when he made a left into an estate two doors north of his residence. I parked the car and ran along an ivy-covered wall to the driveway entrance. The layout looked similar to the Ballington estate, with a detached six car garage to the left, just inside the wall, and the main house in the middle of the property about 100 feet from the entrance. The paved driveway extended along the left side of the house to the backyard. It's the only place the U-Haul could have gone to be out of sight. I walked toward the front door as if I was on official business, in case anyone was watching from inside the house. Upon closer inspection I was convinced no one was watching, so I continued down the right side of the house to the backyard.

I peered around the corner and spotted John carrying a cardboard box toward the rear of the property. He then disappeared over the edge. Rather than chase him into the unknown, it seemed clear that he would need to make several more trips to the truck. I climbed into the back of the U-Haul, sat on a plastic crate in a position where I wouldn't be seen as John approached, and reloaded my gun.

A few minutes later, John rounded the corner and I leveled the gun at his face. "Don't move or I'll shoot," I said in my most authoritative voice.

After he recovered from the surprise John said, "You won't shoot me, Duffy," and appeared to be ready to run.

"You can ask your buddies Donnie Daniels and Luis Hernandez about that when you meet them in hell in a few seconds."

"Luis is dead?"

Tapping my gun, I said, ".38 to the neck, just before you drove by."

"I'm unarmed."

"You paid Hernandez to put a bullet in my heart, and you killed an up-and-coming musician who was also unarmed. Do you think anybody's going to care what happens to you?"

"I didn't kill anybody."

"Then who did?"

"I want a lawyer," John said, and refused to say another word.

I called Shamansky's cell and got voice mail. That was a concern since he was in a gun battle the last time I saw him. I then called Dad, who arranged for a couple of black & whites to join me in Talmadge. Dad hadn't heard from Shamansky either.

When the uniformed officers arrived, they told me Shamansky had been involved in a shootout inside a nursing home and that he was OK. I showed one of the officers where John had disappeared, and they found the box he had carried inside a cave. The cop said he would get a warrant and check it out thoroughly later in the day. In the meantime, one of the uniformed officers would stay onsite.

Chapter 38

I waited in the Metro detective squad room with Dad while Leandra and John were being detained in interview rooms. Shamansky showed up about an hour later.

"What happened to you?" I asked.

"I chased that idiot for three blocks. He ran into a nursing home and cut through the lobby into a dayroom filled with seniors. Then he grabbed a little old man by the neck, put a gun to his head, and started backing up toward a rear exit."

Dad commented, "That guy was really tall. A little old man couldn't have provided much of a shield."

"You're right, Jim. He had to stoop down while he was walking. That's probably why he never saw it coming."

"Saw what?" I asked.

"A little old lady, sitting near the exit, stuck him in the back of the thigh with a knitting needle. He let go of the guy, turned his gun toward the old lady, and I hit him with two in the chest."

Dad said, "I'll bet the press was all over the place."

"That's what I've been doing for the last two hours," Shamansky said.

I said, "It took a lot of nerve for an old lady to do that. Did she say why?"

"She said there are only seven men in the whole facility and Nathan was the best of the bunch. Personally, I think she has a crush on him.

"I'm about to get briefed by the captain on where we're at with the Lundquists. If you can hang here for 15 minutes or so, I'll fill you in when we're done."

After he departed, Dad led us into the breakroom for a cup of coffee. "I read Cory's report from yesterday, and something bothered me."

"What?" I asked.

"It said that in the mid-afternoon, Leandra carried a big vacuum cleaner down the stairs from her apartment and into the main house. He saw her vacuuming in front of the picture window facing the street for a few minutes. Then, about 45 minutes later, she pushed the vacuum cleaner out the front door, across the driveway, and carried it back up to her apartment. I'm thinking maybe she or John used it for the clean-up after Thompson was murdered."

"Shamansky doesn't like Leandra for the murder," I stated.

"Why not?"

"Clean record; long relationship with Thompson; she's a woman; all of the above."

"I heard that room was clean as a whistle," Dad said.

"Not a hair."

"You know a lot of guys with bachelor pads. Are any of them like Felix Unger?"

"Who?"

"Felix Unger. You know − The Odd Couple. He's the guy who kept the place spick and span," Dad said.

"Most of my bachelor friends either have a cleaning lady or live in squalor."

"That's my point. Even in families where the wife has a job, the woman usually handles the detail work when it comes to cleaning. The guy might shampoo the rugs or shake out a throw rug in the backyard, but the woman usually puts on the finishing touches, even when she has a cleaning lady," he said.

"Are you saying you think Leandra did the clean-up after the murder?"

"Why would she bring the vacuum cleaner back up to her apartment? She just lugged it down from there, so the apartment carpet must have been clean. A house the size of the Ballington mansion takes more than 45 minutes to vacuum. It seems to me that she didn't want the vacuum cleaner out of her sight," he said.

"I'm calling Cory." I spent the next few minutes interpreting Cory-speak.

When I finished the call Dad asked, "What did he say?"

"He said it was one of those heavy-duty, industrial-type, upright cleaners with a metal housing. Not the kind of unit you'd expect to sneak into a motel room if you didn't want to be noticed."

"I'll bet it does the kind of thorough job that would pick up every hair."

Shamansky stuck his head in the breakroom and asked, "Ready?"

I asked, "When are you going to search the Lundquist apartment?"

"We're getting the warrant now."

"We think you should include on the warrant a vacuum cleaner or cleaners and their contents," I said.

"The motel room. Good idea," Shamansky said.

"Dad brought it up. What's going on with Leandra?"

"She hasn't lawyered up yet. We're keeping her at a table in an interview room, trying to create the illusion that we're not arresting her. I think we have a shot at a confession, but I want my ducks in a row before I go at her."

"Good idea, Walt," Dad commented.

"I'm going to check and see if John's public defender showed up yet, and get the amendments to the warrant. If you guys want to stick around I'll keep you posted on what's going on."

Shamansky got called into the captain's office to talk about Arnie Augustine.

Dad said to me, "I forgot to tell you, after the pharmacy owner was shot, Arnie picked his gun up off the floor, jumped the pharmacy gate, and ran out the back door. Most of it was caught by the store security camera."

"Did we get him?"

Dad replied, "Chief Carson chased him to the back door and yelled, 'Stop! Police!' When Arnie kept going, the chief air conditioned his ten-gallon hat, causing him to slam on the brakes and signal *Touchdown!*"

"Way to go, Chief. What about the bagman?" I asked.

"In custody, along with the money."

We spent the next half hour debating who killed Garvey Thompson. The more we talked, the closer we came to agreeing.

Shamansky again found us in the breakroom. "I just got out of the interrogation room with Leandra. I was sympathetic and told her we could probably help her out if she cooperates. But getting her to give up a family member won't be easy."

"We think Leandra killed Thompson," I said.

"What? Come on. How did you come to that conclusion?"

I replied, "It started with Thompson having the pharmacy invoice. John's a car thief who works in a garage. Leandra works in a pharmacy."

"It could have been John's idea," Shamansky said.

"That's true," I said. "But all Leandra needed to do was tell him *no* and that would have been the end of it. Besides, take a look at who benefits from Thompson putting out a hit album."

"What does the album have to do with the pharmacy job?" Dad asked.

I replied, "I talked to my friend Calvin Dawson after the party. He's a west coast concert promoter who knows most of the players in the rock industry. He was shocked that The Tactile Tattoo was given a second chance with a major label considering the financial climate of the industry. When I told him the name of the album's producer, he told me he wouldn't trust that guy to tape cable to the floor."

"Is he into drugs?" Shamansky asked.

"Calvin thinks he's been involved in a few payoffs over the years. I'm guessing the drug deal financed The Tactile Tattoo's second chance."

"Where does Leandra fit into your theory regarding the theft of the collection?" asked Shamansky.

"That was John and Donnie Daniels, but couldn't have happened without the information on where Max lives, and where to find the autographed invoice," Dad said.

I said, "You see her as this passive girl being controlled by her brother. We see her as the controlling one. She set up today's deal at the pharmacy so she could control the environment."

"That doesn't make her tough enough to commit murder," Shamansky said.

"She got a career criminal to give up his gun this morning," I said.

Dad jumped in, "Then there's the matter of the motel. There was no sign of a struggle in the room or on Thompson's body. I don't see a big, strong, physically fit drummer letting a stranger shoot him up without a fight."

"He might have if Hernandez was holding a gun to his head," Shamansky said.

I said, "Let me tell you why I discarded that theory. I can see John being in the Hernandez posse for protection while he was in prison. And, I understand why he hired him to hit me on a contract basis. But I don't see the two of them being tight. Hernandez was a hitman for a drug cartel. John's a car thief. I'll bet Hernandez scares the shit out of him. I also suspect that John had no idea Hernandez was going to commit a murder right in front of his sister. I think Hernandez was trying to rip everybody off."

"OK. I'll keep an open mind for now," Shamansky said.

"Has the warrant been served yet?" I asked.

"Let me make a call," he replied, and walked out of the breakroom to his desk. A few minutes later he returned and said, "They just finished. No memorabilia or weapons, but they did get a big old Kirby vacuum cleaner and a new Dirt Devil. They're on their way to the crime lab now."

"Any chance I could head over there and see what comes out of those vacuum cleaners?" I asked.

"I can get you in, but you won't be able to touch anything or transport evidence," he said. "I don't see how it will do any good."

"I'm just hoping they'll process it a little quicker if they see we're anxiously waiting for it."

"I thought you'd want to go celebrate with Max and Ellen. Your job is done."

"I talked Thompson into giving up. I'm convinced he told Leandra and sealed his fate. I want to stay involved until I'm sure she's not going to get away with it."

"Suit yourself. The lab's up in Clairemont. You better get going before the white collars head home."

Dad agreed to stay at Metro and call me if anything significant developed. True to his word, Shamansky greased the wheels and a supervisor gave me a brief tour of the crime lab before showing me to a waiting area. He told me that the collection bag on the Kirby was nearly full, but the one on the Dirt Devil had been removed but not replaced.

"Will you process the Dirt Devil first?" I asked.

"Already on it."

Twenty minutes later the supervisor returned to the waiting area. "There was nothing inside the Dirt Devil, but we did find a single thread at the base of the bristles."

"What did it look like?"

"I'd say a carpet fiber, but we won't know for sure until we do some tests."

"Were there any prints on the Dirt Devil?"

"All over it, but we haven't gotten a hit on IAFIS yet," he said.

"I think the fiber came from the motel room where Garvey Thompson was killed. If I drive over to the motel and get a sample, will you be able to do a comparison?"

"We'll need to send somebody over there later to get a sample we can use in court. But I know Detective Shamansky is holding off on interrogating a suspect until he hears back, so yes, I'd welcome the help," said the supervisor.

I drove eight miles to the motel in rush hour traffic. At first, the clerk wasn't going to cooperate. But as two families lined up behind me to check in, I raised my voice when I said the word *murder,* and the clerk caved.

I rushed the sample to the lab and headed back to Metro. The supervisor assured me it would be processed right away, and he would call Shamansky with the results immediately afterwards.

When I arrived at Metro, Dad was seated in a chair just out of view from the captain's office, and waived frantically for me to join him. I sat in the chair next to him and heard the captain say, "Don't be ridiculous."

Darden was on speakerphone. "I want Duffy's license and I'm not settling for anything less."

I looked at Dad and patted my stomach. He whispered, "He was wearing Kevlar."

Shamansky bellowed, "If your vendetta goes any further than this conversation I swear I'll have you arrested for reckless endangerment and dereliction of duty."

"You might think it's OK to let this guy run your case, but not me. I'm putting that punk out of business," Darden said.

Shamansky replied, "Then let me fill you in on what I'll be saying at that hearing. I'll tell them that as a result of Duffy's involvement we took a murderer off the street, recovered stolen property, solved your case, closed down a bookmaking operation, took the bookie's two enforcers off the street and we're well on our way to solving another murder. I'll also tell them that you nearly got yourself killed and put Duffy and his father in a very perilous situation. By the time I finish with you, you'll be lucky to get hired patrolling the parking lot at Wal-Mart."

Dad laughed and I hoped the captain didn't hear him.

"What do you have to say about this, Captain?" Darden asked.

"I think that if you drop this ridiculous charge against Duffy I might let you transfer out of Metro. But if I have to get in the middle of a pissing contest, you can kiss your pension goodbye," he said, and disconnected the call.

Shamansky walked out of the captain's office and said, "The lab called. It's a match. Do you want to watch me go at the siblings from the other side of the mirror?"

"We wouldn't miss it for the world," Dad said.

Shamansky started with John, since his public defender had yet to arrive. "I know you've asked for a lawyer, but while we wait I thought I'd give you an idea of what we have in case you want to reconsider. If you don't care about what I have to say just keep your mouth shut – no harm, no foul, OK?"

"Whatever," John replied.

In a very calm and systematic manner Shamansky laid out his case for the theft of Max's collection and the pharmacy theft. "I don't believe you were involved in Garvey Thompson's murder. So here's what I'm willing to do. If you give us the name of the meth cook, the DA will give you a pass on the thefts."

"Let's see what my lawyer has to say."

"The minute I walk out that door I'm meeting with your sister. I'm guessing she knows all about your role in this. Somebody's going down for the pseudoephedrine. I'll offer her the same deal. If she takes it I don't need you anymore and you'll do time for both crimes." Shamansky stood up and sang the Roy Orbison line, "It's now or never."

John said, "Put the deal in writing for me and I'll give you the name."

Shamansky grabbed a yellow legal pad out of a drawer, drafted his offer in a couple of minutes and handed it to him. John tore the sheet out of the pad and wrote: *Nelson Tabor – Valley Center* on the next page.

"Nice doing business with you," Shamansky said, and exited the room.

Leandra had lots of time to reflect on her situation. She cried for the first hour over the death of Poppy and the fact that her life had hit an all-time low. She wondered if her brother would do the right thing and take the blame. She wondered if the police would buy it if he did. She wondered what they actually had on her, and if she would be able to explain away her role in today's fiasco. She realized that taking the gun from Arnie in front of the security camera was a mistake.

She spent quite a bit of time trying to rationalize and justify why Garvey had to die. He had promised her a life of luxury as the wife of a rock star. Then he decided to throw it all away by agreeing to confess, and never even asked for her input on the decision. She had totally changed all of her plans for him and remained faithful throughout the relationship. Not only would she lose out on the fabulous lifestyle, she also would have lost her job when Poppy found out about her role in the pharmacy theft. She convinced herself that Garvey had sold her out and was willing to let her life go down the drain. She thought: *To hell with him. He had it coming.*

Leandra had a much tougher time when she tried to rationalize her involvement in Poppy's death. She could barely think about him without crying. When Leandra first started working at the pharmacy she noticed a poorly dressed, 12-year-old girl shoplifting in the candy aisle. She thought Poppy would go easy on the poor girl. Instead, he read her the riot act, brought both parents to the store, and told them she was never to return. When Leandra told him she thought he was harsh, Poppy took the time to explain his views on crime and punishment. He said that if he went easy on her or let her get away with it, he would be reinforcing the behavior and increasing the likelihood that more criminal activity would follow. By coming down hard, he forced her to realistically look at the consequences of being a criminal and make a choice that could have a huge impact on the rest of her life.

Poppy's philosophy made a lot of sense, but the prospects of spending years in prison left her feeling ambivalent about how to proceed with the police. She decided that she needed to be tough on the inside and look like a victim on the outside. Maybe the police would take pity on her and blame everything on her brother. The cop, Shamansky, seemed sympathetic. There may be a way out of it yet, and she wanted to keep the door open to that possibility.

Detective Shamansky returned an hour later carrying a couple of soft drinks. "Let me tell you where we're at and then you can tell me what you want to do."

"OK," she said, and took a sip of the drink.

Shamansky spent the next half hour summarizing everything from the failure of the band's first album, to bribing the executive, to the meth lab connection, to the involvement of

Luis Hernandez. His tone was decidedly non-judgmental.

He took a long drag on his soda straw and said, "You can go one of two ways with this. You can come clean, tell us everything that happened, and be completely honest. Or, you can plead not guilty, deny your involvement, and force the police and the DA's office to spend hundreds of manpower hours going through a jury trial."

"What you described is impossible. I was home watching TV with my mother and my brother when Garvey was killed," she said. "I'll be glad to tell you all about the shows we watched."

"Did you use Tivo, a DVR, or an old VCR?" Shamansky asked.

"Live programming," Leandra replied.

"Did you know that Tivo and DVRs keep a log of all recorded shows? Even video tapes that have been erased, or recorded over, can be recovered to the point where they're admissible as evidence at trial." Shamansky sat on the table. "I really don't think the case against you is so bad right now. It's your brother who should be worried. But if you keep telling lies, I'll stop thinking you deserve a break."

"What's going to happen to me?" she asked.

"If you cooperate I'll recommend a sympathetic DA who can ask for a light sentence. Personally, I'm seeing a girl with no prior arrests who was led astray by her criminal brother. But if you decide not to cooperate with the police investigation, you'll be up against a hard-line prosecutor who will be charging you with murder-one and asking for the death penalty."

"I think I'd better talk to a lawyer."

Shamansky walked out of the interrogation room and into the observation room.

Dad said. "She's nuts to lawyer up after that argument."

He replied, "You never know how these things are going to turn out."

I asked, "Can I go in there with you for the next round?"

Shamansky replied, "We know she'd prefer to see you dead.

But I'm not getting much of an emotional reaction from her. Maybe lighting a little fire might help."

After Shamansky took a restroom break, we sat across the interrogation room table from Leandra.

I said, "Hello, Leandra."

"Go to hell, Duffy." Her affect was still very flat.

I asked, "Do you think Gus Popakalitis is in heaven or hell right now?"

"I don't believe in those places. But if it turns out to be true, I'm sure Poppy is in heaven."

I said, "I believe people live on after their death as long as they continue to influence their loved ones. For the really great people, it goes on for generations. But as soon as their influence ends, they're gone forever.

Leandra put a fist to her mouth and did not reply.

"If Poppy was still alive and sitting next to you, what would he tell you to do?" I asked.

Leandra lowered her fist, opened her mouth, but couldn't speak. She then lowered her head and covered her face with her palms.

I said, "This is your chance to either keep him alive in your heart or drive a stake into his."

Leandra said, "I never meant for Poppy to die."

Shamansky said, "The offer for the sympathetic DA is still on the table." After a brief pause he added, "Last call."

Leandra said, "Okay, I'll tell you what happened."

While Shamansky took her confession, Dad and I walked to China Camp at Fat City for honey walnut shrimp. Shortly after our entrees were presented I asked, "Do you still think my psych degree was a waste of time?"

"I never said that. But I don't think your psych degree had anything to do with that girl's confession."

I asked, "Then what do you think happened in there?"

"I think you finally put in a long overdue appearance at God's house yesterday. He rewarded you by inspiring you to use the power of heaven and hell to get that girl to unburden herself of her sins."

I realized that if I started an argument it would surely be brought home to Mom in a doggie bag. I should have known that in Dad's mind all roads do indeed lead to Rome. I stirred my rice with a chop stick and replied, "Pass the soy sauce."

We brought a take-out order back to Metro for Shamansky. He told me, "John's lawyer finally showed up. You'll be glad to know he's being charged with conspiracy to murder you."

"How are you going to get that one to stick?" I asked.

"We found a *To Do* list in Hernandez's pocket with a checked item that said: *Collect another $700 from John L. for Duffy hit*. It was like the hand of stupidity reaching out from the grave," Shamansky said, taking a bite of shrimp.

"Did you know about the list when you made the deal?" I asked.

Shamansky smiled and Dad replied, "To quote an esteemed colleague, 'Does a bear shit in the woods?'"

"What about Dr. DD?" I asked. "Will the DA be going after him for his role in the bribery?"

Shamansky said, "Very doubtful. We found a recording in Leandra's bedroom that sounded like Thompson giving Dr. DD the payoff. But neither of them mentioned money or drugs or any of the specifics of the deal. A good lawyer would come up with a very plausible explanation at trial. With Thompson dead, it would be hard to refute."

"What about the record executive, Tony Zembrano?" Dad asked.

"I'm guessing that once his boss finds out about it he'll either get fired or promoted. Either way, the DA's office won't pursue it because Zembrano's lawyer will argue that Thompson offered to share costs to get signed."

"What kind of break will Leandra get for cooperating?" I asked.

"We'll probably end up prosecuting her for Thompson's murder without pursuing the additional charges. She'll do plenty of time for that, but won't have to deal with consecutive sentences for the various crimes," Shamansky said.

"I assume her brother gets all of the fruit baskets he can handle," I said.

"They say, be careful what you wish for," said Shamansky.

Chapter 39

On Thursday morning Kelly and I received a dinner invitation from Ellen. I explained that we were staying close to the hospital in case there was a change in Jeannine's condition.

"We'll never be able to repay you for all of your help. You've got a lifetime invitation to our winter weekend party. You'll get to meet quite a few talented musicians," she said.

"That sounds great. I'll plan on being a regular."

"We're also sending you a bonus once the eBay auction is over."

"That won't be necessary."

"You'll change your mind after you look at the online auction. All of the publicity from the killings brought a morbid frenzy of interest from the collectors. The last time I looked the bids totaled over $4,000,000," she said.

"In that case I'll put a tip jar by my office door," I said, and Ellen laughed.

"You certainly earned it."

I said, "I have a question before you go. Kelly was wondering why a beautiful girl like Marni doesn't have a jam-packed social calendar. I know she got pretty close to Pedgy. Did he say anything?"

"Marni grew up as a tomboy, constantly competing with her brothers. She never got into the girlfriends and boyfriends scene. Her life was filled with music, sports, and muscle cars. The bands' girlfriends all tried to help her pick out makeup and clothes."

"Do you think she might be attracted to the girlfriends?"

"She told Pedgy she never lost faith in the idea that she'd eventually become a headliner. She plans to hold off on dating until she can start seeing established male stars, and promote the band through all of the press it will generate," Ellen said.

"Do you believe that?"

"I think she's comfortable being a tomboy and prefers keeping focused on the music. She'll figure it out eventually."

"Is Max going to retire now that he's a man of means?"

"He called the studio this morning to assure them that he intends to play until he's laid to rest," she replied. "What could be better than to do what you love?"

"Not a thing," I replied, and we said goodbye.

On Friday at 3:00 PM Cory drove his van to the facility where Kelly volunteers. I opened the sliding door from the captain's chair behind the passenger seat. Kelly stepped past me, pausing long enough for a quick kiss, and sat in the chair behind Cory.

"Aren't you the guy who drives the neighborhood ice cream truck?" she asked, looking at my all-white uniform.

"Don't laugh, you're going to look just like me in a couple of minutes," I said, and unzipped a gym bag.

"Where's the changing room?" she asked.

"Cory, would you flip your rearview mirror up for a couple of minutes?" I asked, and he did so without a reply.

"No peeking, Cory," she said, slipping out of her slacks and tossing them to me. From the back of the van we heard a noise and Kelly pleaded, "Let me see."

"Keep your pants on. Or, should I say, get your pants on," I said. Kelly pouted.

Cory pulled around back to the service entrance when we reached Scripps Green Hospital. Kelly and I got out of the van, opened the rear door, and removed a canvas industrial laundry basket.

A couple of days earlier I managed to track down an old acquaintance from UCSD who had cornered the fake ID market. As expected, he was no longer in the business, but had passed his craft along to his younger brother who managed to supply us with very credible hospital employee badges.

We made our way up to Jeannine's room, pushed the laundry basket inside, and closed the door. As requested, Mom,

Dad, Michael, Shamansky, and Kerrigan were at her bedside. Assuming we would be on a tight schedule I began giving orders.

"I need Mom, Dad, and Shamansky on the left. Michael, you're at the head on the right, then Kerrigan and Kelly. I'll cover the foot of the bed. Our job is containment and you're going to need to be ready, so bend your knees and put your hands out to the side. Michael, if this works, let me take the lead." Michael nodded.

I tossed the sheets in the laundry basket on the floor, opened the crate below, and lifted out two ten-week-old German Shepherd puppies.

Mom said, "Awww."

Dad followed with, "What the hell is this?"

"Don't worry, Dad," I said in a calm voice.

"You're gonna get us thrown out of here again, and this time they probably won't let us come back," he said, excitedly.

Dad was about to continue arguing when Mom gave him the dreaded lowered chin, raised eyebrows combination. He just shook his head in resignation.

I set the puppies down on the bed, and the one Kelly wanted immediately walked over and nuzzled her hand. The other puppy sniffed at Jeannine, starting at her feet, and made his way up the left side of the bed. Jeannine was lying flat on her back with a sheet pulled up to her armpits and her arms lying at her side, on top of the sheet.

The puppy licked her hand and continued sniffing as he made his way up to her face. After a couple of sniffs the puppy suddenly started licking Jeannine's face, enthusiastically. Jeannine didn't flinch. Just as I was about to ask Michael to pick the puppy up, he stuck his tongue in her ear, and Jeannine bolted upright in the bed.

"What was that?" she asked.

I replied in a calm voice, "That's your new puppy. We got one, too."

"A puppy?" she asked in a bewildered way.

Michael picked up her puppy and put it in her arms.

I said, "He's going to be trained as a guard dog to protect you. You can even bring him to the office with you."

"I can?" she asked, still sounding bewildered.

"That's right," I said. "If anybody ever tries to hurt you again, that dog will be there for you all the time."

"Is that his brother?" she asked.

"Yes, he is," Kelly replied softly.

"Can he come to the office, too?"

I said, "He's going to be at our house to make sure it's safe when Kelly gets home from school."

"That's a good idea," she said. Then, looking up into my eyes she asked, "What happened to me?"

"Luis Hernandez and John Lundquist came to the office and you hid in my credenza. They never found you, but the stress of the situation had a bad reaction with your medication, and you passed out for a few days."

Dad said, "That's what happens when you don't bother to call your bodyguards and go into the office by yourself. You're lucky you weren't killed."

Jeannine looked at me and said, "It looks like you weren't the only one to get a second chance on this case."

I glanced at Mom who was putting her hand on Dad's forearm as I felt Kelly squeeze my fingers.

"What did I miss?" Jeannine asked.

"I'll tell you later. If we don't get these puppies out of your hospital room we're all going to be in a lot of trouble."

Jeannine said, "When I was unconscious, I kept feeling as if I was on the verge of waking up. Then I'd think of a question that Detective Kerrigan asked, and fall back to sleep. Can you answer just that one question for me?"

Kerrigan said, "Shoot."

Jeannine asked, "Does Dolly Parton sleep on her back?"

Mom looked at Jeannine and said, "Yes, she does." Then, glaring at Kerrigan she added, "She's better off with the watch dog."

"OK. Can you take me home now, Michael?" she asked.

"Your doctor will need to check you out first, but I'm sure

he'll send you home soon," he replied, and gave her a kiss.

Kelly and I put the puppies back into the crate and covered them with the sheets. As we were about to leave Jeannine said, "If you see the doctor on your way out tell him I need to go home and take care of my puppy."

Acknowledgments

The author benefited greatly from contributions made by the following people: R. Glenn Cooper, Craig & Janet Correll, Sharon Davis, Carol Gillern, Pat Gillern, Marie Lumsden, Maryann & Mike Nebraski, Donna Riviello, Vince Shumski, Andrea Talarico, and Robbie Walsh. Thanks so much for your assistance, input, and expertise.

OTHER ROCK & ROLL MYSTERY SERIES NOVELS

By RJ McDonnell

Rock & Roll Homicide

Jason Duffy's first murder case could easily be his last. Hired by the widow of a slain rock star, he quickly learns about an unhealthy tie between the victim's recording company and the Russian Mafia. But his suspect list is not limited to the bent-noses of the Borscht Belt.

Midwest Book Review: "A brilliantly told tale of sex, drugs, rock & roll, and the Mob."

Beverly Ford, 20-year veteran Boston Herald crime beat writer: "As an avid reader, I've found McDonnell to be one of the most engaging, enjoyable, and funniest writers I've come across in a long, long time."

BookPleasures.com: "RJ McDonnell's enjoyable style is somewhere between Carl Hiaasen's in *Basket Case* and Michael Connelly's in *Chasing the Dime*."

The Concert Killer

A religious fanatic serial killer, who hates rock music, tries to shut down the concert industry. A group of independent concert promoters hire private investigator Jason Duffy and his staff of former outpatient mental health clients to catch him. The killer believes that God rewards His favorites with the most money, and keeps score of his victims on the back of a dollar bill. Jason uses his background as a counselor and club musician to battle his cleverest and most twisted adversary ever.

The author of the 2010 Mystery/Thriller of the Year, ROCK & ROLL RIP-OFF, once again adds LOL humor in between compelling action scenes. Besides offering readers a backstage pass to the music industry, THE CONCERT KILLER brings to light a potentially catastrophic danger that few have ever considered.

(See excerpt at the end of this book)

The Classic Rockers Reunion with Death

San Diego private investigator, Jason Duffy, travels to
Scranton, PA, in January after his uncle's best friend is
murdered. He learns that Uncle Patrick and the victim were
members of a rock band that nearly made it to the national
scene in the early 1970s, and were about to play a reunion
concert in their hometown when the murder occurred.

The investigation leads Jason back to an "almost anything
goes" era that is exacting a huge price more than 40 years later.
To mix & master this musical mystery, Jason fills in for the
murdered guitarist and soon finds himself struggling to avoid
filling in a cemetery plot.

Someone doesn't want that reunion concert to happen and is
willing to do anything to cancel it forever. The case teaches
Jason how easy it is for all of us to fall victim to our
assumptions. It's a lesson that could exact a tuition that may
never be paid back.

Excerpt from

The Concert Killer

Chapter 1

Virginia Tolliver couldn't stand another day of being known to her classmates as *most likely to become a nun*. Senior year was underway and she was still living up to the first six letters in her name. There was no shortage of opportunities to unlock her chastity belt. Except for a slightly pug nose, she was a natural blond beauty. But high school boys could never satisfy her lofty expectations. She wanted a man whose appeal would rival the hunks in her favorite romance novels. The lead singer in Concierge Lover was such a man. When she read that his band would be performing in the area she invested most of her savings in a beautiful pink mini-dress and a professional makeover. She saw enough groupies on television to know where to go and how to act after the show.

A man with the intense gaze of a hunter sat in his white sedan looking through a small pair of binoculars. He watched six groupies gathered near the stage entrance to the amphitheater where the concert headliner's bus would soon be entering. His eyes were drawn to a blond tart wearing a sheer pink mini-dress. He knew instantly that she would be the one.

He tailed her from a safe distance after the bus arrived. Her outfit made this task exceptionally simple. Throughout the warm-up act and the main show he watched as she drank four beers and danced with rowdy boys and other slutty girls on the lawn behind the permanent seats. When the band finished, she clapped wildly and glanced back at the restroom. He knew that her main concern would be to primp for the band. While the rest of the concert-goers roared for an encore, he finger-combed his brown wig, adjusted the prosthetic breasts he wore under his light gray v-neck sweater, and followed the groupie into the cinderblock women's room. Upon entering, he heard a stall door close, squatted for a moment and, glancing under the stall doors, confirmed that they were alone. He was momentarily disgusted by the array of toilet paper, discarded cups, and paper towels that were strewn about the floor. Before rising, his nostrils flared as he became aware of a puddle of vomit below the sink nearest to him.

He went into the stall at the far end of the restroom so that he would pass the pink trollop as he exited. He sat on the toilet, bent forward, and carefully removed his long brown wig. Underneath was a plastic zip-lock bag containing a pair of latex gloves and a single sheet of paper folded into thirds. After putting on the gloves, he looked down at the paper which displayed the words, "Concerts are Evil," written across the top in newspaper clippings. Below were the headlines of three murders he committed over the past three months. The police were obviously too stupid to recognize the connection, so he decided to point them in the right direction. At the bottom of the note he taped his signature, "The Concert Killer."

He quietly removed four pieces of masking tape from the bag and taped the paper to the back of the stall door, wrinkling his gloves as he smoothed the tape. He placed the wig back on his head, making sure it completely covered his short black hair. He heard the tart's toilet flush and her stall door open.

Virginia was nervous and starting to have second thoughts about turning her fantasy into reality. The beers bolstered her courage, but she couldn't stop thinking about her little sister, who wanted to be just like her. And, did she really want to share this experience with the guy she'll eventually marry? Could she live with keeping it a secret?

Staring at herself in the restroom mirror, Virginia concluded that her plan was a mistake. She focused on her bright red lipstick with the suggestive name, grabbed a tissue, and began quickly rubbing it off, as if once removed she could return to her old self.

From his front pocket, the Concert Killer pulled out a small blackjack that belonged to his grandfather, a deputy sheriff from Eureka, CA. It was about six inches long and was comprised of a leather handle and a small oval of iron wrapped in leather. His grandfather used it to knock out pugnacious drunks who refused to go peacefully.

He slid the metal bar, unlocking the door, and exited. A row of eight sinks and mirrors lined the wall opposite the stalls. He planned on using a diversionary tactic so that the groupie wouldn't see him swing the blackjack. But she was so engrossed in working on her lipstick that the ruse wasn't necessary and she never saw it coming. He connected with her right temple and she dropped instantly, bouncing her chin off of the sink. Holding her by the calves, he dragged her to the stall he had used, circled 90 degrees to his left, and pushed her to the toilet, head first. Noticing that her dress was now up to her waist, the Concert Killer pulled it down over her white panties, flipped her over, and adjusted the back of her dress. He then straddled her, grabbed her blond hair, and shoved her face into the toilet with all of his might. She regained consciousness briefly, but the blow weakened her and he had no trouble holding her down until she was dead. He left her facedown in the toilet bowl.

As he exited the stall he wiped down the handle and inside latch bar that he touched before donning the gloves. Another adjustment to her dress was necessary. He removed the gloves, flushed them down a different toilet, using a single knuckle on the handle, and walked out of the restroom. The band started playing another encore song and everyone's attention was directed toward the stage.

Follow and Friend RJ:

Author website: **http://rjmcdonnell.com**

Facebook:
https://www.facebook.com/profile.php?id=100000152963997

Twitter: @RJMcDonnell7

Goodreads:
http://www.goodreads.com/author/show/1861538.R_J_McDonnell

www.ingramcontent.com/pod-product-compliance
Lightning Source LLC
Chambersburg PA
CBHW060540180626
46817CB00002B/655